The Substance of Shadows

Paul Thomas Holdren

The Substance of Shadows

Olympia Publishers
London

www.olympiapublishers.com
OLYMPIA PAPERBACK EDITION

A CIP catalogue record for this title is
available from the British Library.

ISBN: 978-1-78830-832-8

First Published in 2021

Olympia Publishers
Tallis House
2 Tallis Street
London
EC4Y 0AB
Printed in Great Britain

Dedication

To my wife, Melissa, for all of her encouragement, love and support; to my boys, Parker, Blake and Dylan, for inspiring me to be the best version of myself; and to my mom and dad for always believing in me, even when I didn't believe in myself. And a special acknowledgement to my cousin, Michael Thornton, who was pivotal in helping create this story, and in adapting it into a screenplay.

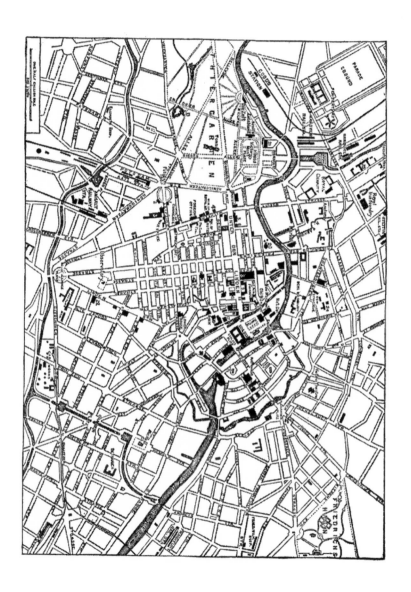

By the winter of 1942, the inhabitants of Berlin could feel the unrelenting burdens of living in a nation which was at war. Over the previous three years, the capital city's demographics had changed dramatically, as much of the adult male population had been sent into service in various theaters of conflict around the globe. They were supplanted by an influx of foreign laborers who had been conscripted to aid in the production of materiel essential to the war effort. For those residents who remained, the days often consisted of dealing with supply shortages, waiting in food lines or seeking gainful employment in a shrinking marketplace. Likewise, the nights were spent under blackout restrictions, battling the frigid winter temperatures with limited coal rations and frequent electrical outages, in fear of the imminent wail of air raid sirens. Under these precarious circumstances, crime soared.

To further complicate matters, effective law enforcement in the city had been severely undermined by the politicization and corruption of the various police forces by their Nazi overseers. Since his appointment as Reichsfuhrer SS a decade earlier, Heinrich Himmler had steadily been increasing his control over the numerous agencies which comprised Germany's ever-expanding police state. In one of his boldest moves as the Head of the German Police, Himmler united the existing criminal police forces (Kriminalpolizei, or Kripo) under the same authority as the highly politicized Secret State Police (Gestapo). He would complete this consolidation of power by bringing the regular uniformed police divisions (Ordnungspolizei, or Orpo), as well as the Security Police (SiPo) and Security Service (SD) intelligence agencies, under the same umbrella. These formerly autonomous and independent police bureaus were now answerable to Himmler and would subsequently be headquartered at a centralized agency in Berlin, known as the Reich Security Main Office (RSHA).

While these developments greatly increased the authority of Himmler and his cohorts, and solidified the Nazis' stranglehold on law enforcement, they wreaked havoc throughout the rest of German society. The politicization, militarization, and corruption of the police forces under the Nazis' authoritarian rule, washed away any remaining hint of the legal precepts of due process, independent courts, individual rights and equal justice. The lines between the different factions in the police state became blurred, causing endless jurisdictional disputes, interagency conflicts, departmental vendettas, and an endless struggle for power.

With the advent of world war, these muddled relationships became further clouded, as special task forces (Einsatzgruppen) were formed from the police ranks and mobilized as paramilitary forces in foreign lands to exterminate or incarcerate German foes. These wartime actions, carried out by members of the various aforementioned police agencies, also aided in the proliferation of the concentration camp system, where 'foreign undesirables', 'ethnic inferiors', and 'enemies of the state' were incarcerated without trial to face the prospects of forced labor, torture and death.

It is against this dark and sordid backdrop that the following story unfolds.

Prologue

Will this be the way it ends? Then why am I not afraid? Even the nest of rodents living behind the wall know enough to be unnerved by the trembling of the ground. Their anxious rustling and screeching remind me that this is no time for sleep, no matter how tired I am. It reminds me that unless I find a way out, they may have more to live for than I do. Either way, this will be my last night here.

My last night to breathe in the cold winter air, if I press my face hard enough against the narrow crack in the stone wall. It hurts like hell when a jagged edge rubs against the open wounds, but it's worth it. Anything for a fresh breath. There's just enough of a gap between the stones to glimpse the starless sky, lit up by tracer fire. Just enough space to inhale the outside draft and exhale the damp stench of excrement and urine. Something nearby is on fire. Smells like gas.

I hated that smell as a child, running past the gas works on Danziger Strasse on my way home from school. Trying to reach the grass field on the other side of my parent's house, the one where the neighborhood kids gathered to play stick ball, just to get beyond the reach of that repellent smell. That very same gas works. What I wouldn't give to be able to run past it to my home now.

But what would I find? Would anyone still be there? If not, then where am I to go? To St Michael's Kirche? Where else?

The church was my last point of contact before the arrest, the place where everything went off the rails. It's where they tightened the noose around my neck. Around all of our necks. Verdammt! My family awaits my return in desperate peril, and I'm left to rot in this cell. Left to count the numberless hours and days by the sound of air raid sirens and church bells.

I'm a number, not a man. Not anymore. It doesn't matter that I fought for my country, or that I patrolled this city's streets. I'm prisoner #616. Cell #26. What was it the arrest warrant read? 'Herr Nomen Nescio?' Herr Name Unknown. I'm nameless. But they know who I am, and what I'm capable of if I'm freed. And that's why I won't be. Because I know too much, have seen too much. I know who they are, what they've done, and where they live. But if they're so untouchable, then why do they need to have me permanently out of the way? What else do they have in mind for me? For my family? I can't know until I get out. And that's why it has to be tonight, unless the bombs finish the job for them first.

So why haven't they already come for me? 78 hours and counting! I've scratched a mark on these walls for every bell that's chimed since I arrived. What's the delay? They have to know I'm here. They're the ones who put me here. The ones who set up everything to happen just the way it did. That has to be the reason I'm the only prisoner in solitary confinement, and the only one with a permanent guard. I can hear his lumbering pace in the hall right now. His breathing is ragged. He's anxiously waiting for this air raid to end, so he can make his nightly visit. He's built like a tree trunk, with sledgehammers for fists, but a sledgehammer takes time to swing. He has his vulnerable spots.

But will my own hands be up to the task? I barely

recognize them through the swelling and cuts, covered in mud and stone dust. How can a part of me that I've known and relied upon every day of my life, look so foreign? But never mind my rambling. My shackles are loose for the first time, and this length of chain can hoist a shorter man right off the ground, given the right leverage. I can see my pulse pounding beneath the scrapes on my wrists. The earth-rattling concussions are growing more intermittent, and distant. It could be any time now. Gott, if you're up there, grant me the strength to do what needs to be done tonight. And forgive me for what I've done after I'm finished.

Why can't it be as simple as the stories my mother used to read to me as a child? The ones my wife reads to our children now? They were all the same. The unjustly imprisoned victim prayed to Gott for deliverance, and the wheels of heaven turned, and the captive would be set free. That's why they're called fairy tales. In the real world, hardened and cruel, there are no such interventions.

That was the moment the explosion occurred in the prison courtyard directly outside cell #26.

Chapter 1

SS Hauptmann Ernst Keppler furrowed his prominent brow. His vacant eyes strained to decipher the details of the folders spread across his dimly lit government-issued desk. He shifted uncomfortably in his chair, feeling constricted by the narrow confines of his office. Then again, the squalor of his quarters was fitting, given how far, and how fast, he had fallen from grace at the bureau. Last year at this time, the young captain and his colleagues had been the guests of *Reichsfuhrer* Himmler himself, at a winter retreat hosted in Wewelsburg Castle.

Now, he spent his days shuttling back and forth between this ramshackle outpost, and the one-bedroom flat he rented across the bridge in Wedding. Why had he been singled out? Where would he go from here? All hopes of promotion, or advancement beyond the pay grade of captain, had been permanently dashed. And he had been an ambitious man. Perhaps, given the gravity of his offense, he should just be glad that his penance wasn't worse.

He had learned that there was a pecking order to Berlin's ever-widening grift scene, and he and his colleagues had run afoul of it. His comrades, being of superior rank and connections, had offered him up as a sacrifice. As punishment, he had been banished to this remote station, and relegated to spending sleepless nights poring over an endless procession of files and dossiers. He had been cast out of his orbit around the Reich's inner circle and been forced to grovel in the darkness. And what's worse, he had come to embrace it. The demotion, which his superiors had intended for his extinction, had instead allowed him to flourish. He had read about plant species that blossomed the more tightly they were confined, and he could relate. Here in the grit and grime of Berlin's Moabit district, Ernst Keppler finally felt alive.

He had further discovered that the bleak winter months in a city distracted by the depravations of war, afforded great opportunities to those who preyed upon the unsuspecting masses. This backwater industrial ward on the far reaches of the Westhafen Canal, cloaked in perpetual darkness, granted him unfettered access to countless illicit ventures. The thought of his newly discovered license caused him to smile perversely, in spite of himself.

The captain reined in his wandering mind and returned to his drudgery. He adjusted the bulb in the flickering desktop lamp and dabbed at the perspiration on his forehead with the grimy cuff of his uniform sleeve. He needed to focus: *The files.* They were the one fixed constant in the shifting landscape of his life, the one connection between his former existence and his current position.

He rubbed the bleariness from his eyes and turned his attention to the array of documents scattered across the surface of his desk. With a methodical rhythm, he resumed the process of stamping and sorting the personnel folders. The minutes turned into hours. Occasionally, he would pause to take a draft from the glass decanter of whiskey he kept in the bottom drawer, and a hurried drag from the dwindling cigarette waning in the ashtray. The muted light from his desk lamp created unusual shadows on the peeling walls, while illuminating the slender pillar of smoke that drifted towards the stained ceiling.

He stamped each document with the official seal of the Reich Security Main Office, which was the department acronym 'RSHA', superimposed by an eagle clutching a wreathed swastika. The stamp left behind a raised, red imprint, and a wax-like residue that stuck below his fingernails. The files were then sorted to a folder earmarked for 'Relocation.' He hated that phrase. Who were they fooling? It may have started that way, back when they were relocating city residents to make space for *Minister* Speer's grandiose architectural designs, but all of those areas had long since been cleared. The mass transports east had commenced months earlier, when *Reichsmarschall* Goring had brought an official halt to emigration. And no one in Captain Keppler's department was still operating under the illusion that they were involved in a routine resettlement project. Regardless, it wasn't any skin off his back.

He hadn't always been so detached. He remembered how his hands used to tremble as he brooded over these folders. He would scrutinize the photos and case details of every assignment. He had shuddered when he first considered that his mundane duties were consigning others to a terrible fate, from the comfort of his bureau desk. The faces from the photographs of the countless subjects who inhabited the folders had haunted him. At night, they would rise from their paper dwellings, their features contorted into expressions of despair, which refused to vanish when he closed his eyes.

That was then. He coldly surveyed the mound of files before him. He no longer felt any such pangs of sympathy for the plight of those scheduled for the transports. Not even on that rare occasion when the deportee happened to be someone he knew. He was immune to it now. He had seen worse. He had done worse. He'd become accustomed to trafficking in the trade of life and death and had come to realize that in Berlin's current climate, human life simply wasn't such a valuable commodity.

A distinctive rustling pierced the still silence of the room, startling the captain from his reflections. He raised his head abruptly and leaned forward to peer into the darkness of the desolate hallway. Everything was still. He checked his watch. Aside from the security desk, the government building would be deserted at this hour, unless he had issued a special security pass for one of his regular late-night *gaste*.

The guests. They were one of the reasons Keppler's initial feelings of humiliation and disgrace over his exile had long since passed. There were numerous perks associated with the captain's increased latitude, and the most enjoyable of these gratuities invariably took place under the cover of night. He allowed his mind back off of its leash. He relished those evening vigils and the forbidden visits from…

That instant he didn't hear the rustling, so much as he felt it. It was a swirling flurry of sound and motion that had already overtaken him. Over the captain's left shoulder, a figure had swiftly emerged from the shadows. Keppler glimpsed a tattered greatcoat, dusty black military boots… *und ein Licht?* A glint of light reflected from the blade of the dagger being brandished by his obscured assailant. *That's SS issued.*

Keppler had barely managed to turn his head in response. He sat paralyzed, rooted to the spot as the dagger deftly approached his throat. The brief, cold touch of the blade to his skin evoked emotions he believed to be forever buried in the recesses of his soul. Longing... desperation... regret, all quickly yielded to resignation. And to a realization: life was much more valuable than he had imagined.

Moments later, Ernst Keppler's lifeless body lay slumped across his cluttered desk. A pool of his blood cascaded over the congregation of personnel files, mingling with the rabble whose lives the captain had previously presided over with such indifference. In the torrential flow of blood from his gaping neck wound, a small tributary of the florid liquid diverged from the mainstream, slowly filling in the borders of the raised red seal on the last folder he would ever stamp.

Chapter 2

Earlier that evening, at precisely thirteen minutes before midnight, special unit *IzB* had gone active. *IzB* had rarely been utilized since their return from the Eastern Front, as only the most critical security breaches required the services of the elite task force. Less than a month prior they had still been attached to *Einsatzgruppe C* under *Brigadefuhrer* Otto Rasch, and stationed with the Sixth Army outside Kiev as part of Operation Barbarossa. There, General Rasch's unit had been tasked with flushing out Soviet infiltrators and operatives in the occupied territories, and eliminating them by any means necessary.

Elimination: it was both their job description and their specialty. The squad's unparalleled proficiency in this arena had earned them the attention of someone far up the *SS* chain of command, who had envisioned a use for their lethal skill set back in Berlin.

But who? Who had the power and authority to disband an essential wartime unit from their Russian outpost, and reconstitute them as a privatized killing squad? They didn't know the answer themselves. They had bypassed the normal period of debriefing and decompression. They still took orders directly from their commanding officer, but who was he ultimately answerable to? Did even *Obergruppenfuhrer* Heydrich, the man in charge of the Reich's vast *SD* intelligence apparatus and the supreme commander of all of its Einstazgruppen units, know of their existence? Not likely. They only knew that their chief handler identified himself by the call sign *die Schlange* — the snake. Otherwise, their task force operated off the grid, leaving them beyond the reach of any single Nazi agency.

This covert anonymity and immunity had led the members of *IzB* to dub themselves *der geist kader* — 'the ghost squad'. Shortly after their return to Berlin, they had eviscerated an underground network of bomb makers intent on assassinating the Fuhrer. They razed the would-be assassins' base of operations to the ground without a hint of blow back from high command, or a whisper of the operation reaching the ears of *Doktor* Goebbels and the press. And the moniker had stuck.

Tonight, der geist kader had been mobilized with a straightforward objective: locate their target, and remove him from the field of play. It was an objective for which they were ideally suited. The unexpected twist, and incentive, had come from the unlikely identity of their mark. The target was an escaped Jewish convict planning to make an attempt on the life of an *SS* officer assigned to the Moabit industrial complex. One day prior, an unidentified explosion outside a high-security prison had sprung this fugitive from Gestapo custody, and now the powers that be wanted him eliminated at all costs.

In the killing fields near Kiev, it had been customary for them to act as the judge, jury, and executioner of their captives, but the legal process normally demanded different protocols here in the capital city. Perhaps that was why their services had been enlisted this evening. After all, in a city nearly purged of Jewish influence and resources, what manner of Jew was capable not only of freeing himself from the Gestapo's grasp, but of subsequently targeting a German officer? Regardless, whoever their target was, and whatever he had done, their superiors had no interest in his apprehension. They wanted him dead and forgotten.

The unit descended upon the blighted industrial island that jutted out into the Westhafen Canal with covert precision. One detachment docked in the freight slips and fanned out past the endless rows of harbor cranes to prevent the fugitive's flight in the direction of the inland port. The main contingency had taken rooftop positions encircling the compound. Their orders were to avoid engagement with the mark, and to elude detection by the *SS* guard detachment posted at the facility. That wouldn't be a problem, as there was no visible security presence. It was immaterial anyway, as this kill was to be carried out at distance, and there were no obstacles between the unit and their amphibious extraction point. In and out.

Like clockwork the target had appeared at the expected hour, deftly navigating the nuances of the facility's perimeter. He had been there before, and knew where he was going. They would only have a matter of moments to take him down before he vanished into the maze of halls within the main building.

The unit's first marksman positioned his elbow on the roof ledge, and closed the breech of his field-issued Mauser Karabiner 98K bolt action rifle. Unlike its standard-issue counterparts, the rifle had been modified by the company machinist, and fitted with a telescopic sight. For this occasion, the sniper had also attached a *HUB-23* suppressor, to decrease the rifle's sound signature. Such measures hadn't been necessary when they had been death marching scores of Soviet and Jewish infiltrators to target practice above anti-tank trenches miles beyond earshot in the Russian wilderness, but here in the city, certain adjustments to their procedures were required.

Across the courtyard a second marksman, the fail-safe, took up an adjacent rooftop position in the event that the primary missed his mark. He never missed. They waited in silence for the signal from their radio operator. Then they received the transmission of a two-word order from dispatch that they had never heard before, at home or abroad: "*Steh auf!*" Stand down?

Chapter 3

The police cruiser crossed the Konigsdamm Bridge, and slowly merged onto the unpaved access road. The streets were void of traffic at this early hour. The car's frame rattled jarringly as it jostled across the network of rail lines that stretched out like tentacles in the direction of the port. Through the low-lying fog, a line of emergency vehicles became visible, littering the median of the north shore entrance. The driver brought the car to a rest along the shoulder of the road. His door stuck defiantly in response to the frigid temperatures. The only thing *Kriminalsekretar* Anton Faber hated more than the cold was rain. Today the aging sergeant had already been blessed with both. He forced the door open with a nudge from his shoulder, and grudgingly exited.

He pulled his coat up around his neck to shield himself from the unforgiving elements, peering through the freezing mist at the dilapidated complex of warehouses and office buildings that dotted the shoreline. On the opposite riverbank the iron foundry exhaled murky columns of smoke towards the kindred overcast sky. Faber's weathered face involuntarily winced, as he inhaled the noxious stench of the Moabit warehouse district.

The sergeant braced himself against the cold and trudged towards the drab entrance of the government building. He wordlessly flashed his *Kriminalpolizei* ID to a uniformed police officer standing watch at the exterior door, and crossed into the maze of interior hallways. He briskly swiped the rain from his jacket, attempting to shake the lingering chill of the morning air. He surveyed the entry. A vacant security desk was situated at the threshold of the building's east wing. The sight lines between the sentry post and the main door were severely obstructed, making the guard station little more than window dressing. *Why even bother?*

The watch post's barren condition stood in stark contrast to the frenetic motion of the police personnel coursing throughout the rest of the facility. Faber observed their aimless movements with an air of disdain. They were a tumultuous colony of under-trained worker ants swarming in every direction, without any awareness of jurisdictional protocols and procedure. The Reich's numerous overlapping law enforcement agencies, each answerable to a separate government department, had created a Gordian knot. *One that would be far easier to cut, than untangle.*

A young corporal from the Hannover precinct approached him with a look of recognition on his boyish face. Faber couldn't say the same.

"*Heil Hitler,* Sergeant Faber," he beamed, drawing himself to attention. "I'll let Sergeant Roth know that you're here."

Faber nodded. His gaze followed the corporal's path towards a series of glass-encased cubicles, which had been transformed into makeshift interrogation rooms for the building's tenants. There his eyes came to rest on his fellow sergeant, engaged in a somewhat heated exchange with a prospective witness. He strained until he could isolate Sergeant Roth's distinctive voice rising above the din of activity in the hollow chambers. Faber shook his head and smiled at his young comrade's enthusiasm. He had always had a penchant for theatrics, so a good interrogation was right up his alley. In the adjoining office, the other workers who had been detained for questioning did not seem to share his amusement, as they awaited their interviews with expressions of agitation and concern.

Faber turned to a window overlooking the canal. A small barge pushing containers of coal was setting off from the port in the direction of Wedding. *Coal in the winter it makes a home glow.* He recalled the advertising jingle his mother used to hum when he was a child, as she lit the kitchen stove. With the shortage of coal rations and the severity of the weather, there wouldn't be many homes glowing in Berlin this winter. Dozens of deadly cases of exposure had already been reported in recent weeks. *People dying of cold right in their own homes. Maybe the war effort isn't going as well as we're being led to believe?*

He reflexively lit a cigarette, and stared vacuously at the rain spattering against a pane of glass. A rivulet of water flowed steadily through a leak in the window frame, further discoloring the faded wall. He heard Roth's approaching footsteps, followed closely by his booming baritone.

"Anton. I'm sorry to call you out so early."

"What do you have so far?"

"A single homicide. One victim, named Keppler..." Roth said, pausing, *"ein SS Hauptsturmfuhrer* Ernst Keppler."

"An SS Captain!?" Faber asked, unable to hide his surprise.

Roth nodded, motioning towards a staircase at the far end of the entrance hall, "His body was found in a third level office, throat slit. A member of the building's janitorial crew found him a little before 6am, and alerted the security desk. An Order Police corporal out of the Moabit precinct was the first to arrive on the scene, and then *Orpo* called it in to us."

Faber sensed the familiar ring of warning alarms echoing in the back of his head. His mind wrestled with the identification of the victim. The murder of an *SS* captain was disconcerting. He tried to focus, "Why would a *janitor* have to find the body in a building with its own security detachment? They asleep at the switch?"

"Good question," Roth shrugged. "The building's security is commissioned by the *SS*, and they work in eight-hour shifts. The guard on duty said he saw Captain Keppler working at his desk during a routine walk-through around midnight."

They ascended the ensuing flights to the third story in silence. The fragile hand railing shuddered at their touch, its mounts pulling free from the stained walls as they climbed the last row of stairs in the untended stairwell. For an outpost quartering *SS* personnel, the complex was in an appalling state of disrepair. It didn't add up.

"What in the hell was an SS officer doing working in a derelict building like this anyway?" Faber fumed.

"We haven't been granted access to his personnel files yet, so we don't have much to go on," Roth answered. "Captain Keppler had a flat across the bridge in Wedding, so I sent a few of our agents to check his place out, and talk to his neighbors…"

The young sergeant's briefing was interrupted by an excited shout echoing up from the first floor. Faber recognized the voice as that of the young Orpo agent who had met him at the entrance.

"Sergeant Roth?!"

"*Ja?*"

"Excuse the interruption, Herr Sergeant, but Captain Keppler's secretary has arrived," the agent bellowed up the stairwell.

"*Gut,* I'll be right down," Roth called back to him, his anticipation evident. "I've been waiting for her to show. Go on up, Anton, Sergeant Lang is canvassing the scene. He can show you around."

Faber nodded. He watched the young sergeant exuberantly descend the stairs two at a time. *Youth, whoever said it was 'wasted on the wrong people' didn't know Emil Roth.*

Faber continued in the direction of the voices echoing from the far end of the third floor. The hallway's high ceiling and narrow walls, absent any external windows, created a disorienting tunnel-effect. The main corridor opened into a sequence of small, nondescript offices, configured in similar designs. Each featured a single door off the main hall, and a sealed two by three-foot window, which, depending on the side of the building, overlooked either the canal or the port warehouses. Grime and soot had collected on the windowpanes, until they had turned opaque. Keppler's generic quarters would have been nearly indistinguishable from its counterparts, if not for the collection of police personnel huddled around its entrance.

Faber instantly spotted Sergeant Lang, his gaunt, spindling frame towering a full head taller than the rest. He was in the midst of an animated exchange with a squat Orpo photographer. The photographer disdainfully held his ground, despite giving up nearly a foot in height to the sergeant. Lang's posture gave him the appearance of a long-necked mother bird trying to placate her quarreling chicks. Faber liked Lang. The rest of the group he recognized as technicians from their forensics lab.

At the sound of the sergeant's approach the heated confab quickly dispersed. The photographer hastily retreated with his equipment into the vacant office across the hall, as Lang greeted his superior with an overly ceremonious show of attention.

"Heil Hitler, Kriminalsekretar Faber," he bellowed. "Orpo sent a photographer over to document the crime scene, but I told him no pictures until you give the say-so."

"That's alright, let him come in."

Faber didn't recollect this particular photographer, but he knew the commanding officer at the Schumannstrasse Orpo branch. They ran a tight ship, and were always cooperative. Didn't hurt to throw them a bone. He liked to accommodate professionalism, and found that professional courtesy had a way of coming back around.

Lang opened the door to Captain Keppler's suite, holding back to allow Faber time to gage the layout of the office, before following him in. Lang was closely shadowed by the small detachment from the lab, and the Orpo photographer who tentatively brought up the rear.

"Alright, have at it," Faber barked. "See what prints you can pull from doors, drawers, handles. Photograph the body and scene from every angle and take note of anything that appears to have been pried, moved, or gone missing."

Faber moved towards the corpse, as the agents sprang into action. His eyes settled on the body sprawled awkwardly across the desk at the center of the room. Moving closer, he crouched beside the desk, and tilted his head upwards to better survey the captain's fatal wound from below. The distractions of the surrounding activity faded into nothingness, as he scrutinized the gash. *His death would have been nearly instantaneous. One blow finished this encounter.* At length, he sensed Sergeant Lang hovering over his shoulder. Lang cleared his throat before breaking his superior's concentration.

"We estimate his time of death to be somewhere between 1:00am and 3:00am this morning, probably on the latter side. Building security reported seeing him working during a sweep they conducted around midnight."

"Sounds like 'building security' consists of one guard, who may or may not have narcolepsy," Faber offered without looking up. "Of course, if I were assigned to this dump, I might consider sleeping through my shifts too."

"Undoubtedly."

"Between 1:00am and 3:00am? What business was so pressing that it had the Captain here logging such hours? Doesn't sound like the MO of your standard *SS* bureaucrat to me. Anyone else see him late last night?"

Lang hesitated, "A call operator working late in the office across the hall stated that she saw Captain Keppler on the phone when she left around 10pm, but that she thought nothing of it. She said it wasn't unusual for him to keep such late hours, or even sleep at the office."

"*Wohl*, this was his last office sleepover."

Faber stood up. His eyes squinted at the interval flicker and glare of the police photographer's recurrent camera flash. He turned his attention to the documents littering the table's surface around the victim's body. They had overflowed the boundaries of the desk in every direction, spilling onto the office floor. They poured out of desk drawers and filing cabinets alike, covering the floor like blood-stained patches of snow. The files had obviously been rifled through with painstaking attention, but otherwise there was surprisingly little site disturbance. *The office isn't in disarray because of a struggle — there hadn't been one — but you'd never know by the looks of it. The culprit must have turned the place upside down after killing the captain. And with hours between when Keppler was last seen alive, and when his body was found, he'd have had plenty of time to look. But what was he looking for?*

"This was quick and clean. The victim most likely never saw it coming, and wouldn't have been able to do much about it even if he had," Faber concluded. "The assailant was skilled in the use of the murder weapon, most likely a long knife or dagger. After dispatching the victim, the perpetrator exhaustively scoured the contents."

Faber paused, the delivery of his postmortem interrupted by the heavy reverberation of fast-approaching footsteps in the hallway. The rapid footfalls heralded the return of Sergeant Roth at the open door. The sergeant's expression was visibly unsettled. He gestured to Faber in an agitated manner, that belied the hushed tone of his voice, "Herr Kriminalsekretar Faber, I need to have a word with you, *bitte.*"

Faber ignored the questioning stares of the other agents, and followed his colleague out into the hallway. Roth closed the office door behind them, and anxiously scanned the corridor, before speaking.

"We've got Captain Keppler's secretary downstairs," he started, breathlessly.

"Right?"

"Turns out Keppler wasn't just some low-level *SS* officer

toiling in obscurity out here in the sticks. He was just transferred here from the Gestapo two months ago!"

"He's Gestapo?"

"And before his recent demotion he had attained the rank of *SS Sturmbannfuhrer*, serving as a chief liaison between the Gestapo and *SS* Administration," Roth continued, pausing briefly to take a breath. "He's also got a high-level security clearance, which makes…"

"Makes this crime scene *klassifiziert*." Faber interjected, grasping the potential repercussions.

"And sets us up for *eine Holle* of a jurisdictional dispute with the Gestapo," Roth added. "Not to mention, there's a distinct possibility that the documents on display in his office may require a clearance we don't even have."

Faber quickly weighed the information. *Never a dull day.* He rubbed his forehead forcefully, wishing he could physically wring the solution from his mind. When in doubt, he preferred to err on the side of decisiveness. Half measures always left one of your flanks exposed.

"Alright, send one of your men to Kripo headquarters to inform *Kriminaldirektor* Brunner. Better yet, go yourself. I don't want the chief to be blind-sided by any of this. I'll assume active control of the site, until I hear back from you."

Be deliberate while making a decision, but once it's made, be bold. That's what his first commanding officer had always told him, and he had rarely regretted it.

He pushed open the door to Keppler's office with purpose, not hesitating long enough to witness Sergeant Roth's acknowledgement of his orders, or his hasty departure. Lang's agents hadn't bothered to resume their canvassing since the interruption. The collective expectation was visible in each face.

Faber motioned for Lang, "Sergeant Lang, change of approach. I want the entire building sealed off and regarded as a crime scene. No law enforcement admitted from any agency until I get word from the Kriminaldirektor."

"*Verstanden.*"

"Anyone reporting for work has their work pass and identity papers checked, and is detained for questioning. Verstanden?"

"Of course, Herr Kriminalsekretar."

Faber noticed the look of doubt lingering behind Lang's words of consent, and he understood. Sealing off the building to other agencies of interest, even in the short-term, was no small task. His orders could trigger a firestorm that spread far beyond the reaches of Kripo, but he felt confident in Lang's compliance and abilities. And at the end of the day, his job was to preserve evidence and the integrity of the crime scene. He was too old to care about interagency disputes. He never had a nose for politics anyway. He was a police officer.

He turned to admonish the remainder of Lang's unit, his voice rising to the occasion, "Alright, clear the room. Access to this office is restricted to Kriminalpolizei brass only, until further notice. You'll receive appropriate clearance when, and if, it's granted."

Faber spotted the Orpo photographer, hurriedly packing up his equipment, and singled him out to Sergeant Lang, "And get him out of here. Some of these files may be klassifiziert!" Professional courtesy only extended so far.

The photographer flashed a brief glare of discontent in the sergeant's direction, but quickly conceded the battle and turned to follow the other agents into the corridor. His hasty retreat was met at the door by Faber's unyielding, outstretched arm.

"*Und die Kamera* stays!"

Ears still ringing. Vision is blurred, or are my eyes just caked with dust? My body is riddled with too many pains to single one out. But none of the wounds are lethal. It's good to have the cover of darkness. It hides my bloodstained face, and my debris-covered clothes from the prying stares of every passerby. Would they even notice? Amidst this chaos and carnage would I even stand out? No matter, I'll be off the main streets soon. What is it, another five kilos? But it will take longer in the dark, especially if I wind my way through the back roads and along the rail lines.

The acrid smell of burning gas is getting stronger. I'm heading the right way. They finally hit the gas works, after how many attempts? But what had caused my explosion? My explosion? Was it mine? Was it meant for me? The blast that crumbled my cell wall, and left the prison guard unconscious? Or was he dead? I didn't bother to check. The explosion radius, and the size of the crater it left in the prison yard, was caused by a large ordnance, but not large enough to be a bomb. So, what was it? A flak shell that had misfired and failed to detonate at altitude? It wouldn't be the first time. Flak fire was causing more damage to the city than enemy bombs of late. But what were the odds? Right at that moment? Right outside my cell? Coincidence? Nein! The margin for error in matters of life-and-death was too close to write off events as coincidence. At what cost have I finally learned that lesson? It had to be a flak shell. How fitting would that be?

How many times had I cursed the construction of the concrete monstrosity whose massive footings had been laid in the park that spring? The maples and oaks leveled. The park grounds cleared. All to better support the buttressed concrete walls that housed the behemoth's system of bunkers and shelters and command posts. Its permanent cranes marred the skylines. Day and night their tentacles hoisted the endless supply of building materials, and then munitions, up to the platforms atop the vast fortification. Then over the past months, the tetrad of gun towers that rose some six or seven stories above ground, had emerged from behind the last of the park's remaining trees. All within earshot, better yet eyeshot, of my home. Our home. I hated that commotion. Hated that our neighborhood park, where meine familie picnicked and meine kinder had learned to swim, had been transformed into a military installation.

Had those repellent 128cm anti-aircraft guns, encircled by their contingency of ack-acks, now been the source of my deliverance? The same guns that nightly rattled my house, and every home in the district, to their very foundations? Had one of their shells returned to the ground undetonated until the moment of impact? And within moments of my twisted attempt at a prayer? Nein! Even more than coincidence, I can't abide the idea of divine intervention. Not after what I've seen. If my deliverance came from above, it came from six or seven stories high, and no more!

Chapter 4

The *Kriminaldirektor* ran his hand through the silver locks of his receding hairline, while the briefing from his adjutant Major Kaufmann faded to a distant drone. He swiveled his leather chair to look out the window of his fifth story office overlooking Werdescher Market. The ornate seat had been a gift from his wife on his promotion to department chief last winter. The plush reupholstered chair, dating from the Wilhelmine era, was the one luxury he afforded himself in his otherwise austere office. *A man had to have a comfortable place to sit.* From his vantage point he could see that the Reichsbank was opening for business, and the streets of the financial district were slowly coming to life on the cold winter morning.

He had started the day like every other, with a predawn walk along the Spree Canal, and a stop at his favorite coffee house. He was a creature of habit and routine. He liked his coffee black, no sugar, no cream, and certainly no ersatz substitutes. From there he had walked through the streets of the old market, stopping to study the twin-towered facade of the Friedrichwerdersche church. He no longer attended services there, as that sort of sentiment was frowned upon by his superiors.

He didn't mind. He prided himself in his adaptability to change. It was this adaptability that had earned Oberst Karl

Brunner the nickname 'the chameleon', and more importantly had allowed the colonel to survive and advance through nearly a decade of purges and regime change in the police bureaucracy. He had been a witness to it all. Power struggles and interagency battles of will had been waged to gain control of Germany's formidable police apparatus, and in the end Reichsfuhrer Himmler, and his confederate Obergruppenfuhrer Heydrich, had emerged victorious.

Brunner's predecessors had largely either been sacked, jailed, or killed, but he had been promoted. That sort of intrigue didn't matter much to him, and maybe that's why he had always emerged unscathed. He was a policeman, not a politician. And even though he had risen to a position where he now answered only to Germany's most senior Kriminalpolizei officer, Arthur Nebe, whose perpetually vacant office sat just across the hall from his own, Brunner still remembered himself as the young patrolman who walked the beat in this same district decades before. That was how the people of Werdescher thought of him too, he liked to imagine. That was how you survived change without selling your soul. *Adapt to your environment, but remain the same man on the inside.*

A knock at the door interrupted Brunner's reminiscences. He had anticipated the arrival of Sergeant Roth, and knew that he was to be the bearer of bad news. He reminded himself of the old adage about not killing the messenger. He liked Emil Roth. This precinct could use more like him. He also prided himself on knowing the personal situation and circumstances of each of his men. Sergeant Roth was no exception. The young, recently married homicide inspector had just welcomed his first child into the world, a baby girl. *Emily, or was it Amelie?* The family hoped she would be the first of several additions, but Roth hadn't allowed anything in his personal life to distract from his job. Brunner appreciated that. Roth had a shrewd mind for detection, but his biggest assets were his heart and his sense of loyalty. If he could steer clear of the political pitfalls that cluttered the landscape of this job, the young master sergeant had a bright future.

"Sergeant Roth, I understand you've had an eventful morning?" Brunner said, motioning for the sergeant to join them.

"That would be safe to say, Herr Colonel."

"Major Kaufmann has already briefed me on the details of Captain Keppler's demise. But I'd be interested in hearing your initial findings?"

"This is Kriminalsekretar Faber's preliminary report from the scene, at this stage it's pretty bare bones," Roth responded, placing a folder on the edge of Brunner's desk.

"Do you have any background information on the victim, aside from his official dossier?"

"We've petitioned the Reich Security Main Office for release of the victim's *SS* personnel folder... so far, without success."

Brunner nodded knowingly. He didn't expect the RSHA to be overly cooperative, and had already caught wind of the looming jurisdictional dispute. Gone were the days of law enforcement agencies sharing information, and of old-fashioned police work. But he still knew where, and how, to pull the appropriate strings. He glanced absently through the contents of the file.

"I'll have Major Kaufmann contact 'Personnel' to solicit any pertinent files on Captain Keppler."

36

"Thank you, Herr Colonel."

"An *SS* office located off the grid, whose existence we didn't even know about?" Major Kaufmann interjected. "How is it secured?"

"Minimally, Herr Major. There's an ID checkpoint at the entrance, manned by a rotation of *SS* guards. The guard desk kept a written log of all authorized office personnel and visitors."

"You've taken this log into evidence?" the major continued.

"We have, but by all accounts, it wasn't well maintained, and there were numerous ways around it."

"Such as?"

"Well, according to his co-workers, Captain Keppler frequently issued 'guest passes', which could be shown at the desk in lieu of producing proper identification. This allowed him to circumvent the clearance process, and undermines the reliability of the log."

The sergeant's briefing was derailed by the sounds of a loud verbal exchange in the hall. A rapid procession of knocks ensued, and the door to the office swung sharply open on its hinges. Leading the incursion were regional Gestapo chief *Standartenführer* Victor Schonbern, and his adjutant Major Weskamp. A small contingency of Gestapo agents followed closely in their wake. Colonel Schonbern scanned the proceedings with a glare, and hastily dismissed his agents back into the corridor with a wave of his hand. He ceremoniously removed his black cap and gloves in silence. His tall, lithe figure cast an imposing shadow over the office. The Gestapo colonel's piercing deep-set eyes, framed behind aquiline features, surveyed the contents and inhabitants of the office haughtily.

"Heil Hitler!" Kaufmann and Roth offered in unison, vaulting to attention.

"Heil Hitler," Schonbern nodded distractedly, extending his hand to Brunner.

"Let's dispense with the formalities. Shall we? Karl, it's good to see you. Forgive our abrupt intrusion. You remember Major Weskamp."

"Victor, Major Weskamp," Brunner nodded, offering a welcoming smile, as if unaffected by the affront. "I believe you've both met my adjutant, Major Kaufmann. And this is Sergeant Roth."

"Gentlemen."

"Sergeant Roth, that will be all for now," Brunner said, with a wink, before returning his attention to his uninvited guests.

"Karl, I came here in person, to avoid any confusion. I'd like to extinguish any potential inter-agency disputes, as quickly as possible," Schonbern resumed, taking a seat across the desk from Brunner.

"We're in total agreement," Brunner concurred. He always liked to accommodate the first point of any negotiation.

"There's no need to further escalate the already heightened tensions between our departments. However, this morning several of my agents were restricted from inspecting the site where one of our own officers was slain last night."

"Herr Colonel, if I may," Major Kaufmann intervened. "Restricting access was simply a temporary procedural measure taken to protect the integrity of the scene. Since our men were the first to respond, we felt that our jurisdiction..."

Schonbern flinched in his seat. His eyes darted in the

major's direction like a rabid wolf eyeing a rabbit that has unwittingly crossed his path. He managed to halt Major Kaufmann's response as much with his scowl as with the interposition of his rising voice.

"I see where you're heading Major, but let's set aside your claims for now," the colonel exclaimed, his face reddening. "Because, at this moment, a former *Gestapo* officer lies brutally murdered, amidst a mountain of classified *Gestapo* documents, on the premises of a *Gestapo* outpost! So, pardon me if I don't give a warm handshake in hell about your 'procedural measures' or claims of 'jurisdiction!'"

"Victor, let's keep this civil," Brunner interceded, his voice as placid as his pale blue eyes. "Major Weskamp, would you and Major Kaufmann excuse us? I'd like to speak to Colonel Schonbern, alone."

Brunner could see that his adjutant was visibly shaken by the exchange. It was best to extricate him from the situation. Major Weskamp sat motionless, eyes fixed on Schonbern like a schoolboy waiting for permission to go to the urinal. The colonel muttered his approval. Both officers exited hastily, without making eye contact. A silence settled over the chamber.

"I apologize for the outburst, Karl."

"It's alright. I expect that you're already taking a lot of heat over this, and I can imagine why."

"What do you mean?" Schonbern asked.

"Well, obviously, anytime a high-ranking officer is killed in a secure location, there's going to be scrutiny from above."

"Of course, but I'm not sure I'd call Keppler 'high-ranking.'"

"No? I was under the impression that until recently

Keppler had attained the rank of full major?" Brunner responded. "Before his demotion and dismissal from the Gestapo for 'misconduct' that is."

Schonbern shifted uncomfortably in his chair. Brunner pretended not to notice that his sleight of hand had caused the colonel discomfort. Information could be used for leverage, even when it was incomplete. If he was lucky, Schonbern might just fill in the outline for him in the process.

The Gestapo colonel hesitated before he replied, "That's right, he was dismissed in light of his activities in *der Schwarzmarkt.*"

The black market? Brunner could smell the manure Schonbern was stacking. A Gestapo officer involved with the black market was as commonplace as flies in a barnyard. There was bound to be more to Captain Keppler's dismissal, but Brunner didn't want to press his hand further. He went into every situation with an idea of what a tactical victory looked like. In this case, that would be an easing of tensions with the Gestapo, even as he convinced them to cede control of the investigation. Given Schonbern's apparent unease with Captain Keppler's past transgressions, he saw an opportunity for the desired outcome, and angled for it.

"So, what's your primary concern, Victor?" Brunner probed. "Do you think that my officers would use this information to paint a picture of rampant Gestapo activity in der Schwarzmarkt?"

"Any number of possibilities exist given the discord between the agencies. It wouldn't be the first time one aired the other's dirty linen."

"The details of Captain Keppler's discharge won't see the light of day, except in relation to the case. The men I have assigned to this are focused on criminal detection, not propaganda," Brunner replied pointedly.

"Of course," Schonbern assented. "Listen, Karl, I don't know who wanted to eliminate Ernst Keppler, but I do know that his dealings with the criminal element in der Schwarzmarkt made him enemies within the Gestapo, and the underground."

"I imagine it would."

"All I'm asking is for some discretion from the officers handling the investigation. Grant me that assurance, and I'll defer to your judgment."

"You will?"

"For now," Schonbern affirmed, managing a thin smile.

Brunner returned a broad smile, and extended his hand across the desk, graciously accepting the colonel's concession. Then he played the card he had been holding close to his vest, the one he had always intended to lay down last.

"As chance would have it, we have a skilled young *Kriminalinspektor* transferring into our department this week. His father and I served together, before he was killed in the line of duty, so I can personally vouch for him. You want an outsider to agency politics who doesn't have an axe to grind, and I want a newcomer whom I can control. As it happens, Lieutenant Konrad Brandt is both."

Chapter 5

The unwelcome visitation had plagued Konrad Brandt's dreams with increasing frequency. It was always the same. No matter how he would try to quiet and clear his mind before closing his eyes, it arrived veiled in a customary shroud of inscrutable fog. The shapeless, ghastly haze issued forth from the land it inhabited between the last moments of wakefulness, and the promised respite of sleep. The vapor emitted the same pale, sickly light found in that forsaken hour where night gasped its dying breath, before reluctantly giving way to the dawn. *The same time of night I got the call saying Papa had passed away.* He shivered in his sleep. The fog made him feel cold and sterile, casting its dreary pall over everyone and everything within the landscape of his dreams.

The obscuring mist receded, allowing him to gain a sense of his surroundings. He was overlooking a schoolyard. His eyes strained to bring the images into focus below him. He pressed his face against the frosted windowpane, peering out onto the school terrace. The glass was cold against his cheek. Through a curtain of sleet and snow, he could make out a solitary figure hanging from a steel beam in the yard. It was a young man. His battered face was twisted in an agonizing grimace as he writhed. A pair of black-uniformed sentries monitored the proceedings from his dangling feet. Brandt felt himself shudder again. He recognized the young man. He tried to move towards him but couldn't. He was rooted to the spot. The more he strained to draw close, the more distant and detached he became. He felt a shifting sensation, as though the ground were moving beneath him, and heard a sharp metallic, grating sound. He startled, awake.

Brandt stirred from his troubled slumber, roused by the slam of a compartment door. The resounding thud chased the haunting images away. He closed his eyes tightly, and fought to bring the fading impression back into focus. He now strained to summon the return of the faceless silhouettes and the impenetrable gloom he had previously wished to banish. As was often the case with his dreams, his efforts achieved the opposite effect. The more he labored to recall the details of the vision, the more clouded the scene became. He wondered if the blinding barrier of fog wasn't an invention of his own mind? Perhaps it was a defense mechanism his subconscious had adopted to protect him from confronting the traumatic spectacle? *Had it been foggy that day?* There was so much that he couldn't remember. *Or wouldn't?* Perhaps he didn't really want to recollect the morose details in the first place? *What am I hiding from?*

His thoughts were interrupted by the jostling motion of the train as it ground to a slow halt. *Another stop?* Brandt straightened himself, trying to relieve the discomfort in his neck. His head had been resting awkwardly against the window, his face pressed against the glass, just as it had been in his dream. He raised the blackout curtain slightly. The darkened landscape crawled past his window beneath the clear winter sky. He looked at his watch. It was the middle of the night. *We're still hours from Berlin.*

He lowered the curtain, troubled by the lingering effects

of the dream. He ardently rubbed his weary blue eyes, as if he could wipe away the vision once and for all. He squinted, acclimating himself to his surroundings.

An elderly porter had entered the darkened train compartment. Row by row, he roused passengers in the front of the car to check their tickets. The old man's task wouldn't take long, as this section of the train was half-empty. The overnight line from Munich to Berlin didn't draw much traffic in the dead of winter, especially in wartime. Brandt ran a hand through his closely cropped blonde hair in frustration. At their current rate of travel, he figured the aged ticket collector could probably outpace the train to Berlin in a foot race.

As the porter approached his seat Brandt reached inside his jacket to retrieve his stub. His movements exposed the Kriminalpolizei warrant disc attached to his belt. His eyes tracked the old man's gaze as it settled on the badge. The night porter briskly withdrew his hand and offered Brandt an awkward smile. As the smile faded, he mumbled an inaudible benediction in a thick Bavarian accent, and gestured that there would be no need for him to present his ticket.

"What's the delay, Herr *Schaffner*?" Brandt inquired, as the man shuffled past.

"Bombing raid took out a section of rail up ahead. We're being rerouted."

"That's a little close for comfort," Brandt replied.

"You're telling me, I work this route five days a week," the old man muttered, returning to his duties.

"What's our new arrival time?"

"We're scheduled to arrive in Berlin, by way of the Anhalter Bahnhof, around daybreak," he replied over his shoulder without looking back.

Brandt continued to watch the peculiar envoy, as his

unsteady gate carried him into the adjoining compartment and the next stop on his late-night paper collecting pilgrimage. The Brits' bombing raids had been less frequent near the capital so far this winter. The number and severity of the raids had decreased from the high watermark of the previous year, but they still happened with enough regularity to create a constant sense of unease in the minds of the German people. Goring and Goebbels had taken to the airwaves in broadcast after broadcast, assuring them that no bomb would ever touch Berlin's civilian population. That fragile illusion had been shattered last December when convoys of British Whitleys and Wellingtons had appeared over the capital city in force. A defensive liability by daylight, the British bombers had resorted to long-range nighttime raids. The long winter nights gave the Brits extended periods of darkness to launch their nightly sorties. For hours the air raid sirens would resound most evenings, as the fleet of bombers dropped their massive ordinance around the capital. No district of the city had escaped unscathed, and everyone had been on pins and needles ever since.

The lights flickered in the compartment as the train lurched forward. *Finally.* Brandt lifted the curtain, and glanced at his watch. *4:15am.* Any of the raiding parties would have ended hours ago, and the *'alles klar'* would have been given for people to return to their homes. He closed his eyes. His mind wavered between his anxious thoughts and exhaustion. Fatigue quickly won the battle. Above all else, he felt tired. Sleep had not come easily of late, nor had it arrived bearing the customary gifts of comfort and restoration. Tonight, had been no different. He felt the car sway as the locomotive began to gain speed. He reclined his seat, and restlessly waited for the motion of the train to lull him back to sleep.

Chapter 6

After hours of delay, the southern boroughs of Berlin were finally materializing through the morning fog. Brandt shifted expectantly in his seat. The passing scenery became increasingly developed and familiar. With the familiarity came a flood of memories and emotions. Travel on the rail to Berlin was a trip he had always made with his father. Remembering was bittersweet.

As the number of tracks increased south of the city, he could see Viktoria Park off in the distance. He had hiked to the top of the park's Mount Kreuzberg countless times with his father as a child. Upon reaching the top, they would visit Schinkel's War Memorial, where his father would marvel over the monument's design and regale him with tales of the Prussian generals who had defeated Napoleon at Leipzig. William Frederick III had renamed the mount — and in the process the entire district — Kreuzberg out of deference to the massive iron cross protruding from the hilltop monument. *Cross Hill.* Standing on that hillside with his father, taking in the sweeping views of the city, and filled with thoughts of nobility and valor, Brandt had known that the world was a beautiful place. Now, he wasn't so sure.

He sat back in his seat, lost in his thoughts. When the train passed beneath the Monumenten Strasse overpass, he craned his neck to make out the outline of two U-shaped sandstone buildings emerging from the tree line. There was the Kesseldorf Strasse police precinct, where his father had been stationed for as long as he could remember. Across the street from the precinct-house was the cemetery where he had been buried. Brandt felt numb, no less so than the day it had happened. *If I went to his office would everything look the same? Aside from a plaque on the wall, would there be any sign that he'd ever even been there? The place he'd given his entire life to?* He pushed these thoughts out of his mind and tried to focus on his impending arrival and re-assignment.

The tracks widened further still as they passed the Anhalter freight and goods stations, and the train veered slowly and jarringly to the westernmost line of rails. Watching supplies being loaded onto the freight cars, he was again reminded of one of his father's history lessons. "Berlin has always been a city of walls and soldiers," he'd say, quoting some historian whose name Brandt couldn't remember.

The city had once been encompassed by a customs wall with 18 gates serving as points of entry and exit. These gates allowed the authorities to levy taxes upon citizens, while protecting the city from smugglers. As a child Brandt had thrilled to the stories of bandits and smugglers being chased through the city gates and apprehended. Perhaps it was then that he had first dreamed of following in his father's footsteps and becoming a police officer?

Here at Anhalter, where one of the city's original gates had been placed, now stood one of the world's largest train terminals, the Anhalter Bahnhof. The city gate that once granted access and exit to hundreds of German peasants a day on the road to the tiny town of Anhalt, was now a portal for millions to all points south across the entire continent of

Europe. *Or at least it had been prior to the outbreak of war.*

To the east, Brandt saw a clearing where multiple tunnels had been burrowed for a proposed *U-Bahn* connection. Those tunnels were intended to further enhance Berlin's already unequaled system of elevated and underground trains, but the project looked as if it had been abandoned. *Another casualty of war, like so many of the Reich's other grand aspirations.* Just a few years earlier Albert Speer had publicized his lofty plans for re-branding Berlin as the architectural capital of Europe. Designs had been drafted, plans had been submitted, land had been cleared, and swaths of the population had been relocated. But as the war entered its fourth year, those plans now sat as dormant and abandoned as the unfinished train tunnel. And Speer had since traded in his title as the Reich's chief architect to become Minister of Armaments and Munitions! *That says it all.*

Across the Landwehr Canal the imposing train shed of the Anhalter Bahnhof came into view, eclipsing the horizon with its enormous vaulted roof. After what seemed like an eternity, his train grudgingly drew to a halt at the platform. He quickly exited the near-empty car and followed the signs towards the baggage compartment. The rows of empty platforms seemed inordinately desolate, giving the terminal a hollow feel despite all of its splendor. *Winter and wartime, the two great enemies of leisure travel.*

Most of the terminal's passengers that morning appeared to be Berliners taking city trains to work. Brandt felt a vague sensation of being out of place, like accidentally walking into the wrong store when shopping. He brushed off the fleeting impression, and with a shake of his head moved to retrieve his luggage. A young porter handed him his bags, in exchange for his claims ticket, and Brandt barely broke stride as he exited platform B in the direction of the main portico. The hands of the ornate clock above the exit indicated it was 11:15am, nearly four hours past his scheduled arrival time. *The Fuhrer may have gotten the trains to run on time as the saying went, but the war had other ideas.*

Brandt exited the terminal onto Askanischer Platz. A two-tiered bus was emptying its passengers onto the sidewalk in front of the ticket-window. He moved past the growing crowd towards the median in search of an on-duty transit cab. Across the bustling Saarlander Strasse, a row of green city cabs lined the entrance of the Hotel Excelsior. Word was that the owner of the luxury resort had fallen into the bad graces of the Fuhrer himself and had fled the country, leaving the hotel to be operated by the Reich. *If the war goes badly, they can always open up an inn.* His eyes scanned the building's impressive stone edifice. In his peripheral he caught sight of an officer moving intently in his direction, flanked by two soldiers.

"Lieutenant Brandt?" the officer called down the sidewalk.

"Yes, Herr Major?"

Brandt couldn't hide his expression of surprise at being recognized in an unfamiliar city. He felt a flush come over him, as if the approaching officers had overheard the irreverence of his running internal dialogue. He lowered his bags to the sidewalk to offer a salute.

"I'm Major Kaufmann from Criminal Police headquarters. I'm Kriminaldirektor Brunner's adjutant," the major smiled, extending his hand. "My men can see to your bags."

"*Danke,* Major," Brandt managed, releasing the handles

to his baggage. "But I wasn't expecting to report until tomorrow."

"It was originally our intention to give you more time to get acclimated to your new surroundings," Kaufmann nodded, gesturing for Brandt to follow him back across the street, "but a matter has arisen which requires immediate attention. In fact, if you'll accompany me, we have a car waiting."

Brandt cast a last uncertain glance back at the Anhalter terminal. Brunow's sculpture of *Night and Day* looked out over the city from their rooftop perch. The youthful personification of Day trained his eyes hopefully upwards in the expectation of blessing from the heavens, whereas his cloaked counterpart Night closed her downcast eyes in a sullen expression of sleep. *Or was it despair?* Brandt wondered apprehensively what this day held in store for him.

Chapter 7

Brandt followed Major Kaufmann across the busy Saarlander Strasse intersection. A black Mercedes staff car idled on the curb in front of the Excelsior. He had looked right past it in his search for a cab. He chided himself for his uncharacteristic lack of observation. As they approached, a staff officer emerged from the driver's seat, and briskly opened the rear driver's side door. The major gestured for Brandt to enter first.

Angling into the back seat, he became aware that someone else was already sitting on one side and adjusted to take the seat opposite. He found himself under the scrutinizing gaze of a distinguished looking older officer with searing grey eyes and a distinct receding hairline of matching grey locks. Brandt immediately recognized him from photographs he had seen.

"Lieutenant Brandt, this is Colonel Karl Brunner, Kriminaldirektor of the Berlin Kriminalpolizei," Kaufmann said, as he entered from the passenger's side.

"Heil Hitler, Colonel," Brandt stammered, instantly feeling ill-prepared for the meeting.

Brunner nodded in a manner that conveyed understanding and gave a signal to the driver. The Mercedes started with a jolt and merged into the steady flow of traffic on Saarlander Strasse in the direction of the city center.

"Lieutenant Brandt, I've been looking forward to meeting you. I had a great deal of respect for your father. I'm sorry for your loss," Brunner said, with a warmth that Brandt interpreted as genuine.

"Danke, Herr Colonel."

"I hope you'll excuse the unorthodox welcome to Berlin but given the nature of the events which have transpired over the past 24 hours, it was advisable for us to brief you in the most expedient manner possible."

"What events are those?"

"The events surrounding your first assignment as a member of the Berlin Kriminalpolizei. Major Kaufmann has a copy of the preliminary report for you," Brunner replied, waiting for his adjutant to present the file before continuing. "This morning an *SS* Hauptsturmfuhrer named Ernst Keppler was brutally murdered in his office at a Reich Security outpost. A declassified background file on Captain Keppler is contained within your report."

Brandt nodded. He felt the world spinning around him. The lurching motion of the train throughout the night, the zipping of the car through city streets, the whirring of Colonel Brunner's words and the gravity of the situation, all conspired against his ability to concentrate. He tried to focus, but his gaze distracted him.

Through the rear window, he could see the distant outline of the Reich Security Main Office peering out from behind the Ministry of Labor as their vehicle crossed over Prinz Albrecht Strasse. The building of this command center had signified the consolidation of all of Germany's police, security, and intelligence services, into a single apparatus answerable to one man: The Reichsfuhrer, Heinrich Himmler. That coup had created a massive centralization of power, and a logistical nightmare for the average police officer his father had said. *I wonder if Colonel Brunner shares those sentiments. He knew my father. Even so, neither would ever acknowledge it to anyone beyond their closest confidant.* He returned his focus to the file on Ernst Keppler.

"Your men move fast, as it appears Captain Keppler has been dead less than 12 hours," Brandt responded.

"Working in a security building may have led to the quick discovery of the victim's body. The lead investigators on the scene to this point, have been a pair of sergeants from our precinct, Kriminalsekretar Faber and his partner Sergeant Roth. They already know the lay of the land. So, they'll remain on the case, but under your coordination. *Verstanden?*"

"Of course, Herr Colonel."

Brandt hoped his calm demeanor concealed the internal turbulence he felt over the abruptness of his first case assignment. *The murder of an SS officer no less! Why me, the most junior Kriminalinspektor in the precinct?*

"We'll drop you at Kriminalpolizei headquarters, where Sergeant Roth is waiting to accompany you to the SS complex in Moabit. We've designated it as a crime scene, and restricted access for now. I wanted you to have a chance to examine the premises for yourself while the trail is still fresh, so to speak."

As if on cue, the vehicle turned and headed north on Hermann Goring Strasse. Brandt hadn't spent much time in the city since he had been a young boy, but he recognized that they were taking the 'scenic route' to their destination, winding through the formidable gauntlet of buildings in the government sector. *Is this for my benefit, to make an impression on me? Or is there more to this briefing?*

Colonel Brunner interrupted his thoughts, "Between the report, and Faber and Roth's guidance, you should have everything you need. Again, I apologize for the trial by fire initiation. I realize this is a lot to absorb, but the circumstances dictated that it be handled this way.

"I understand, Herr Colonel."

The car stopped at the intersection of Hermann Goring Strasse and Unter Den Linden. Brandt couldn't help leaning imperceptibly towards his window. This was the crossroads of Germany's military and diplomatic history and splendor.

Their car idled in the shadow of the fabled Brandenburg Gate, the most notable and ornate of the city's original custom gates, turned triumphal archway. Sitting atop the classical columns, was the sculptured *Quadriga*, which the winged heroine Victory pulled forever onward in her horse-led chariot. Napoleon had once carried this coveted prize away to the Louvre as the spoils of war, but it had been returned to its place of prominence atop the gate following his defeat at the hands of the Prussians and General Blucher in 1814. That was when the Iron Cross had been added to the sculpture's laurel wreath. Brandt's thoughts drifted back to the Iron Cross atop the monument at Kreuzberg. *Our greatest victories often follow our most devastating defeats.* It was a thought that gave him hope.

Their vehicle turned right onto the Pariser Platz and proceeded past the series of diplomatic embassies housed in the former royal quarter of the city.

"There is one other issue which makes this case potentially sensitive," Brunner resumed, interrupting Brandt's internal sightseeing tour. "In the months preceding his murder, Captain Keppler, underwent review and dismissal from the Berlin Gestapo on charges of misconduct."

Brandt felt himself involuntarily wince. *There's the hook!*

He shifted uncomfortably in his seat. He could feel the Kriminaldirektor's piercing eyes searching him intently for a reaction. He remained passive and silent.

"Those facts alone add a volatile dimension to our investigation," Brunner continued. "But don't be concerned, Lieutenant. I'm fully aware of the events which transpired during your brief detachment with the Munich Gestapo, and I trust that this won't be an impediment?"

"Nein. Not at all, Colonel," he managed.

"You can rest assured that we've been granted complete autonomy to conduct this investigation. You'll be acting solely under my authority and will have my full support. I have every confidence in your abilities as a Kriminalinspektor, and in the experience of the men you'll be working with."

Brandt was uncertain how much comfort to take from the Kriminaldirektor's assurances. They sounded like a dreaded *vote of confidence* before his investigation had even gotten underway. He felt adrift in a suddenly muddled stream. He needed some time, and privacy, to process the array of information his mind was trying to sort through.

"I appreciate your confidence, Herr Colonel."

Colonel Brunner reclined in his seat, seemingly content. The last blocks ensued in silence. They passed the Spree Canal and turned right on Oberwall Strasse. At the intersection, Werderscher Markt Five came into view, the site of Berlin's main Kriminalpolizei branch. *My new home away from home.* The driver pulled to the curb adjacent to a row of police vehicles and allowed the staff car to idle.

Major Kaufmann broke the dead air, "The duty officer will direct you down to the motor pool, where Sergeant Roth is waiting. Once you've familiarized yourself with the basics at the crime scene, go home and get some rest. We know you've had a long trip. When you report to headquarters in the morning, we'll get you settled into your office in a proper fashion."

"Danke, Herr Major, Herr Kriminaldirektor."

Brandt retrieved his bags and Weskamp closed the door behind him with a nod. He watched as the Kriminaldirektor's staff car departed in the direction of the Schleusen Bridge. The magnificent snow-covered dome of the Schloss glimmered in the distance as a shaft of late morning sunlight broke through the winter clouds.

They say that guilt is the most agonizing emotion to endure, but they're wrong. The pain of betrayal is far worse. Guilt is not an isolated feeling. It is a verdict. It is the mind's response to something you have done, to a choice you've made. Guilt is self-inflicted. It is the fruit harvested in kind from the seed that you've sown. You feel guilty because you are guilty.

But betrayal? It is unmerited, unwarranted, and undeserved. It is injustice meted out to us when we least suspect it. It is ill-intent imposed upon us by those we've trusted. Nothing is more bitter. You plant goodwill and reap destruction.

I've been betrayed by men I've known. Betrayed by those whom I've worked with to make the best out of bad circumstances. They've seen my efforts and know the work I've done. But my assistance has been met with treachery. And now it is extended beyond me to reach meine Familie! I should never have cooperated with such men, even if it seemed the lesser of evils.

Guilt! It is a weak prescription. The men who betrayed me are guilty, but do they feel it? Does their conscience bother them? Does it cause them to even lose a moment of sleep? Nein! Then neither will I feel guilty for what I've done, or for what I have to do. This is personal. Isn't betrayal always the most intimate transgression? Judas's kiss? Antony's dagger?

My dagger. It wasn't issued to me, but how the wood handle between its nickel cross guards conforms to the curves of my hand. It is as if it had been crafted with me in mind. The glint of light from the streetlamp reveals the inscription on its blade. Mein ehre heipt treue. Honor and loyalty as part of the SS credo. How fitting, knowing what I now know of its previous

57

owner. A nine-inch blade. That's just enough. If betrayal is the most intimate offense, then so should be its repayment. There is only one remedy that can soothe this lethal sting I've suffered, and that's to see the look in the traitor's eyes, as his blood spills over my blade. I've felt this balm, but I need more.

Chapter 8

The overcast gloom that enveloped Berlin in the early morning hours caused Brandt to doubt if he had ever actually fully awakened from the ashen landscape of the previous evening's dreams. His first night of sleep in his new lodgings had been short and fitful. The recurring vision that chronically haunted his slumbers had joined forces with the gruesome photographic images from Captain Keppler's murder, which he had fallen asleep sorting through.

He had been placed in a rundown one-bedroom flat in the Humbolt district, which was still furnished with the belongings of a family who had recently fled the city. *Or perhaps been forcibly removed?* He had awakened with a kink in his neck from falling asleep on the sitting room sofa, covered in photographs from the crime scene. *At least what was left of the scene.*

In advance of his inspection, the Gestapo had already arranged to have Captain Keppler's body transferred to their own branch coroner's office. Likewise, all of the captain's classified office files had been spirited away to an unspecified Gestapo-controlled storehouse. *For security purposes, of course.* In essence, he had been left to examine a crime scene absent a body or any residual documentary evidence. *So much for the promise of autonomy and agency cooperation.* Fortunately, he still had two elements working in his favor.

First and foremost, was Kriminalsekretar Faber's firsthand inspection of the untainted scene. Faber had already demonstrated himself to be a true professional, with a keen eye for detail. And secondly, a developed roll of film from an Orpo photographer, which the Gestapo had inadvertently overlooked in their quest of mass confiscation. And it was the contents of that roll of film that now had him heading into the city at the first hint of dawn.

Traffic was light as he headed towards the government district on the main artery of Konig Strasse. He merged into the flow of vehicles at the circle street at Alexander Platz, where brake lights suddenly slowed his progress to a crawl. A traffic officer directed cars towards the far outside lanes, away from an area being tended to by a road crew.

As he drew closer, Brandt could see a crater of smoldering bomb wreckage near the Alexanderplatz U-bahn station. *The Brits managed to place one in the heart of the city on their overnight run. I must have slept right through the air raid sirens.* Workers hastened to remove rubble from a damaged tunnel and lined sandbags along the roadside to stem the flow from a burst water main. One of the U-bahn terminal canopies had been converted into an aid station. In the midst of the mayhem, he noticed a tall dark-haired man in priest's robes, moving from tent to tent, and coordinating the relief efforts in the rain.

As the gridlock eased, he exited the damaged roundabout and took the first left on Magazin Strasse. The grim stone police branch spanning five stories, and much of the block, was the cross street's lone distinguishing feature. Brandt parked the sergeant's car along the curbing and entered the building past the pair of stone lions that stood like twin sentinels at the main entrance. Today had been designated as a day for him to get acquainted with the facility, and settled into his new office, but he approached the duty officer with other ideas.

"Sergeant Roth's office?"

"Homicide is level two. Roth's office is to your right at the top of those stairs."

Brandt nodded. He took the stairs two at a time. As indicated, the sergeant's office was the first in a series of small offices along the south corridor of the second level. The door was ajar. Brandt knocked twice out of courtesy, and entered without waiting for a reply. Roth smiled broadly as he stood up from his desk.

"*Guten Morgen*, Lieutenant Brandt. You're up early! Ready for the grand tour?"

"Perhaps later, sergeant," he said, more sternly than he had intended. "I want you to take a look at this photograph and tell me what you see. Or rather, don't see."

The young master sergeant was visibly intrigued. Brandt pulled a black-and-white print from the folder he had tucked under his arm, and placed it on the desk for closer inspection. The Orpo photographer had struck gold with a photo he had taken from the larboard side of the deceased's body. Brandt watched as Sergeant Roth scoured the details of the print, shaking his head in frustration.

"Do you have a magnifying glass?"

"Ja, in my desk," Roth affirmed, hurriedly reaching into his top drawer, and returning his concentrated gaze to the image.

"Look at the Captain's cuffs," Brandt instructed, tapping the bottom of the photo. The sergeant leaned closer.

"There's a patch missing from his sleeve," Roth noted. "His *SS* cuff band has been removed, you can see the discolored outline of where it used to be."

Brandt smiled. Sometimes detection was more about noticing what was missing, than what was present.

"And can you make out the lettering of the outline?"

Roth squinted moving the lens closer still. He looked up at Brandt, his eyes widening.

"*IVB4!* That's Jewish Affairs!" he stammered. "Keppler worked in the Department of Jewish Affairs while with the Gestapo?"

"*Exakt!* But there's no record of it. It appears his personnel files have been scrubbed of any reference to his time at Jewish Affairs."

"Why?"

"That's the question," Brandt concurred. "Before his demotion, Captain Keppler was a Gestapo major, assigned to one of the most influential policy departments in the Reich, and that's been completely removed from his records?"

"Who would do that?"

"That's what you're going to find out for me."

"Me? How?"

"I was hoping you'd ask," Brandt smirked. "The Kriminalpolizei branch on Pottsdammer Strasse has an office that liaises with Jewish Affairs. They keep records of every case referred by JA. in their archives. I want you to drive out there and request every case referred by Captain Keppler in the past two years."

"You think they'll just hand those over?"

"It's worth a try. Use the Kriminaldirektor's name if you have to."

The sergeant's hesitance, even of invoking the name of Colonel Brunner, was apparent.

"Look, whatever agency, or entity, scrubbed Keppler's personnel file, did so for a reason. We need to review what kind of cases Captain Keppler handled at Jewish Affairs before they erase any trace of that as well."

They both started slightly at the unexpected knock on the sergeant's office door, and exchanged a sheepish smile as they realized it was just the duty officer from the front desk. The duty officer held an oversized envelope high, flapping it in his right hand.

"Inspektor Brandt, sorry for the interruption. This just arrived for you."

Brandt took the envelope from the officer. It had been hand addressed to him, the flap sealed with a Reich insignia that he had never seen before. He could feel Sergeant Roth's bemused gaze peering over his shoulder, as he read the contents of the formal invitation.

Chapter 9

The valet opened the rear door of the Mercedes staff car, and ceremoniously gestured towards the entrance. Brandt hesitated. He shifted uncomfortably in his full-dress uniform, fidgeting with the tight collar. It felt straight out of the box, and he strained to remember the last social occasion he had to wear it. He put his discomfort aside and gazed up at the ornate venue. The building's facade glowed with illumination, and its host of swastika-emblazoned flags and banners flapped triumphantly in the frigid winter breeze. *Apparently, the blackout restrictions have been suspended for the evening.*

A stream of formally dressed officers and dignitaries, and their dates, lined the stairs to the entrance. He felt a tingle of nervousness in his stomach, as he apprehensively approached the front doors of the monumental structure. A uniformed soldier checked his invitation, and offered him a spirited salute, before directing him into the main hall.

"Heil Hitler, Lieutenant! Welcome to the Konzerthaus. Enjoy your evening."

A few couples milled about the entry admiring the opulent engravings on the walls and vaulted ceilings. He passed through the vestibule, and entered the banquet room. Rows of tables encircled a dance floor, where officers swayed with their female companions to the melody of a chamber orchestra. Brandt noted officials from every agency mingling together around the copious perimeter bars. *Free drinks, one of the few principles even sworn enemies can agree upon.*

He gravitated towards a quiet corner seat, and watched the proceedings from the insulated comfort of his new vantage point. He liked to get the lay of the land, especially in unfamiliar social settings, before diving in. Despite his comfortable isolation, relief washed over him as he recognized a familiar face. Major Kaufmann returned the smile as he crossed the room towards him.

"Well, Lieutenant Brandt, a little overwhelming, isn't it?" Kaufmann exclaimed over the din of the crowd.

"Good evening, Herr Major."

"From the stench of the crime scene, to rubbing elbows with the elites of the Nazi party, within your first day," he scoffed. "You must be a quick study."

"Not necessarily by choice," Brandt smiled. "I'm not sure that my attendance tonight was optional. So, what's the occasion?"

Kaufmann pulled up one of the bar stools, and turned to examine the extravagant scene.

"Occasion? There's no excuse needed for a Gestapo spectacle in self-congratulations. However, in this case, one of their own has been promoted. Brigadefuhrer Reinhard Becht, has been named Deputy Inspector of Concentration Camps."

Kaufmann gestured in the direction of the figure standing on the rostrum at the center of the banquet hall. Brigadier General Becht was arrayed in his full, dress uniform, complemented by a flamboyant white jacket that was covered in medals and ribbons of honor. From the platform, his bellowing voice could be heard above the others, as he chatted in animated fashion with a throng of well-wishers. Major

Kaufmann thoroughly examined a provocatively dressed female attendant, before removing a pair of champagne glasses from her tray, and offering one to Brandt.

"Not tonight, Major. I'm still a little drained from travel, and that would put me right to sleep."

"Suit yourself, but you'd be advised to take advantage while you can," Kaufmann said with a nod, as he started to lead the way across the crowded floor. "Tonight, the Gestapo is picking up the tab, and I can promise you that's not usually the case. Come on, I'll show you our table."

Brandt followed in tow. The major deftly navigated between the bustle of the dance floor, and the thick congestion of people hovering around the tables, like a seasoned professional of the banquet circuit. At the end of the trek lay a conspicuously deserted table bearing a placard inscribed: '*der Nord Berlin Kriminalpolizei.*'

"Here's our stop. As you can see, these functions are always a big hit with the guys from our precinct," Kaufmann offered wryly. "I was hoping to introduce you to…"

His words trailed off. Brandt followed the major's distracted gaze until it settled on the figure of a Gestapo officer purposefully approaching their table. Kaufmann shot Brandt a rapid look that he couldn't quite gage. *Suspicion? Forewarning?* The major offered the uninvited guest a muted salute, before turning to introduce Brandt.

"Major Weskamp, this is Lieutenant Konrad Brandt, our precinct's newest inspector."

"I've heard as much, but I haven't had the pleasure," Weskamp replied, nodding in Brandt's direction. "Lieutenant Brandt, my commanding officer, Standartenfuhrer Schonbern would like to have a word with you, at your convenience."

Schonbern? The Gestapo's local bureau chief? What could I have done to merit his attention?

Brandt glanced at Major Kaufmann, halfway hoping for an out, but Kaufmann simply nodded compliantly.

"Now is as convenient as any time, Herr Major," Brandt answered.

"Very well. *Auf Wiedersehen*, Major Kaufmann, enjoy the festivities," Weskamp concluded, having already turned.

The Gestapo major's rapid gate carried them quickly through the compacted aisles, in the direction of the spacious main bar at the rear of the hall. Brandt's eyes had already zeroed in on the formidable profile of the officer he imagined to be the colonel. The officer leaned subtly against the bar, encircled by a small congregation of Gestapo men. *More than the stripes on his uniform make him stand out from the rest of the pack.*

Exuberant laughter emanated from the huddle of agents surrounding him, as the Gestapo chief reached the conclusion of remarks that were just beyond Brandt's hearing. He noted that the colonel appeared to preside over his entourage, like a king holding court. Or perhaps the show was just for his benefit, Brandt surmised, as he watched the colonel adeptly extricate himself from his subordinates, as they drew near.

"Lieutenant Brandt, this is regional Head of Gestapo, Standartenfuhrer Victor Schonbern," Weskamp proclaimed in a ceremonious manner.

Brandt straightened his posture to offer a salute, but was intercepted midway by the Gestapo chief's extended hand.

"Lieutenant Brandt, I've been looking forward to meeting the young inspector, whom my dear friend Colonel Brunner holds in such esteem," Colonel Schonbern cooed. His piercing gaze remained fixed upon Brandt, as he gestured towards a small, deserted table at the end of the bar, "Let's move to a place where we can hear ourselves talk."

Major Weskamp seemed to take this as his cue, bowing slightly as he receded back into the clamor of the crowded hall. Brandt waited for the colonel to be seated, before taking a chair opposite him. The small orchestra had broken into a popular waltz, and a whoop had gone up from the dance floor. An awkward silence settled over the table, as Schonbern peered silently into his glass for what seemed like an eternity.

"I trust that you've had time to familiarize yourself with the details of the Captain Keppler homicide. Do you have any initial impressions?" Schonbern asked, abruptly.

"To be honest, it would be premature for me to even speculate, Herr Colonel."

Brandt wasn't sure what he expected this discussion to be about, but he was caught off guard by the Gestapo chief's lack of subtlety. He was apparently a man who didn't suffer small talk. Brandt found himself equally surprised by the shrill register of Schonbern's voice. It seemed incompatible with the colonel's gruff, worn exterior. He internally chided himself for considering such distractions.

"I see. And do you find it surprising that the Gestapo would defer to the Kriminalpolizei in a matter involving the murder of one of our former agents?"

Brandt searched for the proper words. Laying this subject matter out on the table with such candor was unconventional. He tried to measure his response accordingly.

"Somewhat, Colonel. It's been my experience that the Gestapo usually prefers to conduct such investigations internally".

"I would say that's accurate," Schonbern confirmed. "And has Colonel Brunner informed you of the circumstances surrounding Captain Keppler's dismissal from the Gestapo?"

Brandt heard warning signals reverberating in the back of his mind. He sensed a strong undercurrent residing just beneath the colonel's placid veneer of composure. He had no intention of testing those waters, and even less of placing his own superior in a potentially compromising position. At the same time, he didn't plan to reveal any discoveries his investigation had made into Captain Keppler's background. *Always give your adversary only what he is already certain that you know.*

"I'm only aware that his transfer record states that Captain Keppler received a 'general censure for misconduct.' "

"Well, allow me to save you the leg work. Captain Keppler was transferred because of an increasing pattern of involvement in der Schwarzmarkt."

"I've heard the allegations that he dabbled in black market goods, but that hardly seems cause for dismissal."

"His activity had become egregious, to the point where he had even run afoul of his contacts within *der Untergrund.*"

"Then with all due respect, Herr Colonel, why not discharge him altogether? And why was there no citation of this in his personnel file?"

The Gestapo chief sighed. *Or was it a snort?* Brandt observed closely as Schonbern reflexively swirled his brandy snifter in silence. At length, he noticed the colonel's gaze drift from the bronze liquid contents of his glass, and rest upon the vivid insignia emblazoned on his own uniform sleeve. There was a patch depicting a black spider enclosed within a golden hexagon. Brandt hadn't seen this badge before. *Most likely the crest of an SS order the Colonel belongs to. The SS has a symbol for everything, but the order of the spider? I've never heard of it. And why is he going out of his way to draw my attention to it?*

"Are you familiar with the term 'autotomy', Inspector Brandt?" Schonbern said, leaning towards him conspiratorially.

"Autotomy? I don't believe so, Herr Colonel."

"It's a form of self-amputation practiced by certain species of insects, as a preservation mechanism."

"Self-amputation?"

The colonel consciously rubbed a forefinger across the fabric of the emblem, before embarking upon his exposition. Brandt suspected the lecture that ensued was well-rehearsed.

"That's right. Take the arachnid. It's one of nature's most proficient predators, but on occasion the insect it preys upon may possess a venomous sting of its own. A sting to one of the spider's legs leaves it with two choices. Either it can trigger a reflex, which voluntarily severs the infected limb, or it can keep the appendage and allow the poison to spread throughout the entire body. Parting with the envenomed leg causes no adverse effect to the spider, but failure to detach the limb can result in paralysis and death."

The Gestapo chief halted pointedly. Brandt could feel him searching his expression for signs of comprehension, or reaction, before continuing.

"When faced with a threat from within, especially a threat with an inside track to law enforcement, certain elements in der Schwarzmarkt may have felt compelled to conduct their own form of self-amputation. Sacrifice the poisoned limb to save the rest of the body," he concluded.

"So, you're implying that Captain Keppler's indiscretions may have caused him to be viewed as an 'infected limb' by his comrades in der Schwarzmarkt? An asset turned liability to be disposed of before he could cause permanent damage?" Brandt queried.

It doesn't make much sense. And for that matter, the ease with which the colonel equates the value of a human life with that of an insect leg is a bit disturbing too.

Schonbern shook his head in frustration, "If I knew that with any certainty, we would have targeted the offenders ourselves. And you and I wouldn't be having this conversation."

"Of course, but you think it's a possibility?"

Brandt caught sight of Major Weskamp moving back across the floor in their direction. He noted the perfectly choreographed timing of his return.

"I'm simply informing you that we've witnessed these types of internal purges of egregious offenders, by the leaders in der Schwarzmarkt before. And I believe you'll find that Ernst Keppler fit that profile."

Schonbern inclined his head, as Major Weskamp stooped to discretely whisper his timely communique in the colonel's ear. The Gestapo chief rose hurriedly from his seat and waved his hand in a dismissive manner.

"You'll have to excuse me, Lieutenant Brandt, perhaps we'll have a chance to continue this conversation another time."

"Certainly, Colonel, it was a pleasure," Brandt said, getting to his feet.

The colonel stopped short. He leaned in uncomfortably close, in deliberate fashion. When his voice emerged, it came out as little more than a shrill whisper.

"Oh, and don't mistake my ceding of this investigation to your department for indifference, Lieutenant. I make it a personal policy to bring to account anyone who spills the blood of those who wear this uniform, past, present or future."

Future?

Chapter 10

Brandt watched the waning figures of the colonel and his adjutant, hastily proceed through the assembled crowd, until they emerged at the base of the central platform. The guest of honor, Brigadefuhrer Becht, eagerly greeted their arrival, descending to embrace Schonbern. He directed the colonel to the podium, and helped him adjust the microphone. A moment later the voice Brandt had just heard as a whisper resounded throughout the hall.

"Good evening, ladies and gentlemen," declared Schonbern, a broad grin spreading across his face.

He can smile? The colonel's presence on the rostrum, and the command he conveyed, had been enough to draw most of the boisterous audience to rapt attention.

"I'm glad to see Brigadefuhrer Becht was able to borrow a jacket from a member of the bartending staff for the festivities tonight. Though I'm fairly certain the glare coming off that thing is in violation of any number of blackout restrictions. So, let's hope for an evening free of bombing raids."

Schonbern glanced smugly at the general, and waited for the smattering of laughs and catcalls to recede before he continued.

"Tonight, I'm gratified to have the privilege to introduce a man whose service to the Reich has been unwavering. A man

I've had the honor to serve with as a soldier, as a government official, and as a servant of the German people. And, as I now stand here, heralding his promotion, I do so certain in the knowledge that his advancement makes our homeland more secure in the process. So, without further ado, I present to you Brigadefuhrer Reinhard Becht!"

A swell of cheers swirled through the hall. Brandt used the interlude to begin his trek back towards the Kriminalpolizei precinct table, in hopes of finding Major Kaufmann. *Perhaps he can shed some light on the meaning of the colonel's scripted object lesson.* As the applause subsided, the general wasted little time in regaling the festive crowd with the opening remarks of his acceptance speech.

"Danke, Standartenfuhrer Schonbern! Thank you all! And as for the jacket, it's called 'style', something Victor would know precious little about," Becht announced, blithely. "This evening's ceremonies signify a time of personal good fortune: The fact that my peers and superiors have seen fit to bestow upon me the honor and responsibility of promotion. However, tonight we also share a common thread of good fortune, for we are a generation present to witness the dawning of a new era of power and prosperity for the German Reich."

Brandt located the banquet table, as vacant as when he had first arrived. He planted himself at an end seat, and returned his attention to the stage. Brigadefuhrer Becht's remarks had been interrupted by enthusiastic applause, and howls of support, from a group of officers who had left their tables to congregate in the open area near the base of the rostrum. Their uniforms all bore the markings of camp assignments. They were apparently a collection of the general's associates and peers in the concentration camp system. Or, at least they had been peers before his promotion. *Now they're his constituency.*

"So, tonight is an occasion for celebration, but I would be remiss if I did not take this opportunity to address a peril which even now threatens our stability as a nation. I speak, of course, of the Jewish blight on our society," the general exhorted, pausing for the cessation of responsive jeers. "For far too long, the Jews have acted as a common parasite feeding off the lifeblood of their German host. Lacking the capacity to prosper on their own, and unable to assimilate, they collectively drain the financial, moral, and social sustenance of the German people. My position of oversight in the labor and reform camps has afforded me a special vantage point into the nature of the Jew."

Brandt looked down and rubbed his head in his hands. He had heard this routine before. The Brigadefuhrer's plodding monologue became an indecipherable rumble in the background. *Maybe I'll have that drink after all.* Brandt was pulled from his thoughts by the sound of metal legs scraping across the tile floor. He looked up to see the agent who had loudly requisitioned the empty chair next to him. *A Gestapo sergeant?* The agent took a swig from his drink without saying a word, and flashed a crooked grin at him.

"This seat taken?"

"By all means, make yourself comfortable," Brandt jabbed.

He could tell by the wavering eyes, and by the smell, that the sergeant had already had a few. Overly familiar with drink, the man inclined his long face towards Brandt in an ungainly manner, and spluttered, "So, you're the new Kripo Inspector?"

"And you are…?" Brandt countered, now noticing that one of the Gestapo sergeant's brutish cohorts had subtly flanked him, taking a seat on the other side.

"Sturmscharfuhrer Heller, and this is my partner, Sturmscharfuhrer Kohl."

"Good evening, sergeants. What can I do for you?" Brandt offered, nodding to Heller's unresponsive comrade.

"Messy business, you drawing the Keppler case as your first assignment," Heller said.

The sergeant's gaunt features appeared even more drawn as he narrowed his eyes to study Brandt's reaction. Brandt remained stoic, deciding not to take the bait. He had already played the role of guinea pig once tonight, and that was enough. Heller seemed agitated that his opening gambit had no effect.

"No reason to be so tight-lipped, Inspector," he continued. "We've been fully briefed. You see, Captain Keppler was one of ours. Before we washed our hands of that piece of human excrement!"

"Oh, you knew him?"

"Fritz!" the taciturn agent interjected, reprovingly.

"Alright, alright!" Heller replied. "You want some professional advice, Inspector? Here it is. Try dredging the sewers."

"The sewers?"

"Vice! Skim the records at Vice Squad, they've got a file on Keppler a foot deep."

"And why would Vice be keeping tabs on an *SS* officer?" Brandt inquired. This had the feel of a dog and pony show. *But might as well see where these mutts lead me.*

Heller faltered glancing at his partner. The statuesque Kohl remained expressionless, as though undecided on whether or not to participate.

"Seems Captain Keppler was running a little prostitution racket on the side," he offered, his thick Bavarian accent matching his brooding exterior.

"I expect that hardly makes him unique in your department."

Brandt was immediately aware that his comment had agitated Heller. *Doesn't seem to take much.* He would file that away for future reference. Kohl, on the other hand, only offered a thin smile, before resuming.

"What *was* unique, was the angle he used," Kohl replied. "Captain Keppler's position in the department, allowed him to tab Jewish girls slated for the transports, and in exchange for payment and other 'services', have them Aryanized."

"Aryanized?"

"He'd have them fixed up to look like Germans, and give them the identity papers to match."

"Why? To spare them from being deported?"

"Sometimes, if he had formed an attachment, but mostly so he could prostitute them out to his clients. Guys who had a taste for Jewish flesh, but an aversion to the penalties of getting caught with the Jew."

"I don't know how it is where you come from Inspector, but here in Berlin, we take a dim view of those who flaunt the sex codes with Jews!" Heller crassly interjected.

"Right. The laws restricting sexual activity between Germans and Jews, are strictly enforced here in the capital. So, Captain Keppler created a loophole. He gave himself the ability to offer the forbidden to those who fancied it."

"And this is what put him at odds with his own department?"

"Among other things. Those types of activities earned him

some enemies in the Gestapo and at Vice, but mostly among the lowlife scum he rubbed elbows with in the underground."

Again, directing me towards the black market. Or misdirecting.

Kohl's words halted abruptly. The sergeant's gaze wandered down the aisle next to their banquet table. His comrade's eyes quickly followed suit.

"Talk about someone I wouldn't mind briefing in the finer points of sex crimes," Heller exclaimed.

Brandt looked up as a beautiful blonde, in a flowing red dress, swayed fluidly past their table. She seemed oblivious to the attention she was drawing in her wake. He caught himself following the outline of her curves beneath the thin fabric of her dress, as she made her way towards the balconies outside. She disappeared through the double doors, and a moment passed before Brandt became aware of the awkward silence that had settled over the table. He cleared his throat, and covered his tracks by redirecting the conversation back to the topic of the deceased captain.

"So, you think Captain Keppler's skirting of the Racial Purity Laws made someone want to leave a five-inch gash where his throat used to be?" he asked, skeptically.

"The prostitution racket was just the tip of the iceberg with Keppler," Kohl replied. "Let's put it this way, I hope you're not in a hurry to narrow down your list of suspects, because there's no end to the criminals he crossed, in der Schwarzmarkt, who wouldn't have minded seeing him dead."

Brandt shook his head. *Time to wrap this up.*

"Danke for the background, and for the great company. But I have to ask, why so much interest from the Gestapo in the investigation of a guy you describe as little more than a two-bit grifter?"

Kohl bristled, rising from his chair.

"We're just trying to be good neighbors. Besides, if we were that 'interested' in this case, it would be ours. Come on, Fritz."

"Good night, Inspector," Heller said, drawing out his parting words with disdain. His fetid breath lingered well after his tottering exodus. Before the agents were out of sight, Brandt's mind began sifting through the hearsay, often contradicting, he had been exposed to over the course of the evening. *Why are Gestapo agents tripping over themselves to share information? What seed are they trying to plant?* He could almost feel Standartenfuhrer Schonbern pulling the strings from his seat up on the rostrum. And all the while, Brigadefuhrer Becht's diatribe against the Jews had continued unabated from the dais.

"Even when we send them to labor camps in the hopes of reforming their habits and work ethic, they regress into an almost bestial existence. Our once pristine camps become overrun with every manner of illness, which the Jews, being natural carriers of contagion, communicate back and forth amongst themselves. Epidemics rage uncontrolled within confines which were designed to bring rehabilitation."

The general's words droned on in the background, until they became a low, dull buzz in Brandt's head. He felt restless. He needed some fresh air. His thoughts drifted back to the vision in the red dress. She had stood out like fireworks at a funeral. *Who is she?* He got up from the table and walked through the empty portal leading out onto the balconies beyond the main banquet hall. He pulled against the bronze handles of the rear doors and proceeded out into the night.

A gust of frigid wind greeted him, instantly clearing away the heaviness his eyelids had felt in the stifled air of the ballroom. He walked to the edge of the balcony and rested his forearms against the stone railing. He inhaled deeply. The cold air was invigorating, as was the view of the city enfolded in the wintry mist. He closed his eyes for what felt like little more than a second, before his brief meditation was interrupted by the sound of voices rising from the street below.

The voices were elevated in pitch, raised in dispute. He leaned further over the railing searching for the source of the escalating shouts. Below him, beneath the back portico of the building, he was surprised to catch a glimpse of the woman in the red dress. He moved further down the railing to gain a better vantage point. Another figure came into view, an officer whose dress uniform was cloaked by a long trench coat. The man gestured wildly, obviously engaged in a heated exchange with the woman in red. Both of them exhaled plumes of cold night air that lingered above their heads, as their argument intensified. The officer was now attempting to direct her by the arm, into the back of a staff car that idled by the curb.

Brandt saw the front passenger window of the staff car lower, and noticed the driver lean across the seat to yell something to his entangled comrade. He couldn't make out what was said, but the woman in red took this distraction as an opportunity to pull free from her assailant and walk away. The officer quickly recovered, and reached out to corral her again, but the force of his movements caused her to lose her balance. She slipped and fell awkwardly on the icy sidewalk with a thud. *Did she slip, or was she pushed?* He decided not to wait any longer to find out.

"You, down there! Halt!" he shouted at the officer, as he moved purposefully towards the long bank of stairs leading to the street level portico below. The bespectacled officer looked around in surprise, and shot an angry glare up in his direction.

The man hesitated over the fallen woman for a moment, apparently trying to decide whether to pull her back to her feet for another attempt, or whether to flee. As Brandt closed the distance between them, the officer opted for the latter. He hurriedly jumped into the back of the car and yelled at his partner to drive. The staff car's wheels whirred, and spun on the ice, spitting up a wide swath of slush onto the curb as it peeled away.

Brandt strained to make out the details of the government-issued license plate, as he descended the stairs towards the street. By the time he reached the sidewalk, the car had vanished down the blackened road. The young woman was attempting to get back to her feet, but had stopped long enough to examine the scrapes beneath her torn stockings.

"Here, let me help you, just take it slow," Brandt said, as he helped her to stand. "Are you alright?"

She looked up, as if noticing him for the first time. Her pale blue eyes were clouded with tears, and her cheeks were flushed with color.

"I think so, just a little worse for wear."

Brandt removed his coat and placed it around her shivering shoulders.

"Danke, Lieutenant, is it?"

"Konrad will do."

"Danke, Lieutenant Konrad," she replied offering the first glimpse of a smile.

"Just Konrad, and you are?"

"Erica… Erica Graffe," she offered.

"It's a pleasure, Fraulein Graffe, despite the circumstances. Speaking of which, who was that?"

"That? That was an event planner's worst nightmare."

Chapter 11

Fraulein Graffe's firm was the primary event planning group in the capital, with an emphasis on planning state-sponsored functions. They were currently under permanent retainer to the Reich. Given that virtually every event in Berlin, from speeches to parades to concerts, was 'state-sponsored,' Brandt presumed that her firm didn't lack for business. He had asked if he could escort her back into the gala, to get her out of the cold, but she had declined. She needed to head home by way of her office. Brandt had noticed an off-duty cab driver parked down the block, who had no doubt witnessed the confrontation in its entirety. He offered to hail her a ride home, and she had agreed, on the condition that he would share the ride with her. He agreed, pleased to have a reason not to return to the festival hall, and to spend more time in her company.

Their conversation during the cab ride had seemed a blur to Brandt at times. He had lost count of how often he had caught himself staring at her beautiful profile, losing track of her words in the process. He internally admonished himself to focus more attentively as she openly shared the details of her work.

The officer who had assailed her was an *SS* Major named Kurt Waller, an adjutant to Brigadefuhrer Becht. For the past several months Waller had been the liaison between Becht's office, and Fraulein Graffe's staff. He had been her contact in charge of coordinating the details of the general's big bash. Apparently, at the end of the night, Major Waller had expected her to be one of the party favors. When she had declined, the situation had become heated.

She had turned earnestly to Brandt, and with misty eyes told him how grateful she was that he had arrived when he did. He had muttered something self-effacing in reply, and had purposefully turned away to avoid gazing too intently into her eyes. He was relieved when she returned to the unthreatening topic of her job, and the routine stresses she faced coordinating events for Reich officials. This had brought her to her next admission.

Brigadefuhrer Becht's promotional gala had been an enormous headache for her of late, for more reasons than the uninvited advances of the major. Rather, it had become a big distraction that siphoned time and attention away from her firm's primary assignment, that of planning the concert for the Fuhrer's upcoming 53rd birthday party. Though it was still months away, she shared that the logistical planning for such a state event was exhausting. Her firm had been contracted to decorate the venue, establish the guest list, and most importantly secure the entertainment. To that end she had been in negotiations to have legendary conductor Wilhelm Furtwangler perform at the head of the Berlin Philharmonic. The hopes were that for this historic performance, the Fuhrer would be the guest of honor, and attend along with his entourage of dignitaries and colleagues.

Her enthusiastic description of the details of this epic undertaking had piqued Brandt's interest as well, but for other reasons. Furtwangler's genius as a conductor was known far and wide, as were his well-publicized run-ins with the Reich party bosses. The conductor's international fame preceded the rise of the Nazi regime, and this celebrity had perhaps given him a false sense that he transcended their reach. A power struggle had ensued for the heart and soul of the Berlin Philharmonic, with the Reich using all of the discretionary powers at their disposal to compel Furtwangler to bend the knee.

Jewish members of the symphony had been expelled, numerous other musicians had been conscripted into the military, and the performance of music from Jewish composers, past and present, had been strictly forbidden. Even the portrait of Mendelssohn had gone missing from the pantheon of legendary composers at the Philharmonic's digs at the old symphony hall, but maybe that was just coincidence?

The final straw fell as the Philharmonic began to struggle with financial insolvency and the specter of bankruptcy, due to the deprivations brought about by the war. There wasn't much demand for a national orchestra when the rest of the continent was either aligned against your country, or under its occupation. This turn of events had allowed the Reich to swoop in and bail out the Philharmonic, and in the process to effectively co-opt them as a government-controlled orchestra. Since that time Furtwangler's resistance had largely consisted of token gestures, to the point that he now found himself in annual negotiations to perform as Hitler's birthday entertainment. *No matter how high you ascended up the ladder, there was always someone higher up. Someone who knew how to sound your strings.*

Fraulein Graffe had instructed the driver to pull up to the curb alongside a row of office buildings on Mauer Strasse. Before Brandt could move to assist her, she had bounded out of the passenger side door and scampered across the snow-covered pavement towards a darkened alley. Surprisingly, she showed little sign of ill effect from her fall, as she expertly navigated the icy terrain. She had returned within moments, wearing a long winter coat, and with his jacket and a thick stack of folders tucked under her arm. She slid back into the cab and set the stack of folders between them, as she gave the driver her home address.

Atop the folders fluttered a rough draft sketch of the flier for the celebratory event to be held in April. The evening's festivities at the symphony were to be keynoted by a speech from Dr Goebbels, followed by Furtwangler conducting the Berlin Philharmonic in a performance of Beethoven's 9th Symphony in D Minor. Her eyes gleamed as he examined the flier, but when he looked up her face had taken on a different expression. She flushed self-consciously as she apologized for talking so much about herself and her job.

For the remainder of their drive, she had peppered him with questions about himself. How long had he been in the city? What precinct did he work in, and what was his department like? She had always found criminal detection fascinating. Were there any interesting cases he had been working on? Brandt quickly realized that he felt much more comfortable when the spotlight was on her. But there was something about her manner that put him at ease. It turned out they had a lot in common, including the recent loss of a loved one. In her case it had been the sudden death of her brother on the eastern front. He had felt an instant bond with her over the pain of losing someone in the line of duty. As she shared about her loss, he commiserated, and couldn't help but think of his own. The time had flown by, and he was barely conscious of the fact that she had twice tapped the driver on the shoulder and signaled for him to circle the block again.

As the cab made its last rounds and slowed to a stop against the curb, she tore a strip of paper from one of her notebooks and scribbled her name, extension, and office address on it. She had placed the folded paper in his hand, and allowed her hand to linger an extra moment during the exchange. He should stop by sometime she had indicated, though it was best to call before dropping in at her office, as she was often out on location with clients. He had insisted on getting her car door, and she had given him a quick hug, and again expressed her gratitude. In that moment, he had breathed in the intoxicating smell of her perfume through the frigid night air.

She suggested perhaps they could meet for lunch once her schedule settled down, and with a wave of her hand, and a 'good night', she disappeared down a narrow lane of row homes. Brandt watched her until the last wisp of her red dress and winter coat disappeared into the shadows. He lingered briefly before getting back into the cab, and giving the driver the address of his flat. On the drive back, fatigue washed over him like a flood. He realized that he had spent most of the night running on adrenaline, and more recently, on the pleasure of the fraulein's company. But what he truly needed most was a good night of sleep. Nonetheless, it felt good to know someone in the city. Perhaps once everything settled down, they would have that lunch after all.

Chapter 12

Floodlights pierced the veil of sleet and freezing rain, their beams intersecting as they reflected off the murky waters of the Spree. Armored trucks had been positioned along the east entrance to the Oberbaum Bridge pulled up tight against the sidewalks. They scanned the surface of the river with their mobile searchlights. Brandt merged onto an access road, where a traffic officer wielding a blue flashlight waved him towards the shoreline below the bridge. Emergency vehicles dotted the landscape of the frigid embankment. He brought his car to a halt at a clearing on a treeless stretch of beach, and got out. He peered back over the roof at the bridge.

A pair of massive floodlights had been placed on the decks of the Oberbaum's Gothic spires. They stretched high above the surface of the double-deck bridge. The towers had been designed to resemble the historic fortified wall-tower in Prenzlau, whose origins dated back to the middle ages. And tonight, with the added barricades, Brandt thought it looked every bit the part of a medieval fortress standing guard over the river. The bridge was dual-purpose, and he could see that officials had taken steps to shut down both the automobile overpass, and the elevated U-bahn bridge rail line that ran parallel to it. Not that there was much traffic at this ungodly hour of the morning. *Bad dreams, bad timing, calls in the middle of the night... three days in the city, and I haven't slept through the night yet.*

He rubbed a hand across his face, and scanned the banks of the shoreline. He quickly caught sight of Kriminalsekretar Faber, who had spotted him simultaneously. The sergeant hastily strayed from a group of officers huddled on the waterfront, and trudged up the snow-covered slope in his direction.

"Herr Lieutenant, I'm sorry to call you out in the middle of the night," he called out as he approached.

"Think nothing of it, sergeant."

"I wouldn't have called you without good reason," he said, motioning for Brandt to follow him towards the river.

"What have you got?"

"We drag floaters out of this part of the river routinely. It's just about the widest section of the Spree within the city limits, as it flows east towards the city center," he continued, stopping a dozen meters short of the water. "The location makes it a favorite dumping grounds for both the Gestapo and criminals alike… but this is different."

"How so?"

"A body was pulled from the river around 1am. An Orpo unit was the first to arrive at the scene."

"Who notified Kripo?"

Faber pointed towards an agent at the edge of the shoreline, who was helping to pull a buoy line out into the water.

"Sergeant Wanstedt and I used to work in the same precinct, so as soon as he saw it was a homicide rather than a drowning, he contacted me. Actually, I think he contacted me because of the victim."

"What do you mean, you couldn't already have an

identification?"

"That's the thing," Faber replied in a hushed tone, steering Brandt clear of a passing cluster of emergency personnel. "Wanstedt, and his partner Reardon, were the first agents to respond to the scene."

"Right? Get to the point, sergeant!"

"While they were dragging the body ashore, Wanstedt got a look at the victim, and he maintains that it's... Theodore Goertz."

"Who?"

"*SS* Major Theodore Goertz. You've never heard of him?"

"Should I have? But another *SS* officer? "

"And not just an *SS* officer, a high-ranking cabinet member in the Interior Ministry, and a prominent Gestapo official."

"How can the sergeant be so sure that...?"

"One more thing, if I might, Lieutenant," Faber interrupted. "Before being dumped in the river, the victim's throat had been slit, from ear to ear. And though it's hard to tell with the exposure to the elements, to my eyes it seems consistent with the wound inflicted on Captain Keppler."

Brandt felt a pit form in his stomach, and then begin to spread out like an uncontrolled brush fire. His mind reeled at the improbability. *What are the odds?*

"And how certain is Sergeant Wanstedt on the ID?"

"He's pretty adamant about it. Wanstedt's been with Orpo for a long time, and seen a lot of things. I can't recall ever getting bad information from him. He wouldn't throw out such a high-profile name on a whim."

"Call him over, I'd like to have a word with him."

The sergeant hesitated.

"I have his statement, and he's firm in his identification, so don't you think it's best that…"

"Just call him over Sergeant Faber!" Brandt interjected, his voice laced with agitation.

Brandt treaded slowly down the frozen incline, as Faber retreated towards the riverbank. His feet crunched against the thin layer of ice that had formed atop the shore. He watched the turbulent flow of the glacial waters, and felt the current in his mind coursing in unison with them. *Two murdered Gestapo officials in less than a week, one of them apparently a cabinet minister? What have I wandered into?* It started to rain harder.

Faber returned promptly, followed closely in tow by Wanstedt. The outer layer of the Orpo sergeant's uniform was saturated with water, and a towel hung loosely around his neck. A similarly waterlogged grimace was etched upon the worn features of his face.

"Inspector Brandt, this is Sergeant Johann Wanstedt of the Ordnungspolizei."

"Sergeant Wanstedt."

"Inspector," Wanstedt muttered tersely.

"Kriminalsekretar Faber tells me that during the retrieval process, you believe you recognized the victim. But I imagine there has been quite a bit of decomposition?"

"Well, obviously the body is a little distended and bloated from the effects of the water, but not beyond recognition."

"And you don't think it's premature to make a positive identification before the victim has had a proper examination?"

"Not if you knew the man. Major Goertz headed up our detachment in…" Wanstedt faltered, clearing his throat and glancing at Faber before he continued. "Our intelligence training detachment at the academy. It's been a little while, but there's no mistaking a man like Theodore Goertz."

"Intelligence training? Sergeant Faber indicated that Goertz was with the Gestapo, not with the SD?"

Brandt registered the blank expressions exchanged between the fellow sergeants, and decided not to press their silence any further. He would follow up on the discrepancy later.

"Thank you, Sergeant, that will be all. I'd appreciate you sticking around while we examine the body."

"Of course, Inspector."

"One more thing. Have you told anyone else about the possible identity of the victim?"

"Just my partner, Reardon."

"Good. Let's keep it that way for now, at least until we have some confirmation. If your ID is right, and this is Major Goertz, we want to keep it under wraps as long as possible," Brandt concluded.

Wanstedt assented, snapping off a salute before turning back in the direction of the shoreline. Brandt glanced at Faber questioningly. The sergeant shrugged. *He knows more than he's letting on.* They descended down the slope of the remaining shoreline to the river's edge in silence. A makeshift tent had been erected in anticipation of the medical examiner's arrival. There would be a field examination before the body was moved to the appropriate coroner's office. *That doesn't give us much time.* The coarse black tarp of the tent flapped violently in response to the westward wind gusting across the Spree. The rain had begun to mix with large flakes of snow.

Two uniformed Orpo officers milled around the entrance to the tent futilely seeking respite from the unrelenting elements. They saluted in unison, glad to be temporarily relieved of their post, as Brandt and Faber approached. Brandt entered the tent first. The victim had been covered with a white sheet and was lying prostate on a stretcher above the frozen sand. A field light hung from a line above the stretcher, giving everything inside the tent a sterile glow. Brandt knelt beside the body, and pulled back the sheet. The first glance at a fresh corpse was always a momentary shock to the system. *Especially a floater.* He fought back against his body's gag reflex.

"He's not in too bad shape," he lied.

"For a dead guy," Faber rejoined.

"Either he hasn't been dead long, or the cold water's done a good job of preserving him."

"Maybe both."

"What?"

"Well, if the killings are related, the victims may have died in pretty close proximity to one another."

"What are we, about 72 hours out on Captain Keppler's estimated time of death?"

"Approximately. Hard to tell with the water exposure, but this guy looks like he might have been dumped in the past few days. What about the wound?" Faber queried.

"It's hard to tell much about it, in these conditions, but there could be points of correspondence. This guy's a lot more beat up than Captain Keppler was. We'll have a better idea once the coroner's office gets him cleaned up," Brandt replied, as he tilted the victim's head to more closely examine the multiple areas of trauma. "*What is this?*"

"What?" Faber inquired, stooping for a closer look.

Brandt pointed to a small cluster of lacerations. The

victim had a series of cuts and contusions near the crown of his head, distinct from the primary wounds. *These came before the deathblow. There was a struggle this time.*

"A pattern of abrasions. It looks like small shards of glass are embedded in these cuts between his right ear and the crown of his head," Brandt said.

A uniformed Orpo private poked his head into the opening flaps of the tent.

"Herr Inspector, I'm sorry to bother you, but the medical examiner has arrived and would like to see you."

"Tell him he can wait. We'll be right with him," Faber replied gruffly, his harsh tone enough to send the agent scurrying without further reply.

Brandt covered the victim. He rose from his crouched position, and lifted the rear flaps of the field tent facing out onto the river.

"What's bothering you?"

"I was just envisioning how this is going to play out."

"What do you mean?"

"If the medical examiner confirms that this is the body of Major Goertz, by tomorrow morning the Gestapo, and every other agency in the Reich, are going to be lining up to take this case away from us."

"The Gestapo doesn't get in line," Faber interjected.

"Exactly. Are you willing to just hand this investigation back to them before we've even had a chance to dig into it?"

The sergeant's aged face adopted a stalwart expression. He shook his head decisively. There was no need for words. Brandt felt a strong affinity for Faber in that moment. *He's a veteran, with plenty to lose. He doesn't need this, but he wants it.* Brandt also felt emboldened by the Kriminalsekretar's resolve, a boldness he noticed in his own voice when he resumed.

"Very good! I'll stall the medical examiner on the transfer of the body. You try to get a residential address for Goertz. If he's in the cabinet, he's got to have a place nearby in the city. And pull any background files for him you can get your hands on."

"Straight away."

"Once you have an address, have Sergeant Roth contact the precinct and get a warrant for an immediate search of the property, on the basis that it may be connected to a homicide. Have him wake Colonel Brunner if necessary."

He noticed an immediate change in Faber's demeanor.

"I'll assume responsibility."

"Less than a week in Berlin, and already feeling a little suicidal?" Faber smiled.

"Ask me again, after the search," Brandt smirked. "In the meantime, just get it done. And have Sergeant Roth meet us at the address, alone. If we're going to search the home of a Nazi dignitary, who we aren't even sure is deceased, let's try to do it with some discretion."

"Right, discretion."

Brandt didn't respond. He wandered back through the rear opening of the tent and watched the dark ripples of water lap against the shore. He stared up at the ominous silhouette of the bridge, now barely visible through the sleet and rain. The floodlights on the Oberbaum's towers struggled to pierce the worsening weather conditions. He could relate. A low-lying fog was settling in on the riverbanks, and from the looks of it, it wasn't going to lift anytime soon.

There are moments that change your life forever. Sometimes they pass without your recognition, like the glimpse of a familiar face on a passing trolley. Other times you instantly recognize the gravity of the moment, and that you will never be the same.

Like the morning mein Sohn was born. I still remember everything about that day. Even the shaft of sunlight that broke through the clouds at the exact moment I wheeled meine Frau from the car to the hospital entrance. When the nurse held him up, and I heard that first unimpeded cry, everything changed. Whoever I was, whatever my ambitions had been, however I had imagined spending the rest of my days, had all been swallowed up in those first gasping sobs. My desires and wellbeing were no longer what mattered most. God had given us a child, a tiny being completely dependent upon us for his survival. And then He had given us ein Tochter, and when I looked into her eyes, whatever was left of 'me' had been completely absorbed into a new identity. Had been absorbed into 'us'.

But where are they now? Where was I in their moment of need? And what am I without them? What's worse, what have I become? Without them here there is nothing inside but an unquenchable void. I'm an unwelcome inhabitant in this city. A stranger to the same streets I've known my entire life. There is no friend or agency left to turn to for help. They're all gone. The landscape is the same, but everything has changed. I have no job, no family, no place to call home. I'm even inadmissible to that same hospital, not two blocks from here, where I watched my children be born.

I can feel the stares from every person on the street. They scrutinize my clothing, search my face for any sign of impropriety. It's no longer safe to continue my search aboveground, or to walk in the light. Now is the hour of darkness. It's time to take a dive, and to become a shadow. A time to be seen, and heard from, no more.

Chapter 13

The wiper blades creaked in disapproval as they pushed the icy slush off the windshield, and onto the frigid pavement below. In their wake frozen crystals quickly spread across the glass in starry patterns. The gravel shoulder made a grinding sound beneath the tires, as Brandt edged the police vehicle to a rest along the side of the road in the Friedrichshain suburb. He lowered the frosted driver side window just enough to read the engraved address on the stone pillars: 428 Kurische Strasse. He dimmed the lights and left the car idling.

Brandt peered at the distant house through his binoculars. The damp winter air drafted through the car with a bone-chilling gust that rustled through the folders on Sergeant Faber's lap. His view of the estate was obstructed by a high wrought iron fence, and by the scattered collection of trees that dotted the perimeter with their crystallized branches. There were no lights on, no vehicles in the driveway, and no signs of activity on the property.

"Not bad for a 'second' residence," Faber quipped, his breath visible as he spoke. "Why don't you close that window?"

Brandt obliged, the crank handle sticking and resisting every inch of the way. They had uncovered that Major Goertz's primary home residence was in Hamburg. Since being appointed to a cabinet post, he had recently acquired a house in Berlin, the estate here at 428 Kurische Strasse.

"How long had Goertz lived here, again?"

"I'm not sure the ink has dried," Faber responded, paging through the file.

"The house was previously titled to a David Hedrich, and the transfer of deed to Goertz was completed back in October. The transfer was granted approval by the Interior Ministry."

"Hedrich? Be sure and run that name. And since when does the Interior Ministry involve themselves in residential acquisitions?"

The sergeant shook his head, not looking up from the series of notations he was making on the back of the folder. Something didn't add up in Brandt's calculus. The sudden proximity of landmark events in Major Goertz's career, immediately preceding his apparent demise. It all seemed too synchronized and interconnected to be coincidental. Papa always said that a police officer didn't have the luxury of believing in coincidence.

"The move to Berlin, a palatial new home, a promotion to a cabinet post... Seems that until recently, Major Goertz was having himself a good year. What was his position prior to his promotion?"

"There are some gaps in his file, but it looks like he was stationed with the Gestapo at RSHA."

Brandt turned to face Faber, placing the binoculars on the dash.

"RSHA? Captain Keppler was also stationed at Reich Security Headquarters before his demotion. Did you know that?"

"That's the first I've heard of it!"

Faber leafed back through the contents of the file more

rapidly, his eyes darting searchingly across the pages.

"Goertz was assigned to Department II at RSHA, section A5."

"What are the responsibilities of section A5?"

"I'll have to look further into it, but it says he served as a liaison on the Berlin resettlement projects."

"What type of resettlement projects?"

"His office was working with Inspector General Speer on property requisitions."

"Albert Speer? That's as high up as it gets. But what interest would the Fuhrer's chief architect have in local resettlement projects?"

"I don't need a file for that," Faber continued. "Speer's office has been in the process of requisitioning large swaths of residential property around Berlin for several years now. His office has been empowered to acquire land for numerous Reich building projects. Identified properties are normally confiscated, condemned and then leveled to make way for redevelopment."

"And their inhabitants?"

"Depends on who they are, or *what* they are. But in general, they're relocated within the city, or elsewhere…"

"Ja, 'elsewhere.' I'd heard of the scope of Minister Speer's grand designs, just never really thought about the personal repercussions," Brandt mused. "So where did Major Goertz's department fit into this process?

"Looks like Goertz's office was tasked with seizing properties in Berlin that belonged to Jewish residents for use by the Reich, as well as scheduling their inhabitants for relocation."

Brandt's mind churned, "Just Jewish residents? That's

interesting."

"How so?"

"Well, Captain Keppler's post at RSHA before his transfer had been in department IV B4. The Jewish Affairs desk."

"Are you sure?"

"Positive. I had Sergeant Roth pull Keppler's RSHA file, after we noticed a missing department insignia on his uniform sleeve."

"And what did you find?"

"I haven't had a chance to look at them in detail yet, but they're in evidence. What I do know is that Captain Keppler's office at IV B4 had a particular area of focus."

"What was it?"

"The relocation of Berlin area Jews!" Brandt revealed.

"Good Lord! I realize that's a vast field, but it seems like a strong common link between the victims. More importantly, when were you going to tell me all this? You holding out on me?"

"No, nothing like that," Brandt chuckled. "I just hadn't seen you again until tonight, and we were a little preoccupied back at the river! Speaking of holding out, what was that awkward exchange between you and Sergeant Wanstedt down at the shoreline?"

"What?"

"Don't play dumb with me. That line Wanstedt fed us about Major Goertz at the *SD* intelligence-training academy? He looked like he'd just swallowed a rat sandwich, and he looked to you to see if you'd like a bite."

The sergeant hesitated, fidgeting distractedly with the files, before responding.

"Are you sure you want to know?"

"Of course! Is that even a legitimate question?"

"It doesn't have anything to do with the case."

"Anton!"

"Alright, alright. Well, it wasn't a domestic training academy. Major Goertz was one of the instructors training Einsatzgruppen units for deployment to *der Ostfront*."

"Task forces? For what purpose?"

"The original premise was that they'd serve as an attachment to *Wehrmacht* units, and would stay behind the army's advances to instill order in the occupied territories."

"That makes sense."

"Then somewhere along the way their assignment evolved… into something much more ominous."

"Ominous?"

"Reports started coming back from the east that these units were engaged in liquidation efforts, and mass killings."

"What?"

"The units began to systematically round up Jews, gypsies, foreign operatives in droves and eliminated them."

"*Mein Gott*, Anton! You're telling me that you believe German polizei units are engaging in a policy of mass elimination in the eastern territories, and that Major Goertz helped train some of these units?"

"He didn't just train them, Konrad, he led some of the first deployments to der Ostfront, which means he would have likely directed and undertaken these activities himself."

"The man was a cabinet minister!"

"I'm just telling you what I've heard."

"From whom?"

"Other officers, soldiers."

"Well, that narrows it down!"

"Men who were there."

"Like?"

"Like sergeants Wanstedt and Reardon... among others."

They fell silent. Stillness descended over the vehicle, broken only by the patter of the wintry precipitation on the roof. Brandt took a deep breath. He felt the cold air spread throughout his lungs. *Two murdered Gestapo officers found within a week of each other. Both having sustained lethal knife wounds, and both with ties to RSHA departments handling Jewish resettlement projects. That's a connection far too big to ignore. And now my partner is talking about mass killings being sanctioned by Reich officials!*

A loud thud shattered the silence. Startled, they looked up to see Sergeant Roth peering through the fogged glass. His palm was pressed against the car's icy windshield, search warrant in hand. They exited the vehicle in unison, mildly embarrassed by their jumpiness.

"*Der Dummkopf!*" Faber chided agitatedly.

Roth was smirking.

"Dummkopf? I thought you'd be much more appreciative. You can't imagine how hard it was to get my hands on this at this time of night."

Brandt smiled. He was glad for a little levity, and to be on the move again. He took the search warrant and stuffed it inside his jacket for safekeeping. He led the way across the ice-laden lawn towards the iron gate that secured the driveway. The freezing rain had formed a thin coating of ice above the snow, accentuating their every step with a crunch. Brandt shook the bars of the vehicle gate. It was locked, or frozen shut. Without hesitation he pulled himself up onto one of the stone pillars that book-ended the gate, and lowered himself down onto the estate grounds on the other side. The sergeants followed suit, and the trio soon found themselves moving along the driveway in the direction of the house.

They proceeded slowly. The darkness limited their visibility, and the footing was slippery. Brandt switched on his flashlight, and veered off in the direction of a detached two-bay garage. Through the windows he could see a vehicle parked inside. *Government tags.* There were no tire tracks on the driveway, and no signs of snow or salt on the car. *It's been parked there awhile.*

Brandt trained his flashlight down the cobblestone path that led to the front entrance. There weren't any footprints visible around the yard or flowerbeds. *The snow and ice would have covered anything more than a day or two old.* He stepped onto the front landing, with Faber and Roth closely in tow. He hesitated, noting the shared look of apprehension on his comrades' cold faces. His flashlight beam shone through a row of windowpanes framing the front door. It was pitch black inside. A phrase he couldn't place flashed through his mind on a loop, *"Darkness within, darkness without"* like a nursery rhyme.

The front door had a brass knocker shaped like an anchor. Brandt switched off his flashlight, and steeled himself. *There's no turning back now.* He delivered a series of resounding knocks. They echoed briefly, and were followed by silence. Somewhere in the distance down the street, a dog howled. Sergeant Roth stepped off the porch and began scanning the front of the house. Brandt repeated the exercise with a series of four even more pronounced knocks.

"This is der Berlin Kriminalpolizei!" he exclaimed, trying the door handle. It was locked.

"Lieutenant!" Roth beckoned.

Brandt stepped down from the porch, his eyes following the path of the sergeant's flashlight. Broken panes of glass were visible on a second story window.

"Can't be a point of entry," Faber offered.

"No, it's broken from the inside," Brandt concurred. "But it gives us another cause to search the premises. Let's find a way in."

On his signal, the sergeants fanned out. They trudged through the snow in opposite directions around the sides of the sprawling mansion, leaving Brandt to check the front. He squeezed himself through a snow-capped hedge of tall bushes bordering the house, their frozen leaves felt razor-sharp against his face and neck. One by one, he inspected a series of first floor windows. Each was locked. He heard the crunch of approaching footsteps. A dark silhouette appeared at the far corner of the house. Then there was a glow. *It's Faber.* The sergeant was silently waving Brandt towards him with his flashlight. Brandt extricated himself from the frozen tentacles of the prickly hedge, and followed. Sergeant Roth waited for them at the rear of the property, standing by a large set of French doors off the back patio.

"They were closed, but not locked. There's no sign they've been forced."

Brandt nodded and eased the right door open. The hinges creaked in protest. They found themselves in a large living room with high ceilings. The beams of their intertwining flashlights bounced off the darkened walls, giving them fragmentary glimpses of the first floor. Brandt blinked rapidly, groping along the wall in the darkness for a light switch. Switch after switch offered no response.

"No power?" Roth queried.

"Electricity hasn't been shut off, otherwise it would be freezing in here. Most likely a breaker."

Brandt trained his beam down one of the corridors off the living room. It led towards the entrance hall, and the front door they had been on the other side of just moments before. Stacks of unopened moving boxes lined the walls. *But the rooms are fully furnished.*

"Looks like the major was still in the process of moving in," Faber observed.

"That, or the previous residents never had a chance to move out," Brandt replied, thinking of the abandoned furnishings and belongings left behind in his own squalid flat.

They felt their way along the hallway until it opened out onto the main entry. A massive double staircase led to the second-floor landing above. Brandt turned to Sergeant Roth, "Check the rest of this floor, and see if you can locate a fuse box. Kriminalsekretar Faber and I will take the upstairs."

As Roth vanished into the maze of rooms off the main hall Brandt exchanged a wary look with Faber. *Nothing feels right about this place.* He headed towards the right staircase and began the ascent. Faber shadowed him, a few paces behind. The hardwood creaked beneath their every step. Brandt hesitated at the top of the landing. The long hall branched in opposite directions.

"Let's check the room where we saw the broken window first," he whispered, gesturing down the far corridor.

They edged forward, flashlights guiding the way. A pair of doorways became visible to their right. As he drew close to the first doorway, Brandt stopped abruptly. His beam had settled on a large smear on the white chair railing. *Blood?*

105

He instinctively unholstered his Walther and looked back to see that the sergeant had done the same. The door was slightly ajar, and the surface around the door handle was similarly stained. Brandt pushed the door open with his foot and stepped into the room with a single motion. He could feel Sergeant Faber's heavy breath over his shoulder. The door opened into a large master bedroom. He strained to bring the room into focus. The disarray was apparent even in the dark. Dressers were open, their contents strewn across the floor. The bed against the far wall was stripped bare, its mattress discolored. A shaft of light from the sergeant's flashlight revealed a massive pool of dried blood spreading out from left to right on its saturated surface. An end table and lamp were overturned in the corner, the drapes above them dangling from a broken rod.

They drew closer to inspect the surface of the mattress and recoiled in tandem as the wall behind the bedframe came into view.

"Was in der Holle!" Faber gasped.

Above the headboard large letters were scrawled in blood. By training both flashlight beams on the wall, they were able to make out the words 'Nomen Nescio.' A loud buzz invaded the room, closely followed by a series of flickers. The lights came back on. The broken lamp made a hissing sound in the corner.

Brandt stood motionless, dumbfounded. His head swam, as his vision adjusted to the restored light. The room felt like it was spinning. He briefly closed his eyes. They heard footsteps scaling the stairs in leaps and bounds, and Sergeant Roth's excited voice in the corridor.

"It wasn't an outage. Most of the breakers had been thrown," Roth faltered, as he entered the room. "Mein Gott!"

Chapter 14

They stood in stunned silence surveying the blood-soaked master bedroom. Brandt was the first to come back into focus. They didn't have much time. When he spoke, his voice was noticeably shaken.

"You two check the rest of the upstairs."

The sergeants snapped to action, heading out into the hallway beyond. Brandt edged closer to the wall; his eyes transfixed by the bloody inscription. Nomen Nescio. It was a Latin phrase indicating anonymity, or literally 'name unknown.' *I've seen it used before, but where?* The rest of the room faded from view, as he focused on the brutally crafted phrase.

In the back of his mind, he could hear the clattering of Faber and Roth as they searched the remainder of the second floor. He closed his eyes. *Nomen Nescio, Nomen Nescio... Herr Name Unknown.* A shudder ran down his spine. Brandt knew where he had seen the term before, and wished that he didn't. He purposefully put on his gloves and inspected the stained mattress cover on the bed, before moving to the broken windowpanes. He crouched to examine the fragments of glass littered across the carpet. He hadn't been afforded the chance to examine an uncontaminated crime scene at Captain Keppler's office. So he needed to focus on the details of the physical evidence here, while he had time.

"The rest of the floor is clear," Faber huffed, as he returned. "The only other sign of disturbance is the den at the end of the hall. It's been ransacked."

"Ransacked? Let me guess, Major Goertz's files?"

"Piles of them, spread from here to kingdom come. Now that we have the lights on, I sent Roth back down to check the main floor."

"Good."

"What about in here?"

"Well, there doesn't seem to be any need for speculation about where Major Goertz was killed before his body was dumped in the Spree. And it's safe to say it has happened within the past 72 to 96 hours, which fits our timeline."

"That's two officers murdered at knifepoint in the past four days! You think Goertz was killed before Captain Keppler?"

"It looks that way."

"But unlike Keppler, he must have put up a fight."

"There was definitely a serious struggle between the assailant and Goertz before he was subdued. And look," Brandt gestured, holding up a sliver of the broken windowpane for the sergeant to see. "This explains the shards of glass we found embedded in the major's forehead."

"From a head on collision with the window."

"And once Goertz was lying incapacitated on the bed, he received the lethal slash. Judging from the amount of blood, the assailant left him there to bleed out for a long time."

Faber shot him a troubled glance.

"There's just one problem."

"And what's that, Anton?"

"It's nothing like the scene we discovered at Captain

Keppler's office."

"Agreed. Keppler was killed by such a swift, efficient cut. It was almost clinical."

"And indifferent."

"As if killing the captain was just the means of gaining access to his files. But this…"

"But Captain Keppler was in a public place, and mostly likely taken by surprise," Faber interjected. "Major Goertz obviously saw his assailant coming. Maybe that complicated things."

"Perhaps, but I think there's more to it than that… *dies war personlich*!"

"Personal? How can you know that?"

"Look at the passion of the act, and its aftermath. Whoever murdered Major Goertz almost literally bathed in his blood afterwards, and then used his bedroom as a canvass."

"Before painstakingly disposing of the body?" Faber countered.

"What?"

"The killer takes his time, creates this mess, then takes the risk of being seen removing the body from the premises?"

"I hadn't thought of it that way."

"Why go to the trouble of dumping the victim in the river? Why bother disposing of a body from a scene left in this condition? And how?"

"I don't know why, but he must have wrapped the body in the missing bedding. That insulation, and the fact that he let the victim bleed out for so long, is the only reason the whole house isn't saturated with blood."

"What about the 'Nomen Nescio?'" Faber queried. "'Name Unknown?' What's that supposed to mean?"

"I've seen the phrase before," Brandt hesitated.

"Where?"

"During my time with the Munich Gestapo."

Brandt noted the sergeant's surprised expression, and avoided his inquiring gaze.

"Gestapo? I wouldn't have guessed that."

"Let's just say that it didn't last long, and that it didn't work out," Brandt said, forcing a smile.

"Understood, Lieutenant. So, how did you come across this phrase?"

"I saw it in the field during mass roundups, especially of Jews. When the high volume of arrests made it impractical to process everyone by name, agents would arrest individuals under the pseudonym 'Herr Nomen Nescio'."

"So what's the perpetrator's message here? Gestapo involvement? Or implicating Major Goertz as a Jew?"

"Or maybe that the suspect is a Jew, himself?"

"What?"

Faber's follow-up was derailed by Sergeant Roth's return.

"*Alles klar* on the main floor. No signs of forced entry, or other disturbance. Should I call it in to headquarters?"

"Not yet, let's take a look at the major's study first," Brandt replied. "See what we can make of the paper trail."

The major's office had clearly been originally designed as a home den. Custom-made wood bookshelves, lined with rows of leather-bound volumes, framed both sides of the stone fireplace. The room's transformation into a working office, a veritable repository of files, had apparently taken place only recently. As a result, the comforts of the upscale home library had since been engulfed by a legion of government-issued filing cabinets and vaults. As was the case at Captain Keppler's office, the floor was covered in layer upon layer of rifled files and folders.

"This guy really brought his work home with him!" Roth chirped.

Brandt managed a smirk. *Always trying to lighten the mood.* Faber, conversely, offered the young sergeant the unamused look of a parent admonishing a child.

The orderly lines of filing cabinets were off-center, each showing signs of being rummaged through. The most visibly damaged units, were the pair of cabinets that bracketed the wall behind the major's desk, like two metallic sentinels. Their drawers had been forced open, and pried from the runners, leaving their contents spilled across the Oriental rug below. Each of the drawers of the ornate desk had also been pulled off their tracks.

Brandt leaned down to examine the desk. In the open space below the center drawer, he spotted a small desk safe. Like the rest of its counterparts, the safe had also been pried open. It was empty. *What was he looking for?* Brandt reached down and sifted through a pile of the documents scattered across the rug below him.

"What's this guy after? These are all transfer files," Brandt thought aloud.

"What kind of transfer files?" Roth replied, his voice echoing from a walk-in closet he was inspecting.

"They're labor assignments. Consignment of Jews, foreign workers, and prison inmates to work in German factories and armament plants."

"The major's department in the Interior oversees labor allocation," Faber chimed in, from behind a row of cabinets.

"Is that right?"

"It is, and unless I'm mistaken, those are klassifiziert files," Faber chided.

Brandt flashed him a sardonic smile. The Kriminalsekretar could be a real stickler at times. He absently sorted the files into a stack and set them aside, running his hand across the metal ridge of the pried safe drawer. The wail of sirens could be heard in the distance. The sirens grew louder. Brandt moved across the study, and opened a set of doors out onto the balcony. The sirens pierced the damp night air. A small stream of flashing blue lights became visible through the line of trees, their bleary glare distorted by the rain and ice. He watched the steady advance of the vehicles apprehensively. *Verdammt! This is their destination.*

He returned to the den, and tried to close the doors behind him, but they stuck. A stack of framed pictures had fallen behind a nearby table, and become wedged under the bottom of the door. He pried the frames loose, stopping briefly to examine the family photographs they contained. *This isn't Major Goertz's family.* He was pulled from this distraction by the sound of cars skidding to a halt on the siding of the nearby street.

"The scavenger hunt is over. Let's call this in to headquarters, before our being here raises any further questions."

"Right," Roth responded, already headed for the landing.

Brandt returned to the major's desk. He purposefully avoided meeting Faber's piercing gaze, as he tucked a small stack of the transfer files under his arm and headed out into the hall. The sergeant caught up to him before he could reach the stairwell.

"Lieutenant! Tell me you're not taking those!"

Brandt looked at him intently, a faint trace of a smile bending across his face.

"Do you have any idea the charges for removing classified files from the home of a cabinet minister?"

"A stern lecture from your partner?"

"This is no laughing matter! This residence is about to be declared a capital crime scene, and those files are restricted!"

"Restricted? Restricted to whom?" Brandt snapped, feeling any trace of mirth drain from his expression. "To Major Goertz's killer, who has already had access to them? To the Gestapo? The same Gestapo preventing us from examining the files from Captain Keppler's office?"

"You can't compare..."

"Two former Gestapo officials killed, two completely disparate crime scenes, and two sets of classified documents rifled! That tells me that these files represent our best chance to make some connection between the murders of Major Goertz and Captain Keppler. What do you say?"

Faber was unmoved.

"This is no longer an isolated incident, Anton. And it's not going to stop here. If we're going to prevent a repeat of this bloodshed, I think we deserve a look at the same documents the killer's been consulting. And the Gestapo certainly isn't going to accommodate us!"

Faber stared back at him, stone-faced. The voices of arriving Gestapo agents resounded in the entry below. Brandt could feel the heated flush of blood rising on his neck. He kept his gaze fixated on Faber's, refusing to break contact. He saw a look of resignation, creep across the sergeant's tired features. Brandt's hand slid the files inside the lining of his jacket, ending the standoff just as the sound of footsteps began to ascend the stairwell.

"Now, can you and Sergeant Roth fend for yourselves until some of our own units arrive?"

"Of course."

"When backup from our precinct gets here, brief them and then get out of here and get yourselves some rest."

"Yes, Lieutenant! And what about you?"

"I'm going back to headquarters to file a report for Kriminaldirektor Brunner. I want to let the colonel know what we've found, before he gets the Gestapo's side of the story."

Chapter 15

The precinct building was quiet in the hours before dawn. Brandt entered by a set of side doors off Magazin Strasse, and quickly descended the flight of stone stairs to the basement. He was further relieved to find the lower level vacant, aside from an unfamiliar sergeant at the evidence desk.

In the still confines of the examination room, he wearily collapsed into the wooden swivel chair, glad to be off of his feet. He stared blankly at the documents he had splayed across the desk, and rubbed his burning eyes. It was nearly 5am. *The night that wouldn't end. How many nights does this make without sleep anyway?* He shifted in his chair restlessly. An ache in his back slowly spread up his spine, coming to a rest between his shoulder blades.

He willed himself to concentrate. By his estimate, he had less than two hours to write his report, and accompany it across town to personally brief Colonel Brunner. It was well known that the Kriminaldirektor promptly arrived at headquarters each morning at 7am, and Brandt knew that the Gestapo wouldn't be far behind with the filing of their own grievances.

We needed more time at Major Goertz's estate! Who had tipped the Gestapo off so quickly? The medical examiner? Sergeant Wanstedt?

He straightened himself in his chair determinedly, and systematically began to cross-check the file folders. He scoured the documents he had just checked out of evidence for any points of correspondence with the ones he had covertly procured from the major's residence. He searched for any sign of overlap between the documents and the agencies that issued them. *Anything!*

He shifted his attention to a stack of files obtained from Captain Keppler's office. Each of the folders in the stack was labeled *Arbeit-Dateien: Berlin Juden.*

Transfer orders for Berlin area Jews. A record of each individual's conscription into the labor force, accompanied by the correlating factory assignments. How did these files slip by the overly zealous censors at the Gestapo?

The endless procession of names, dates, and locations became jumbled in his mind, the words becoming increasingly hard to decipher and comprehend. The pain in his back had advanced to the base of his skull. Brandt leaned forward against the table, and buried his head in his hands. He rubbed his temples with his thumbs. He felt the urge to close his eyes, *just for a minute*, but he resisted.

Another folder from Captain Keppler's crime scene drew his attention. It contained a series of photographs from the captain's office that he hadn't seen before. He thumbed through them one by one. *Why wasn't I given these during my initial review?* A detail in one of the photos caught his eye. Behind the deceased victim's slouched body hovered an archaic row of wooden filing cabinets, each drawer engraved with a distinct insignia. *These were long gone by the time I examined the captain's office.*

He magnified the images. Each insignia consisted of the same emblem, *a laurel wreath encircling a skull*. He didn't recognize the insignia. *Where had these filing cabinets been when I canvassed the crime scene? Removed, like everything else, by the Gestapo? But where were they now?* He felt like he was chasing his tail. His thoughts gave way to frustration.

He pushed himself away from the table, and slumped down in the unforgiving chair. He closed his eyes. Images from the night before paraded across the inside of his eyelids. The bloody inscription Nomen Nescio; the major's bloated and brutalized face beneath the tarp; the layers of files strewn across the study floor… Brandt's eyes opened with a start. *The files at the Goertz estate!*

He quickly sifted through the folders he had confiscated from the house earlier that evening, until he reached a familiar folder marked, '*Die Lodenfabrik — Juden Arbeitskrafte.*' The file contained lists of Berlin area Jews conscripted into the workforce of the local Loden Works Factory by Major Goertz's department. *Didn't I just see that same factory referenced in the captain's files?* He leafed back through the labor transfers from Captain Keppler's office, flipping through them rapidly until he came to a tab marked, '*Die Lodenfabrik — Juden Arbeit-Dateien.*'

His pulse quickened, as he surveyed the contents of the folders side-by-side. His index finger trembled slightly as he traced the details of the first conscription order to the bottom of the page. The transfer authorizations contained dual signature lines, *executed by order of SS Hauptsturmfuhrer Ernst Keppler and SS Major Theodore Goertz*! *There it is! There's our connection!*

He felt a shiver pass through his frame. An accompanying surge of adrenaline coursed through his body dissolving his fatigue in the enthusiasm of discovery. He hurriedly leafed through each file in the stack of Loden Werke factory transfers.

Every assignment contained the signed authorization of both Captain Keppler and Major Goertz, as the respective RSHA representatives of Department IV and Department II.

Keppler and Goertz were working together at RSHA on a massive project. Who were they reporting to though? Minister Speer? And more importantly, what connection could it have to their deaths?

He interspersed several of Captain Keppler's files with those from the Goertz estate, and placed them both back into the lining of his jacket, before returning the rest of the trove to evidence. The sergeant at the desk gave him a look that was hard to gauge, but Brandt didn't linger long enough to give it a second thought.

He clambered back up the dark stairwell towards his office. He had to determine what to include in his report to Kriminaldirektor Brunner in order to justify their actions, and more importantly, what to leave out. He heard a door slam, and rapid footsteps descending the stairs from the floor above. He looked down at his jacket to be sure that nothing from his hidden cache was evident. Sergeant Roth nearly bowled him over, as he rounded the corner of the second-floor landing.

"Sergeant Roth? What are you doing down here?"

"Lieutenant! I was looking for you, actually. Kriminalsekretar Faber said you'd likely be down at Evidence."

"Speaking of Sergeant Faber, I told him to send you home to get some sleep."

"With all due respect, Lieutenant, I didn't feel much like sleeping after what we saw tonight. No need to go home and disturb the Frau und Kind at this hour. Besides, Faber wanted me to let you know before you briefed Colonel Brunner that the Gestapo has already revoked our access to the Goertz estate."

"They don't waste any time."

"They've staked jurisdiction, and apparently plan to file a grievance with the department regarding the conduct of our search."

Brandt winced. He hoped they hadn't beaten him to the punch before he could brief the Kriminaldirektor. He felt the packet of folders jabbing against his ribs, through the lining of his jacket, and allowed himself the glimpse of a smile.

"That's unfortunate, but it may have been worth the risk."

"What do you mean?" Roth asked, surprised.

"Some of the files I borrowed from Major Goertz's estate indicate collaboration between Major Goertz and Captain Keppler while they were at RSHA."

"What?"

"They were working in tandem on the requisitioning of Berlin properties, as well as on the conscription and assignment of Jewish laborers to at least one factory location in the city."

"That seems like more than a coincidence!"

"In essence, they were removing Berlin *Jews* from their homes, relocating them to designated Jewish districts, and then conscripting them into factory work. Or having them deported if they didn't meet the factory criteria."

"That's incredible! You think this connection could be a link to their murders?"

"I don't know, but someone has gone to a lot of trouble to cover up the collaboration of their departments."

"What factory were they assigning workers to?"

"A location northeast of the city called the Lodenfabrik.

Have you heard of it?"

"Die Loden Werke? It's a major armaments and munitions plant, located up near Plotzensee."

Brandt glanced furtively up at the landing above, then back in the direction of the basement. He checked inside his jacket and pulled out a pair of folders. He handed them to the sergeant.

"Take these, and keep them concealed. They catalogue the personnel and locations of each labor assignment. I want you to cross-reference them for any more points of overlap."

"Directly, Lieutenant!"

"And Sergeant Roth," Brandt said, halting his colleague's departure. "These files don't leave your sight. I have to head crosstown to brief Colonel Brunner, before the Gestapo can fan the flames any further. I'll also try to contact the Lodenfabrik to get a current roster of their workforce. When you're done with your examination, bring the files to my office, and I'll get them back into Evidenz."

The young sergeant saluted crisply, and bounded up the stairs two at a time, as Brandt turned to retrace his steps down towards the motor pool. Kriminaldirektor Brunner would be in soon, and would undoubtedly be expecting him. *Now for the tricky part.*

Chapter 16

Dawn never really broke that morning, it had simply slowly become less dark. Or perhaps that was just the sensation that accompanied one day passing into another without the interlude of sleep. A fog rolled across the canal, cloaking the Werdescher Market and Kriminalpolizei headquarters in mist. Brandt couldn't shake a strong sense of foreboding, as he was ushered into Colonel Brunner's office. As he briefed the Kriminaldirektor, he realized the colonel's neutral grey eyes were as impenetrable as the fog that enveloped the district. In the end, Brandt had opted to be as forthcoming as possible with the chief about the status of the case, without disclosing the full scope of information at his disposal. After all, if he couldn't trust Brunner, his investigation had been destined for failure from the outset.

Initially, the colonel had expressed displeasure at the amount of heat he was already receiving from higher-ups in the Gestapo in response to their search tactics. However, the colonel's demeanor had visibly softened as he learned of the discovery of an interdepartmental link between Captain Keppler and Major Goertz. By the time Brandt disclosed that the Gestapo's personnel files had apparently been whitewashed in an attempt to cover-up this connection, the Kriminaldirektor's distemper had totally dissolved. Had Brandt even detected a look of pride in the colonel's inscrutably stoic features? It was hard to say. *Maybe that's just what I had wanted to see.* Regardless, Colonel Brunner had worked with his father, and in a way, garnering approbation from the colonel was like a pat on the back from his dad, *in absentia.* And he missed those pats.

At the conclusion of their meeting, the colonel had agreed that Brandt should stay the course with the leads he was currently pursuing, and promised him continued support in the face of the Gestapo's obstructions. Before he had left, the Kriminaldirektor had proffered to look into any areas of overlap between the assignments of Major Goertz and Captain Keppler, and the resettlement projects of Minister Speer. The colonel had then dismissed him with a thin smile, that Brandt had taken as a stamp of approval.

As he climbed the stairs back to his own office, Brandt couldn't help but feel that the briefing had gone as well as could be expected under the circumstances. It felt like the first hint of good news he had experienced in days. *But I didn't leave my office door open.*

He eased the door open gently, and a familiar scent washed over him. He felt his pulse quicken, instinctively. His senses were in a heightened state before his cluttered mind knew the reason why. Across the room, he glimpsed Erica Graffe gazing out of his window, her figure silhouetted by the first rays of the morning sun. He wasn't sure if he was more surprised to see her, or that the sun had broken through the overcast Berlin skies for the first time since he had arrived in the city. Perhaps the two were linked.

"Fraulein Graffe?" he managed.

She turned. Her smile was as radiant as the shafts of light that surrounded her. She wore a blue patterned blouse, which magnified the color of her eyes. She was more stunning in blue than she had been in red.

"Guten Morgen, Konrad!" she beamed. "I was on my way into the city center for a morning meeting, and thought I'd take you up on your offer."

"My offer?"

"To stop by your office. Besides, I wanted to thank you again for your late-night heroics," she smiled, pausing at his apparent confusion. "But from the looks of it, you haven't slept since coming to my rescue."

He suddenly felt self-conscious of his disheveled state. He realized he must have looked, and smelled, like hell on a dirty platter. He rubbed a hand across the stubble on his cheeks, and looked around distractedly. Had he suggested she stop by his office sometime? At least his quarters appeared tidy, a byproduct of having rarely used it since his arrival. Out of the corner of his eye, he spotted a stack of files on his desk, and could make out a handwritten note from Sergeant Roth attached to them.

"Of course. You'll have to pardon my, uh, my appearance, Fraulein Graffe," he stammered, trying to reorient his bearings. "How is your ankle feeling?"

"Much better, thank you," she responded, the lilt gone from her voice.

He recognized a look of embarrassment in her eyes. She had mistaken his momentary disorientation for indifference, and had walked to retrieve her jacket from the coat rack.

"I'm sorry, I've obviously picked a bad time. I should have called first," she said, without looking up. "I wanted to leave you some passes so you could take a proper tour of the symphony hall when you had the time. They're on your desk."

"Fraulein Graffe… Erica, please, sit down. I'm the one who is at fault," he recovered, with a smile. "That's very thoughtful of you. Let me get you a cup of Kaffee and we can talk."

"Are you sure?" she asked, hesitating by the door.

"I'm positive. As you can see, I'm not a morning person, much less when I'm operating on no sleep."

"*Oh mein*! Is everything alright?"

"I'm just recovering from being on call all night. White or black?"

"If you're certain, but I'll just stay a moment," she replied, taking a seat. "And black will be fine."

The phone on his desk intruded with a plaintive reverberation. *Perfekt!* He offered her an apologetic grin, before raising the receiver to his ear.

"*Das ist Oberleutnant Brandt.*"

Kriminalsekretar Faber's agitated voice bellowed from the other end, tinged with concern as it crackled across the distorted connection. *A suspect?? Has Sergeant Roth briefed me yet?* Brandt's excitement was quickly tempered by the instant realization that there would be no coffee date. He briefly lowered the receiver.

"Fraulein Graffe, you'll have to excuse me for a moment. I'm afraid this call can't wait."

She was already on her feet. Her lips curled into a smile at the corners. Her eyes seemed to convey understanding. She wasn't offended.

"I've told you, it's Erica, and I should be leaving anyway. Perhaps another time?"

"I'd like that, Erica," Brandt said, managing a smile, before returning to the call.

The Kriminalsekretar's impatience was tangible as he resumed speaking. Brandt leafed through the files that Roth had left on his desk, as Faber's words reverberated in his ear. Next to the files, a handwritten envelope bulged with the outline of two guest-passes to the symphony hall. Through the turmoil, Brandt heard the door close, and looked up to catch one last glimpse of Erica Graffe as she walked out of his office.

Chapter 17

Brandt hastily approached the briefing room located deep in the bowels of the old stone building, with Sergeant Roth matching him stride for stride. Kriminaldirektor Brunner had issued a search warrant for the Loden Works factory grounds and had assigned tactical support for the mission. Brandt felt a wave of nerves course through him as he took an open seat in the corner. He tapped his foot expectantly. Roth had been called over by a colleague from the tactical team, whose members sat in a tight circle boisterously exchanging jokes. Brandt caught the tail end of one of the offerings from a ruddy-faced young corporal, who tripped over his words in his race to get to the punch line.

"The maid answers and tells him, 'Your wife can't come to the phone, I'm afraid she's in the bedroom with another man.' So the union boss says, 'What?! I want you to go get my gun from the dresser and kill the both of them!' When the maid protests that she can't do that, he tells her, 'Do it now, and if I don't hear the shots, I'm going come home and kill all three of you!' So, she leaves the phone, two shots ring out, and she comes back and tells him she did it. The union boss says, 'Good, now what did you do with the gun?' She says, 'I threw it in the pool.' And the union boss says, 'Pool, what pool? We don't have a pool!'"

Laughter echoed off the stone walls, none more robust

than the guffaws of Sergeant Roth. Brandt smiled, glad for a little levity to temper his anxious state. Amidst the frivolity, the door swung open abruptly, and Major Kaufmann entered the briefing room. Sergeant Faber followed closely in his wake. The major gestured curtly for Brandt to join him at the podium.

"Alright recess is over, take your seats. For those of you who don't know him, this is Inspector Brandt. He'll be your lead on this excursion," Kaufmann announced, above the din of scraping desk and chair legs. Sergeant Faber, if you'll pass these around, we'll get started."

"Certainly, Herr Major," Faber chirped, spring into action.

"This is a photograph of our suspect," Kaufmann continued, pinning a photo to the board. "According to his labor file, his name is Jacob Hirsch, a 46-year-old Jewish male. He's a veteran of the great war, and as far as we know, he has no prior record. He was assigned to the Lodenfabrik in March of this year. The factory transfer is his last known placement, and where we lose track of him."

The major reached down and picked up an oversized scroll of paper he had propped against the wall. He meticulously unrolled it until it was flat against the board, pinning it at the corners next to the photograph of Jacob Hirsch. Brandt could make out architectural drafts of property lines and floor plans on the document, and a crest at the base of the blueprint bearing the words *'die Loden Werke'*.

"Excuse me, Major, but if the suspect is part of the Lodenfabrik workforce, why not use the factory's security detail to locate and apprehend him?" a young tactical officer in the front row interjected.

The question earned the officer a withering glare from the

major. Brandt hadn't seen the business end of Major Kaufmann before, and quickly noted that he was not one to be trifled with in these settings.

"Due to an increase in deportations over the past six months, the factory's workforce has become increasingly transient. Gaps exist in our personnel files too, which impedes our ability to track the movements of certain individuals. As a result, we can't confirm whether the suspect is still assigned to the plant without going in ourselves."

"Understood," the officer quickly replied, swallowing hard.

"And as Jacob Hirsch is wanted for questioning in relation to an ongoing homicide investigation, apprehending him is exactly what we intend to do," Kaufmann concluded, firmly.

"Major, a question?" inquired a deep-set voice from the far corner of the room. It belonged to the tactical unit commander, Kommandeur Rausch. "If the suspect has been assigned to factory labor for the past six months, how could he be involved in a homicide that happened outside the compound?"

"That's an excellent point, Kommandeur. According to his transfer file, the suspect has a Jewish work pass from the Reich Labor Bureau."

A pass that was granted by one of the victims! Had Captain Keppler unwittingly signed his own death warrant when he issued the pass that granted Jacob Hirsch the ability to move about the capital freely? Hirsch had combat training and experience to boot.

"This work pass allows anyone who possesses it to commute to the Fabrik on a daily basis from their local districts. So, like many other Jewish workers from the Berlin area, he has not been restricted to the factory premises over the period of time that he's been assigned there," Kaufmann concluded, turning his gaze to Brandt. "Is there anything you'd like to add Inspector?"

"Just one thing, Herr Major. You all may be wondering why we have asked for tactical backup in this situation. Major Kaufmann has advised me that the Lodenfabrik is in close proximity to nearby Jewish relocation settlements, as well as foreign worker camps. Those factors have made the surrounding areas a breeding ground for violence and pockets of resistance. This is why we requested your support. We don't anticipate being met with opposition, but if we are, we want to be prepared for it. So, be alert."

"Correct. We don't have any record of the suspect being affiliated with organized resistance groups, but we want to take every precaution," Kaufmann affirmed.

"Otherwise, our objective is precise. We're there to conduct a quick sweep of the factory compound, and to apprehend the suspect if he's present. No detours." Brandt concluded.

"There you have it. Move out. *Die Fabrik Wache* have been made aware of your impending arrival. Kommandeur Rausch will direct you to the motor pool."

Chapter 18

They jostled roughly in their seats as the transport truck downshifted and diverged from the main avenue. Looking out the rear window, Brandt could see the other vehicles in their small convoy exit onto an unpaved dirt access road. For a stretch they mirrored the bends of the nearby river. He could smell the acrid scent of the factory, as the first stacks became visible above the tree line. Soon, billowing plumes of smoke swallowed the horizon, adding another layer of gloom to the bleak morning sky.

"You think this is our man?" Faber asked above the roar of the engine."

"I don't know, but he certainly fits the profile."

"There are a lot of points of connection."

"Agreed. Hirsch was conscripted into the workforce by Captain Keppler, and assigned to the Lodenfabrik by Major Goertz. His labor transfer was signed by both men, and the travel pass allowing him to live off premises was granted by Keppler."

"And Hirsch's name shows up all over the visitors log at Captain Keppler's office, right up until the week of his murder."

"Right, the log is what separates him from the other potential suspects. That gives him first-hand knowledge, access, and motive. And what's a Jewish factory worker doing visiting an *SS* Hauptsturmfuhrer on a regular basis?" Brandt concluded.

But where was his prior record? Why did Hirsch's personal history vanish into thin air outside of the transfer files and visitors log? Just like everyone else in this investigation.

Their truck accelerated, closing the distance between them and the lead vehicles, as they veered away from the river and towards a widening set of train tracks on the perimeter of the factory grounds. They passed the entrance to an iron foundry and an assembly plant, before taking the fork in the road marked "*Lodenfabrik — Zugang Verboten.*" This 'closed-access' route led them to a service entrance near the worker's dormitories. The guard post barriers stood open and unmanned, in anticipation of their arrival.

Their vehicle ground to a halt, and they quickly filed in with the officers from the tactical unit. The agents from the truck ahead of them had already disembarked, and were flowing through the factory gates. Brandt felt a sudden rush of adrenaline in his torso that spread out towards his limbs. A pair of factory guards at the service entrance waved them through the gates without delay. Their arms extended in a formal salute, as Brandt passed through the checkpoint and joined Kommandeur Rausch at the head of the detachment. Brandt gestured for the task force to close ranks. The agents huddled around expectantly.

"We'll divide into two units, one group with Kommandeur Rausch, one with me," he instructed. "Starting here in the dormitories, we'll sweep one level at a time. Once this area is clear, we'll move to the factory floor, and then out onto…"

His directives were cut short by a shrill report that pierced the dry hum of the factory machinery. His head turned on a swivel. *Gunfire?* His fears were quickly confirmed, first by the look of shock on Kommandeur Rausch's face, and then by the echo of another gun report, followed by another.

Before he could make sense of the situation, he found himself on the move, signaling for the detachment to follow him. *Those reports came from the northeast side of the factory.* He recalled the floor plan to his mind. The reports had come from the vicinity of the main entrance and the offloading courtyard.

He spotted a staircase that led to an elevated walkway spanning the length of the main building. He sprinted up the stairs, the footsteps of the legion of agents behind him echoing in his ears. He ran along the length of the exterior brick wall on the east side of the factory, past rows of windows that looked down onto the machine room floors. He caught glimpses of workers running about in confusion. Up ahead, he could see where the walkway opened onto a large observation deck. He reached the landing first, and leaned over the railing to behold the unfolding chaos in the terrace below.

A black mass of Gestapo troops streamed into the courtyard, spilling from the row of parked military trucks that surrounded the factory entrance. The first arrivers among the Gestapo agents had already begun haphazardly rounding up workers in the yard, creating hysteria and causing violent exchanges to break out with their aggressive tactics. A random warning shot was fired up into the air, by a stone-faced corporal at the man gate, accompanied by the shrieks of some nearby female workers.

Jesus Christus!

He located a stairway leading down from the landing onto the terrace level. Within a moment, he found Kriminalsekretar Faber and Kommandeur Rausch hovering just over his shoulder, and motioned them both towards the stairs.

"Someone obviously tipped off our friends at the Gestapo, but let's try to put a halt to the aggression before it escalates any further. Kommandeur, you and your men attempt to restore order among the workers. Sergeant Faber and I will handle the Gestapo."

"Immediately, Lieutenant!"

Without waiting for further reply, Brandt rapidly began to descend the stairs. Across the courtyard he saw a scuffle break out, accompanied by sobs and shrieks. A pocket of Gestapo agents, were roughly corralling some women laborers, separating them from their children in the process. Several male workers had broken away from their grouping and were trying to help the women. Brandt heard a shot, and saw one of the men fall to the ground. More shouts and screams ensued. *This is spiraling out of control!* He was running now, pushing his way through the crowd in the direction of the chaos.

Another shot was fired into the air, and the workers pulled back. At the center of the crowd Brandt could see a Gestapo agent forcefully pulling a sobbing woman away from a young boy. As he drew closer, Brandt watched the boy pick up a rock from the ground and sling it in the direction of his mother's assailant. It struck the agent on the cheek below his helmet. Brandt pushed himself to run faster.

The stricken Gestapo agent had released the woman. She dropped to the ground, and instantly scurried across the dirt to cover the child. The agent's hand was pressed against his face, where a bright red stream trickled through his fingers. Then the agent's hand was on the rifle strapped across his back. He slung it around his body and strode towards the woman and child. He raised the butt of his rifle high into the air. *No!* Brandt could now feel his hand moving to unholster his own weapon, still in full stride, his mouth shouting above the din.

"Halten!"

Brandt pulled up 10 meters from the officer, halted by a blur of motion in his peripheral vision. A tall, strapping worker came running free from the crowd, his broad shoulders sending the Gestapo agent forcefully to the ground. The fallen agent's rifle clattered across the dirt floor of the courtyard towards the crowd. *Scheisse!*

Another nearby officer instantly responded in force, swinging the butt of his rifle, and striking the worker in the back of the head. The man fell to the ground in a clump. Brandt stood rooted to the spot, watching the exchange dumbfounded. But now he moved again. He saw that the first Gestapo agent had regained his footing, and had drawn his firearm to take aim at the fallen worker.

The fallen man didn't even raise a hand in his own defense. He peered up from the ground with unsteady eyes, his expression a mixture of resignation and contempt. Brandt stepped in between the agent and the crouching worker, and forcefully pushed the Gestapo officer's pistol to a lowered position.

"What do you think you're doing? Holster your weapon, corporal!"

"That Jewish swine! He put his hands on a soldier of the Reich…" the agent fumed.

The agent glared at Brandt. He was shaking with rage. He had murder in his eyes, as he again moved forcefully towards the fallen worker.

He'll be dealt with!" Brandt responded, using his leverage to hold the corporal at bay. Out of the corner of his eye, he could see Faber arriving at the edge of the growing crowd of onlookers, accompanied by several members from the tactical unit. "Sergeant Faber, remove this man," Brandt yelled, gesturing towards the injured worker.

Faber swiftly obliged, and Brandt watched as he attempted to wrestle the dazed worker to his feet. The aggrieved Gestapo agent had been pulled a few feet away by his comrade, who along with several other agents had stepped in to intervene. He still glared menacingly, his eyes darting between Brandt, and his Jewish assailant.

"I don't care about your rank, Lieutenant! We have jurisdiction here!" the agent sputtered, dabbing his hand against his lacerated cheek.

"Jurisdiction?" Brandt fumed. "We're here to serve an arrest warrant signed by the Kriminaldirektor, himself! So, this is now our jurisdiction, and if you have an issue with that you can take it up with Colonel Brunner's office!"

The gathering Gestapo agents looked at him questioningly. He felt his anger rising. The Gestapo's heavy-handed tactics had likely flushed out Jacob Hirsch, ruining any chance they had of taking him unawares. He also felt further emboldened by the arrival of more and more agents from the tactical unit.

"We were under orders to apprehend a suspect in a series of capital homicides, and your arbitrary blundering has all but assured his escape."

"Lieutenant!" Faber leaned in confidentially, the worker in tow "you shouldn't stir up the hornets' nest."

"I'm not going to preside over an investigation where innocent women and children are trampled in the pursuit of the guilty, Sergeant Faber!" Brandt snapped.

"Innocent?!" the Gestapo corporal scoffed.

Brandt didn't respond. He was too distracted by the sight of the injured Jewish worker in the sergeant's custody. Gone was the man's veneer of passive resignation. He stared wildly at Brandt, resisting Sergeant Faber's efforts to move him away from the fray, with renewed defiance. But there was something else in his look, something that Brandt couldn't place. The sounds of the continued clamor and disorder throughout the courtyard brought him back to the matter at hand.

This is a powder keg with a short fuse, that needs to be doused right now.

"Corporal, have your men stand down!"

The disconcerted agent glowered in his direction, unbowed.

"You're directly obstructing an investigation authorized by *der Chef der Berlin Kriminalpolizei*. Have your men stand down, now!"

The corporal wavered, then looked towards the factory entrance. Brandt followed his gaze. Sturmscharfuhrer Fritz Heller had moved into view, standing astride the running board of a black Gestapo truck at the main gate. *I might have guessed. Schonbern's trained dog.* Heller offered Brandt a familiar, disdainful smirk, before signaling for his men to withdraw.

He gruffly barked out an accompanying command that resounded across the terrace, "Clear the yard!"

As he watched the Gestapo agents disengage and recede back in the direction of the main gates, Brandt allowed himself to momentarily exhale. *This will be a temporary retreat. The Gestapo never pulls back for long.*

Kommandeur Rausch's men took their cues from the Gestapo's withdraw, and began to disperse throughout the courtyard. The workers who needed medical attention were moved to the factory infirmary. Within moments, the plant's guards and orderlies began to cautiously reemerge, directing the shaken laborers back to their work stations. Brandt watched from a distance as order was slowly restored at the Lodenfabrik. *What a debacle. Kriminaldirektor Brunner will not be pleased.*

Across the terrace, he saw Sergeant Faber engaged in an animated conversation with a group of factory orderlies. The pack of orderlies all wore machinist bands around their arms. Brandt tracked the sergeant's rapid movements around the yard with interest, as he disengaged from the orderlies, and quickly directed a pair of nearby agents to begin cordoning off tables in an adjacent workstation. Once his rounds were completed, the sergeant trudged back across the courtyard in Brandt's direction.

"I thought that went well," he chided, as he approached.

"Do you think so?"

"When you're ready, we're designating an area to conduct interrogations of some of the workers."

"You work fast."

"Not fast enough. Trying to extract the suspect after a debacle like that, *eins zu einer Million*. Not to mention, I have a factory orderly who says that Jacob Hirsch was transferred out of here months ago."

"Months ago? Do you believe him?"

"I don't see a reason not to, people in here can't afford to stick their necks out."

"True. What about the worker who attacked the corporal?"

"That was suicidal!" Faber exclaimed. "He's in the infirmary, and he'll be fine, but there will be hell to pay for that."

"I expect so. I want to talk to the orderly."

"I thought you might, I'll bring him over."

The sergeant returned momentarily, with one of machinists Brandt had seen him talking with before. The man had a doughy face that framed his abrasive expression. Brandt couldn't tell if the worker was upset at being detained for questioning, or if his face always bore the look of disdain.

"Lieutenant Brandt, this is Kirk Daschle. He's the factory machinist supervisor. He was the head orderly of Jacob Hirsch's department here."

"Was."

"Yes, Lieutenant. As I mentioned, he claims that Jacob Hirsch was transferred some time ago."

"That will be all, sergeant."

"Good luck with this one," Faber muttered under his breath, as he retreated back in the direction of the cordoned-off tables. Brandt returned his attention to the orderly, who continued to stare at the ground.

"Ordonanz Daschle, is it? How long have you been assigned to the Lodenfabrik?"

The orderly remained silent. The dull features of his rotund face were unmoved, except for a slight quiver of his cheeks. *Nervous*? But when he looked up, Brandt could see that his eyes glistened with nothing but contempt.

"'About a year," he sputtered.

"And you maintain that your former co-worker, Jacob Hirsch, is no longer assigned here? When did his transfer take place?"

There was a protracted silence.

"Don't recall."

"You don't recall? And why would Jacob Hirsch be transferred so quickly from a plant he was just assigned to this spring?"

"The way you shuffle workers in and out of here like cattle... I can't keep track of them all. All I know is that he hasn't been working here for months."

"You supervised his unit, and yet you can't tell me exactly where he was transferred, or when?"

"I'm telling you that I don't know."

Brandt felt his already depleted reserves of patience wearing thin. It had been a hell of a night, and an even worse day. This orderly's sour attitude and dead-end answers were the final straw. He drew closer.

"Here's what *I'm telling you*... I expect you to cooperate to the fullest extent right now, or we can continue this line of questioning in an interrogation cell."

He noticed Daschle's eyes shift with discomfort, and the slight twitch in his cheeks return. The orderly's dour expression softened.

"What do you want from me?"

"As an orderly, you're accountable for the workers in your department, right? If one of them goes missing, you're the one who answers for it."

"So?"

"So, you must have some recollection of the timing, or location, of Hirsch's transfer. You didn't just let someone on your watch go unaccounted for without asking why."

The orderly shifted uncomfortably on his feet, rocking slowly from side to side.

"What's it going to be, Ordonanz Daschle?"

"Someone higher up must have been looking out for him. Not long after he left, there were rumors he had landed a position as a grounds-keeper at some *Kirche* in the city." *Transferred to a church?*

"When did this happen?"

"It was a few months back, I don't remember exactly."

"Anything else? *Die Kirche?*"

"St Matthew, St Michael, something like that. That's all I know."

Brandt looked Daschle hard in the eyes. His scrutiny of the orderly was interrupted by the commotion of raised voices near the entrance of the courtyard. He looked up to see Fritz Heller's colleague, Sturmscharfuhrer Kohl approaching him on foot. *That ceasefire was even shorter than I imagined.* Over Kohl's shoulder, Brandt could see a long, black staff car idling outside the front gate. The rear window was lowered just enough to reveal the profile of Major Weskamp. *Schonbern's adjutant, and odds are he's not here to invite me to another banquet.*

Brandt turned back to Daschle, who looked increasingly anxious to leave as the Gestapo sergeant approached.

"You can go, Herr Daschle, but we'll keep in touch," Brandt said, dismissing him with a wave of the hand. The orderly hurried away in the direction of the factory floor without looking back. *I wouldn't have thought he could move that fast.* Sergeant Kohl was in spitting distance now, which seemed appropriate to Brandt.

"Sergeant Faber," Brandt called across the yard to his startled comrade. "You and Kommandeur Rausch finish things up here, and I'll see you back at the precinct."

I think I have other plans for the afternoon.

Chapter 19

Prinz Albrecht Strasse 8 was one of the most imposing addresses in the city center, perhaps more so psychologically than architecturally. The collection of properties bearing the name of the royal family, had undergone numerous transformations in the years since they had been turned over to the city. But none of those changes were starker than those at #8, where the classical structure that had once housed the School of Industrial Arts and Crafts, had since been re-purposed to serve as Gestapo headquarters.

After Reichsfuhrer Himmler had settled himself into Prinz Albrecht Strasse 8, the migration had begun in earnest. One after another, the stately land and buildings that had once served as palaces, guest homes, parks and museums for King Frederick II and his royal descendants, had been appropriated by the Nazi security and police apparatus. At Himmler's prompting, the *SS* leadership had annexed the adjacent Hotel Prinz Albrecht. As the last piece of the puzzle to fall in place, Obergruppenfuhrer Heydrich had appropriated the royal palace, to house the ever-expanding domain of his security and intelligence services, more commonly referred to as the *SD*.

Ultimately, the entire royal quarter of the city had been carved up, and requisitioned, by either Reichsfuhrer Himmler or Reichsmarschall Goring. These properties were now being utilized to realize their vision of centralizing the Gestapo, *SS* and *SD* into a single entity. *And why not? Himmler, Heydrich, Goring, Mueller... these were the new kings. Have I not been summoned by Schonbern, like a commoner to the royal court?*

Brandt kept pace with Major Weskamp's determined stride, as they entered through the doors off Prinz Albrecht Strasse and into the vaulted ceilings and archways of the main hall. A vast series of stairwells led to the offices above, and to the ground floors below. Brandt peered over the railing towards the basement. The lower level had originally consisted of a series of artist studios, but the entire level had since been converted into the Gestapo's subterranean house prison. Nearly 40 isolation cells and interrogation rooms had been constructed to hold political prisoners of the Gestapo for questioning, until they could be shipped off to a nearby prison or camp. *If they survived their interrogations.*

Weskamp snapped off a smart salute as they passed the marble busts of der Fuhrer and Reichsmarschall Goring on the landing, before wordlessly leading them up a stairwell towards the offices on the top floors. The long drive from the factory had been similarly void of conversation. *Who salutes a statue, but doesn't talk to another human being?* Brandt sensed that there were no grey areas in Major Weskamp's world. He simply carried out the bidding of his superiors without blinking. *Standartenfuhrer Schonbern had summoned me, and Major Weskamp being a point A to point B type of guy, had made it happen. The rest was silence. What else was there to talk about?*

That was just as well with Brandt. He hadn't missed the major's riveting conversational skills, and the quiet had allowed him time to process what had transpired at the factory. Scenes from the violent melee played on a loop in his head during the drive. With great effort, he had managed to force the images aside, in order to mentally prepare for what Standartenfuhrer Schonbern had in store for him. Nonetheless, there were unresolved questions that had to be answered.

What was the Gestapo doing at the Lodenfabrik, and how had they timed their arrival simultaneously? Do we have a mole at Kripo? Our intentions must have been telegraphed by a mole in the department? But who could it be? Someone planted on the inside, or someone keeping watch on our movements from the periphery? Moreover, did we really discover the trail to Jacob Hirsch or were we pointed in his direction?

At the end of the third-floor hallway, Major Weskamp gestured towards a row of seats just outside a large corner office.

"*Warten Sie hier,*" he ordered, before disappearing through the outer door.

Pleasure as always.

Brandt took a seat as Weskamp had instructed. He felt aches in his body that he didn't know he had. His mind craved sleep. He was running purely on the leftover adrenaline from the botched factory raid. One scene from the Lodenfabrik continually returned to the front of his mind: The chaos in the courtyard preceding the Gestapo corporal's separation of the mother and child, culminating in the reckless intervention of the Jewish laborer. *Why did he intervene when no one else would? What would his punishment be? Would he end up in one of the prison cells below? Worse?*

He recalled the feverish expression on the man's desperate face, and the wild stare. It troubled him. *What about it though*? He heard a door open in the distance, down an

144

opposite corridor.

A brief wave of shock passed through his frame. *Is that...
Erica?* He found himself involuntarily rising from his chair,
but an invisible weight rooted him to the spot. Rather than her
customarily fashionable attire, she wore the drab grey uniform
of Gestapo Administration. She glanced down the hall in his
direction. Their eyes met. For the first time her eye contact
brought with it, not a sense of enticement, but rather of dread.

He thought he saw a brief shadow of remorse cross her
face. Or did he imagine it? Her features were as lovely as ever,
but her expression was cold and lifeless. She turned away and
walked hurriedly down the hallway in the opposite direction.
He felt sick to his stomach. *Suffice to say she isn't here to plan
Schonbern's retirement party.*

His feeble attempt at wit brought him no relief. Heaviness
descended and wrapped around him like a blanket. *Every word
that she had spoken had been part of a calculated ruse. Never
mind what she had said to me, what had I said to her? I let my
defenses down and let her in. But how deep had she burrowed,
and what access had she gained? And not just to me, but to the
investigation. Is she the mole who had tipped-off our
movements to the Gestapo? She was in my office earlier this
morning before the raid. And Roth had left classified files out
on my desk, including the transfer records for Jacob Hirsch.
No wonder the Gestapo knew where we were going, and when.
Mole or not, she's just another one of Schonbern's puppets,
and he wants me to know it.*

Chapter 20

Major Weskamp reemerged, short-circuiting Brandt's ability to track his troubled thoughts to their logical conclusions. The major waved him through the door with a wry look of satisfaction. *Whatever the fraulein's role was, they must not have a use for her anymore. They wanted me to see her leave Schonbern's office. Every detail is always perfectly rehearsed, and timed with Schonbern.*

"Colonel Schonbern will be with you presently."

Brandt heard the door close soundly behind him as the major hastily departed. If they had wanted to rattle him before the colonel's cross-examination, they had succeeded. He needed to re-orient himself.

He took a deep breath, and walked around the spacious room, trying to acclimate to the new surroundings. The colonel's office was spacious and ostentatiously decorated, a testament to opulence and splendor. It's high vaulted ceilings, and elaborate sculptures and paintings made it a perfect contrast to Colonel Brunner's austere chambers at Kripo headquarters. The space seemed more befitting the quarters of a nobleman than those of a state police colonel. *The new royalty.* Brandt's gaze settled on a detailed relief painting hanging directly behind the colonel's desk, fortuitously placed to draw the visitor's eye.

The vivid engraving depicted the buildings of an ancient

city ablaze in a sea of fire. At the center of the blaze, a temple was encircled by the howling multitudes of a religious order. The host of rabbis and priests were being slaughtered by Roman soldiers in the most gruesome manner, until their blood flowed like a river through the city. *Israel.* He heard Schonbern quietly enter the room behind him and turned to salute.

"Heil Hitler, Herr Standartenfuhrer!"

"I see you've discovered one of my favorite pieces," Schonbern mused, ignoring the formal greeting.

Discovered? How could I have missed it?

"Driven to exasperation by the endless depravity of their rebellious *Jewish* subjects, the Roman General Titus, and his battle-hardened legions concluded their siege of the Temple Mount in this orgiastic rampage of mass slaughter."

He stared wistfully at the engraving, and then at Brandt. His mouth curled into a sardonic grin before he resumed.

"Those were times when generals were empowered to do what had to be done, but do have a seat Lieutenant Brandt. You must be tired after this morning's activities."

Brandt wordlessly complied.

"Do you think that the German Reich is the first government that's had to take drastic measures to protect itself from Jewish infection?" Schonbern continued, his relish for the subject apparent.

"I'm afraid I don't follow, Colonel."

"The Jews have been expelled from virtually every civilized nation in Europe. At some point in their national history Spain, France, Italy, even England, all found it imperative to exorcize their borders of the Jewish menace. Were you aware of that, Herr Oberleutnant?"

"No, Herr Colonel."

He felt like he was back in the midst of Brigadefuhrer Becht's promotion speech. *No wonder they're so close.*

The colonel looked displeased, "Let this be a history lesson, then. After all, isn't it always advisable to know the history of one's adversaries?"

"In my field, the 'adversaries' come from a variety of backgrounds."

"Is that so?" Schonbern inquired. "Nevertheless, my point is that the Jews have been a blight upon the welfare of every society which has tried to assimilate them, including our own. If we can't assimilate them, where is the Reich to turn?"

"I'm not sure what you're asking me, Herr Colonel."

"Mass segregation? Forced emigration?" the colonel continued unabated. "As we expand our borders to acquire more living space for the German people, we find that even those measures aren't effective. So, what alternatives are left to us?"

"Elimination?"

Brandt heard the words stumble across his lips before he could pull them back. He quickly realized the gravity of his mistake, as he watched the storm clouds spread across Schonbern's face. The colonel's eyes darkened visibly beneath the veneer of a thin smile. *Damn Faber and his conspiracy theories!*

"An official government policy of elimination? I see that the rumor mills have spread even to Polizei barracks," Schonbern admonished. "I've spent a great deal of time with our forces in the East, Lieutenant, and I can assure you that such rumors are purely the figments of fevered imaginations, lies spread by our enemies abroad!"

"Of course, Herr Colonel!" Brandt conceded. "It wasn't my intention to imply otherwise. I was just playing des Teufel's Anwalt."

Playing devil's advocate with the head of the Berlin Gestapo on matters of international policy? What am I saying? I have to steer clear of this minefield.

"Despite our disdain for the negative effect the Jews have had on society, above all, the Reich is extremely practical. We have no intention of depriving ourselves of the labors of the Jewish workforce, especially during a time of war, when production is at a premium. So, I don't expect to hear that manner of slander uttered again."

"Of course, Colonel!"

Schonbern leaned back in his chair, seemingly appeased for the moment.

"Our only goal is for the relocation and resettlement of the Jewish population outside of Germany proper," he concluded. "And while there may be some ancillary loss of life in the process, or the occasional atrocity in the course of wartime, there is no design to 'eliminate' even a single individual."

"Understood, Herr Colonel," Brandt apologized, seeing an opportunity to change course. "But I can't imagine this is why you wanted to speak with me."

"Quite right. Though it occurs to me that this habit of playing, what did you call it, '*des Teufel's Anwalt*', might explain why you interfered with my men at the factory today."

"Interfered? With due respect, you've only heard one side of the story. The tactics employed by your men at the Lodenfabrik were unacceptable."

"Unacceptable? If you find my methods of handling the Jewish work force objectionable, it's only because you lack my experience in dealing with them!"

"I'm not concerned with the Jewish work force, I'm troubled that the actions of your men purposefully impeded the objectives of our investigation."

"You should consider that perhaps the Gestapo has our own investigative objectives in this matter, Lieutenant."

"Kripo coordinated a tactical raid between two agencies to go into the factory in an attempt to apprehend a specific suspect for interrogation. That's a legitimate objective. Your men, on the other hand, seemed more interested in arbitrarily inciting violence and chaos."

"Perhaps our actions aren't as 'arbitrary' as you think."

"How so?"

"Inspector Brandt, it's well known among the Berlin Jewish community that Major Goertz headed a department that oversees the assignment of Jewish labor to many of our most vital armament factories. And nearly 90% of the work force at the Lodenfabrik is Jewish."

"And how is that relevant?"

"If we catch wind that someone assigned to the factory may be involved in his death, or that the actions taken against Major Goertz may have been a sign of retribution or resistance… Then our response will be to send a counter message of reprisal on the factory population, as a whole."

"Even if it means disrupting the apprehension of the actual perpetrator?"

"If necessary!"

The colonel's voice had risen to a shout. He rose abruptly from his seat, face flushed. His hands clenched tightly against the edge of his desk, as he glared at Brandt.

"You're not seeing the big picture here, Inspector! In your

job, you can afford to focus on the actions of individuals, whereas mine requires regulating the movements of thousands. I don't have the luxury of viewing the Jewish situation through the narrow prism of a single investigation!"

"I hadn't considered that, Herr Colonel."

Brandt realized that his exchanges with the colonel oscillated rapidly between instigation and appeasement. This had seemed to be a moment that called for further appeasement, but he quickly realized from Schonbern's change of expression that his most recent act of contrition had arrived too late.

"When you say, 'actual perpetrator', are you implying that the Jewish worker you were seeking in the factory raid is a primary suspect in these killings?!?"

"I don't follow…"

"The individual you were trying to apprehend, you referred to him as the 'actual perpetrator.' "

Brandt felt as though he had wandered back into the minefield, not knowing how he had gotten there, or how to get out. Perhaps disorienting him had been the goal of the colonel's meandering dialogue about the Jewish situation all along. He tried to recover his footing.

"No, I was speaking hypothetically."

"Hypothetically? Another case of playing des Teufel's Anwalt?"

"Not at all, Herr Colonel. We don't know who perpetrated the murders. I was simply asking if 'sending a message' was worth derailing our lead."

"Verdammt! Don't parse words with me, Lieutenant!"

"That's not my intention, Colonel."

"These aren't peasants we're talking about. I've got two

murdered Gestapo officials to account for," Schonbern fumed. "That alone is enough to have Obergruppenfuhrer Heydrich and Oberhaupt Mueller breathing down my neck. Can you imagine the backlash if it turns out a Jew is involved in these murders? And a factory grunt of a Jew at that? Now, what are you sitting on? "

"I see your concern, Herr Standartenfuhrer, but we've got nothing to indicate any direct involvement by a Jewish worker."

"Nothing? I expect it takes something fairly substantial to embolden a newly appointed inspector to conduct an unauthorized search of a Nazi cabinet minister's residence in the middle of the night, and to follow it up with a raid of a major armaments plant!"

It was Brandt's turn to feel his gall rising, and a flush spreading across his face. *So, this was the trap the colonel's been baiting for me. Put me on the defensive, as if our procedures have run afoul of the chain of command. Leave me feeling that I've been compromised by his undercover agent, Fraulein Graffe. And then, isolated, and indebted, with nowhere else to turn, he can hang me out to dry for information about the case. He's the one who has been pulling all of the strings, and I'm tired of the charade.*

"Our search was unauthorized? We had a body, a witness identification, and reason to believe that a homicide had taken place at Major Goertz's residence. That was enough to qualify his premises as a potential crime scene!"

"I'm aware of your findings."

"That's called doing your police work!" Brandt continued, picking up steam. "Did your men have any of those things before they stumbled into Major Goertz's residence? Or

152

before botching the raid at the Lodenfabrik for that matter? Of course not!"

"That will do, Lieutenant," Schonbern admonished.

"And we were right on all counts. Homicide is our domain—that's what we do! As for our procedures, neither search was undertaken until we had a signed warrant from the office of Kriminaldirektor Brunner, and I was under the impression that you had ceded him the jurisdiction in this case!"

"I said that will be enough!"

The room grew still. Brandt could feel the palpable tension hovering in the silence between them. The colonel rose from his seat and moved towards the window. A light sleet pattered against the glass. Brandt wondered if he had gone too far. He thought of Erica Graffe. *If that's even her name.* He could see clearly through her façade for the first time. She had lured him in as a hapless victim, had used information from his personal background to establish a bond, and then she had used that closeness to worm her way into his investigation. *All at the behest of Colonel Schonbern.* The rising flood of anger accompanying these thoughts assured Brandt that he hadn't gone far enough. He pressed further.

"As long as we're reviewing my procedures, perhaps I could operate more openly, if I didn't have to worry about my office phone being wired, and your agents shadowing my every move!"

He saw the colonel wince in the reflection from the window.

"As I said, Lieutenant, the bottom line is that two Gestapo officers are dead, and Major Weskamp is pushing hard to have you removed from the case in his stead. Based on your erratic behavior, I'm inclined to agree with him."

Weskamp? He doesn't have a thought in his head that you haven't planted there. You can do better than that.

Brandt cleared his throat, and started to object, but the colonel raised his hand authoritatively, halting him in his steps.

"However, your instincts have proven accurate so far, and as you said, have managed to keep you one step ahead of my men. So, given the gravity of the situation, I'm stuck with you for now," he continued. "Therefore, I suggest we consider our disputes up to this point as *Wasser unter der Brucke*, and start working together to prevent further bloodshed."

"What kind of cooperation are you suggesting?" Brandt asked warily.

"A joint investigation. Unfettered sharing of resources and information. You will continue to head-up the investigation, under the condition that you involve our agents, and periodically report your findings directly to my office."

"Herr Standartenfuhrer, I obviously don't have the authority to agree to that without Colonel Brunner's..."

"Colonel Brunner has already granted his consent," Schonbern smiled, his victory complete.

Brandt felt like he had been punched in the gut. A familiar gnawing sensation returned in the pit of his stomach. He could feel the colonel's eyes on him, searching for a reaction. This was the coup de grace Schonbern had been waiting to serve all along. If Erica Graffe had been the stab in the back, this was the twist of the knife. *He's ultimately in control of not only me, but of the entire investigation. He's letting me know that I can't trust anyone, can't turn to anyone, can't even confide in anyone. This. This is what Schonbern had been angling for the whole time.* The colonel's searing gaze was unblinking. Brandt decided not to give him the satisfaction of an adverse response.

"In that case, it sounds like we'll be working together, Herr Standartenfuhrer" he replied.

"Very well," Schonbern cooed, looking mildly disappointed.

The colonel opened a file that sat in the center of his desk.

"Now, in that spirit of collaboration, let's get right to business. What was the name of the Jewish worker you were seeking at the factory?"

"The name?"

"Yes, the name. You see, the Gestapo has extensive personnel files on individuals who've been conscripted into labor programs, which may be of assistance in tracking his whereabouts. Let's start with his name, and how he's connected to your case."

There's no way to withhold it from him. He may already know Hirsch's name anyway, and just be using it to test me.

"His name is Hirsch, Jacob Hirsch."

For an instant, Brandt thought he detected a hint of recognition register in the colonel's downcast eyes. It was brief, and vanished as quickly as it had appeared, but it was there. *Or is that just what he wanted me to see? Either way, why not turn it to my advantage?* He cast out a line of his own.

"We ran a background check on him at the joint archives, but came up empty. He's a ghost; no paper trail at all. That means he's most likely either a transient who's slipped through the cracks, or…

"Or what?" Schonbern queried.

"Or he's connected to someone high enough up the food chain to make any trace of him vanish."

Schonbern involuntarily winced again. *Bull's-eye!* Brandt

leaned back in his chair and allowed the colonel to hang in the breeze for a change. *What does he know about Hirsch, and about the gaps in the files? Hirsch's transfer file was among the declassified documents the Gestapo permitted us to retain. That's odd. Surely the colonel is aware of that.* He decided that he would follow up on that later. For now, he had to focus on guarding his own information from the colonel's prying talons.

"The former most likely, the labor relocation filing system is notoriously unreliable. But without personnel records, how did you make any connections between this 'Jacob Hirsch', and your investigation?"

"The visitor's log at Captain Keppler's complex. Hirsch's name appeared on numerous dates, despite the fact that he had been assigned to a work camp. So, we were following that lead."

"I see."

"Normally, that transfer would be accompanied by numerous background files, but as I mentioned, Hirsch's have either been pulled or misplaced."

"So, you said, and who do you ascertain would have an interest in pulling them?"

"That's the question."

"Is there more? Anything that directly ties Hirsch to either victim?"

"No, Herr Standartenfuhrer, that's all we have to go on so far."

"And now that your search of the factory failed to produce him, any leads on his whereabouts?"

"We have conflicting reports, and aren't sure about the reliability of any of them."

"Conflicting how?"

"My chance to properly interview laborers from the factory was cut decidedly short," Brandt prodded. "But from our initial findings, there was speculation among his fellow workers about whether Hirsch may have been transferred to another factory, a nearby prison camp or even deported. We haven't had time to confirm any of it, so it's all conjecture at this point."

"That's unfortunate. You're undoubtedly aware that with emigration closed, mass transports of Jews have increased for destinations in the East, as part of our program of 'resettlement and relocation?'"

"Certainly."

"As you might expect, many of the Jews are intent on avoiding this process, and in an attempt to evade these transits have become 'divers.' "

"Divers? I'm afraid I'm not familiar with the term."

"Diving below the surface to live a fugitive existence in the Berlin underground."

"And you think it's possible Jacob Hirsch may have taken this route?"

"It's possible. And if that's the case, we have a technique which might prove to be particularly effective in locating him," Schonbern concluded, emphatically closing the file with a flourish.

Chapter 21

The black staff car passed through an arched gate, before pulling into the portico of the hospital compound. The rows of red brick buildings that littered the property had likely once been impressive, but they now looked dated, and had fallen into a state of disrepair. The grounds had been left untended, to the point where weeds and underbrush had engulfed their surroundings. Several worn emergency vehicles and ambulances sat idle in their stalls beside a closed-off garage entrance.

Parked or abandoned? Is this place even operational? On the drive from Gestapo headquarters, the normally taciturn Major Weskamp had undergone a transformation, suddenly becoming an endless font of information. *Or more likely disinformation? And from the man who wanted my job!*

In the abandoned waiting area, a diminutive, balding man, with spectacles shuffled towards them expectantly.

"Major Weskamp!" he called out, shrilly.

The man wore a wrinkled white doctor's coat, which whisked against his pants as he walked. Brandt noted the Star of David badge, inscribed Jude, affixed slightly below the left lapel of his dust-covered jacket. The doctor approached Major Weskamp submissively, with an air of doting attentiveness.

"*Willkommen, Herr Major, willkommen!* We've been expecting you," he chirped, undeterred by the major's indifference. "Per your request, Fraulein Weiss has been moved to a holding room."

Fraulein? Schonbern's diver is a woman?

"Very well."

"She's located in the south wing of the hospital, room 131. Do you know the way, or would you like me to direct you there myself?"

"That won't be necessary," Weskamp responded with a dismissive wave of the hand. He looked as if he was trying to shoo away a bothersome gnat.

"If there's any way, I can be of further assistance…" he called after them.

The major ignored this final plea, as they headed down the hall, winding their way through the sterile grey corridors of the main ward. They passed by a set of open exam rooms, followed closely by a series of empty operating rooms. This ward of the hospital was well staffed, but seemed to be lacking one thing: patients. A doctor passed them with a train of nurses in tow. Their heads were lowered deferentially, and each wore the same large yellow star on their outer garments.

"Is this place staffed entirely by Jews?"

"By Jews, and for Jews. You're witnessing one of the last remaining traces of Jewish autonomy in all of Berlin."

"How's that?"

"The RSHA is running the show, but the hospital is staffed and operated entirely by Jewish doctors and nurses for the exclusive treatment of Jews."

"To what end?"

"Until the city is officially cleansed of its Jewish population, we have to provide the wretches somewhere to go for medical attention. Don't we?"

"Of course, but that's not what I meant…"

"Given the way they spread disease, left untreated, they'd create an epidemic. You can't expect a German doctor or hospital to treat them, so Obergruppenfuhrer Heydrich allows them to keep this place functional, at least for the time being. They'll be the last to go. The last rats on a sinking ship."

The major stopped abruptly and offered a perverse smile. Brandt had never seen him so animated, and talkative. *Or for that matter, smile.* He rather preferred the silent treatment. They descended a stairwell and found themselves in a series of tunnels that ran below the hospital.

"All of the hospital's wards are located in separate buildings," Weskamp said. "They're connected by tunnels, so that patients aren't exposed to the elements when they are transferred from one ward to another."

Brandt nodded. Sections of the tunnel had been reconstructed to serve as bomb shelters for the various wards. They ascended another set of stairs back to the floor above and passed through a door marked 'Neuropsychiatrie'. Observation rooms, with oversized window boxes, faced out onto the hallway. These rooms stood in stark contrast to the rest of the hospital, in that they were filled to overflowing with patients. The frenetic buzz of voices vibrated through the corridor accompanied by an almost palpable air of panic. Brandt was startled by a loud thud against the glass as he passed close to the observation window of the last room in the ward. A man wearing nothing but a hospital gown, and a desperate expression, pressed himself hard against the glass. He mouthed two inaudible words over and over, 'Help me.' Brandt quickened his pace.

"Don't be alarmed, Lieutenant, they're harmless,"

Weskamp chuckled. "The patients in that room were transferred here after the SS shut down most of the city's Jewish mental asylums. It's just a temporary layover station until they're deported. This entire ward is being used as a holding camp for a number of patients awaiting deportation."

Why would the SS close down an entire city's mental health system? How can you deport people who are in need of constant medical attention to concentration camps? Maybe Faber is right about what awaits those headed east on the transports.

"Here we are. It's this way," the major indicated. "We've had this wing of the psychiatric ward converted into a secured area for Jewish prisoners who need medical treatment, before being released back into our custody. Fraulein Weiss fits into the latter category. She was slightly banged up during her apprehension, but mostly just in need of a convenient way to be removed from circulation."

The guard rose from his seat and snapped to attention as they approached a series of exam rooms.

"Heil Hitler, Herr Major. She's in triage but should be done in a moment."

Major Weskamp turned his back to confer with the guard, as Brandt walked a few paces ahead. He saw the triage lounge and leaned forward to look through the curtains. A young woman sat on the edge of an examination table. She spoke inaudibly to a Jewish nurse, who was attending to an injury she had sustained to her arm. He heard the major, concluding his whispered discussion, and moved back away from the curtain to join him.

"Corporal, have the prisoner brought to us when they're finished with her," Weskamp said, opening the door to a conference room.

The major directed Brandt to a seat opposite him at the long wooden table. He pulled out a cigarette, and opened a personnel file, spreading the contents across the table in front of them. He inhaled deeply and breathed out a plume of smoke into the air above them.

"Since we began tightening the screws on Jewish emigration, swarms of Jews have gone into hiding in attempts to avoid the transports east."

"Colonel Schonbern mentioned that they try to evade detection by going underground."

"Right," Weskamp nodded. "And in those cases, we've found that the best way to find a Jew, is with a Jew. For some lost fugitive residing in the shadows, there's nothing as alluring as a fellow outcast promising access to the light."

"And this attracts them?"

"Like moths to the flame…"

"And how does it work? Why would a wayward Jew voluntarily track another Jew?"

"I wouldn't say it's always voluntary," the major smirked. "But when we find a viable tracker, we provide them with certain 'incentives', which motivate them to hunt down their own kind."

"Such as?"

"For example, in exchange for their services, we exclude them from the transports, for as long as they remain useful. The Jews call these agents *greifers*."

Grabbers?

"And when the greifers realize that you're only offering them a temporary reprieve?"

"You'd be surprised what lengths condemned people will go to buy themselves some more time."

"How about when their cover is blown? I'd think they would have a pretty short shelf-life before their identities were exposed and circulated to rest of the community."

"That's true enough. But in that case, Fraulein Weiss is different."

"Different in what way?"

"Her father was a *Rabbiner*, one of the leaders in Berlin's Jewish Community. He was trusted by the Jews. So, when we applied the pressure to him, he made overtures of cooperating with Colonel Eichmann in 'facilitating' the deportation process."

Eichmann?

"Facilitating?"

"Yes, said he was interested in 'making the transition easier on his people'. So, he cooperated with us, but it turns out the rabbi was aiding the flight of fugitive Jews left and right," Weskamp sneered.

"You mentioned, Colonel Eichmann? He's the head of the Jewish Affairs Desk, Department IVB4, correct?"

The question earned him a withering scowl from the major, one that confirmed Brandt's inquiry. *The same department Captain Keppler had been dismissed from in the run-up to his murder, and the same department Major Goertz had been utilizing to expedite his relocations.* He filed that connection away, evading the major's scrutinizing gaze with a follow-up.

"So, what happened with the rabbi?"

"He unknowingly offered assistance to one of our undercover agents. And when he figured out that we were onto him, he sent the rest of his family into hiding."

"And Fraulein Weiss was one of those family members that was apprehended?"

"That's right. As for the rabbi, he was arrested and interrogated about the details of the fugitive network, and when we couldn't wring anymore information out of him, he was shipped to Chelmno."

"Chelmno?"

"A bone mill in Poland where they likely would have ground him into dust, if he hadn't died in transit," Weskamp concluded with a twisted grin.

A bone mill?

"And then, last week, we found the rest of his family holding up in a relative's basement in the Friedrichshain district."

Friedrichshain? That was Goertz's neck of the woods.

There was a knock at the door. The guard escorted the female prisoner into the room, and pushed her roughly into the open seat at the head of the conference table. The woman had been issued a hospital gown in place of her own rumpled clothes. Her hair was untamed and disheveled. She sat with her eyes downcast, looking at neither of them. Despite her condition, and what had likely been weeks of living like a fugitive, Brandt couldn't help but find her striking.

"Rebecca Weiss, this is Inspector Brandt of the Kriminalpolizei. We're working on a case together, and believe you could be of some assistance to us."

"How so?" she asked, without looking up.

"In helping us make contact with a Jewish fugitive. We believe the missing person in question worked, and possibly lived, in the district where your father presided."

She flinched in her seat at the mention of her father. Brandt observed the brief crack in her otherwise impenetrable facade. Her eyes flitted briefly in his direction. He saw in her glance a momentary expression of inexpressible sorrow, which was replaced instantaneously by a blank stare. The mask returned as quickly as it had dissolved.

"There are many 'missing persons' in that district," she replied, her voice tinged with sarcasm.

Brandt saw the gall rising in the major's face. He redirected the tension, by sliding a photograph from the open folder across the table in her direction.

"Fraulein Weiss. This is the suspect we are looking for. Do you recognize him, or the name Jacob Hirsch?"

She looked up at Brandt, as if she was taking note of his presence for the first time. He felt her searching gaze, and cleared his throat reflexively. Her eyes wandered briefly to the photo.

"No, I don't recognize him."

"You may want to reconsider the terms of our agreement," the major growled, "and take a closer look at the picture!"

He pushed the photograph towards her, but she remained detached. Enraged, he forcefully thrust his chair away from the desk. He leaned closer to her, his face hovering uncomfortably close, a cigarette dangling from his clenched lips. He jerked her head into position by her hair, compelling her to view the photograph more thoroughly.

"You recognize him now?"

"Major, why not let it go for now?" Brandt interjected. "She'll have plenty of time to familiarize herself with the target while she's on the mend."

"This dog needs to start upholding her end of the bargain!" he snapped.

"It doesn't help our cause to place her back in the community looking like damaged goods."

Weskamp grasped her hair more tightly, and then released her head with a shove. Brandt tried to coax the major's attention back to the case.

"What's the next step in getting her back into circulation?"

"We'll set her up in a flat in a different section of the Jewish district from where she was picked up. No longer than she's been off the street, it's likely she hasn't been missed."

"How do you spread the word?"

"We'll have contacts and informants circulate that she evaded the dragnet which ensnared the rest of her family, and that she's still a source for obtaining illegal papers, and the like. After they find out that..."

An urgent rap at the door interrupted the conclusion of the major's plan. The corporal leaned his head through the crack, visibly agitated.

"Excuse the interruption Herr Major, but there's an urgent call for Lieutenant Brandt. It's coming through on the house phone from officers in the main hospital ward!"

Brandt rose briskly and stepped into the hallway, carefully avoiding the major's suspicious glare. He picked up the receiver of a phone attached to the wall of the adjacent nurse's station. He heard Emil Roth's boisterous words crackle through the distortion on the other end of the internal line, and was glad to hear the familiar voice. Roth's message was brief and to the point.

"We've got a location on Hirsch!"

Chapter 22

Had the factory orderly's tip checked out, or had Standartenfuhrer Schonbern's involvement really moved the needle this quickly? Perhaps both. Either way, Brandt found himself staring up at the impressive stone facade of St Michael's Kirche, the same church where Jacob Hirsch had allegedly received his most recent work transfer. *Strange, there was still no written record of it.*

St Michael's had apparently been the target of several recent run-ins with the Gestapo, so Brandt persuaded his new shadows, the four agents headed by the venerable Sergeant Heller, to wait outside. He likewise signaled for sergeants Faber and Roth to remain in the vestibule, as he checked out the sanctuary.

A familiar looking priest quietly held conference with a group of men sitting on pews towards the front of the nave. The hushed tones of their confab reverberated softly off the church's stone walls. The priest made eye contact with him, and gestured that he would be right over. *He's the priest I saw manning the relief tents outside the train station after the bombing raids.*

Brandt surveyed the painstakingly ornate architecture of the church, and the visual splendor of the sanctuary's design. *How had German architects and craftsmen possessed the skills to produce such an elaborate edifice some 300 years ago?*

Could they do the same today? Would they even want to? Of course, it was nothing new, compared to the wondrous structures of antiquity, but it always amazed him just the same. His parents had routinely taken him to an old protestant church when he was a child, and he had always marveled at the beauty of the building's neoclassical lines. *I can't remember now when we stopped attending, or why?*

At length, his gaze settled on a vibrant tapestry hanging on a nearby wall. Its colorfully detailed weave portrayed a boy being hastily lowered into a well by a young man, as nine other men of varying ages watched in states of great agitation and provocation. He became absorbed in its intricate detail, trying to place the story it depicted.

"It's a fascinating tapestry, isn't it? I've become lost in the intricacies many times myself."

He was surprised that he hadn't heard the priest's approach. His voice had a soft and harmonious quality to it, but Brandt was startled at the unexpected nearness of it. He turned to see the priest standing a few paces behind him, head uplifted, as though admiring the tapestry for the first time.

"It's a depiction of Reuben and his brother Joseph at the well. Are you familiar with the story?"

"No, but I'm not here to..."

"Reuben is the one attempting to protect the child from the murderous intentions of his brothers, by sheltering him in an underground cistern. It's a tale from Genesis, one of refuge and redemption, and a source of great inspiration to our congregation during these trying times," he concluded, with a smile. "But as you were saying, I realize you're not here to discuss spiritual matters. I'm *Pfarrer* Eckhardt."

"Father, I'm Lieutenant Brandt of der Kriminalpolizei,"

Brandt replied, taking Eckhart's extended hand.

"Der Kriminalpolizei? What brings you to our sanctuary, Lieutenant?"

"We're trying to locate the whereabouts of a man named Jacob Hirsch, and the last records we have indicate that he received a work transfer to this location some time ago?"

"Yes, Jacob Hirsch," Eckhardt responded, readily. "He was transferred here earlier this year by the Reich Labor Bureau to serve as a church sexton, and to help tend to the church grounds. But I'm afraid he hasn't shown up to perform those duties in months."

"Months?"

"Yes, I would say it's been at least several months."

"According to our information he was only transferred here a few months ago, and you're saying he hasn't been to work in months? Are you sure about that?" Brandt pressed, skeptically.

"Well, I, can't be certain of the exact dates from memory, but he stopped showing up shortly after his transfer."

"And did you report his absence to the Labor Bureau?"

"No. We don't make a habit of..."

"You have a conscripted worker assigned to you by the Reich Labor Bureau, and yet you don't bother to report his disappearance? He's required, by law, to be here every day!"

"With all due respect, Lieutenant," the priest countered. "We would have inquired more thoroughly into his absence, but given the frequency with which people go 'missing' in Berlin these days, especially Jewish workers, I can't say we were surprised by his sudden departure."

"And you know nothing about the reason for his departure, and nothing of his current location, or address?"

"Nothing. I wish I could be of assistance, but he wasn't with us long, and his disposition was mostly to keep to himself when he was on the church grounds."

"'When he was on the church grounds?'"

"That's right."

"Wouldn't his work order as sexton, necessitate that he spends all of his time on the premises, including having a residence on the premises? His travel pass would have been revoked when he was transferred here."

"That's correct," Eckhardt faltered. "I simply meant to imply, that he kept to himself, and was something of a loner."

"So he did live on the property?"

"During his time here, he lived in the sexton's quarters on the grounds behind the church. When he left, he took what few belongings he had, and certainly didn't offer me the courtesy of a forwarding address."

Brandt noticed that the priest's tone had become somewhat indignant and defensive, but he sensed something else behind the facade. His mouth sounded dry, and his initially placid gaze had several times been overcome by an involuntary eye twitch. Given his apparent discomfort with this line of questioning, Brandt decided to press deeper, adopting an increasingly confrontational edge to his inquiry.

"Father Eckhardt, in the event that you may privately sympathize with this man, or that you may be covering for him, you should know that Jacob Hirsch is wanted in connection with the murder of two prominent government officials."

"I can assure you that's not the case..."

"And here I find myself standing face to face with the man who was not only his last known employer, but also his landlord, so I'd expect you to be a little more forthcoming. As from what I understand, you don't currently reside in the good graces of the Gestapo, as it is."

"Lieutenant, I…"

"If you'd prefer that I yield the questioning to them, I'll be more than glad to oblige, as they have agents currently sitting on your front doorstep. Otherwise, I expect your complete cooperation, because I have a feeling, they're going to be a lot less understanding than I am."

"Lieutenant, I had no idea about the murders, and am more than willing to share any information that can be of assistance. But I certainly don't sympathize with Hirsch!" Eckhardt volunteered, visibly agitated.

"No?"

"No! He wasn't hired by me, or sent here by my request. In fact, he was placed here by the Reich Labor Bureau, against my wishes."

"Against your wishes?"

"That's right, if anything he was viewed with apprehension and suspicion!"

"Why would that be?"

"Many on my staff feared he was planted here as *ein Informant*."

"*Ein Informant*? What's to be gained from planting an informant in a church?"

"That's not for me to say," the priest replied, casting a fleeting glance towards the entrance. "However, there are certain parties who have a vested interest in ensuring that church doctrine and practice conforms to Reich policy. And though it's accurate that we've had some conflicts with the Gestapo, it's been due to matters of political orthodoxy, not of

171

harboring criminals. So, as I said, I'll be more than happy to cooperate."

Brandt had pushed the priest for answers, but they had not led where he had expected. *Who has the time, or motive, to spy on a church? It seems absurd.* But Father Eckhardt's weary tone had an earnest quality that convinced Brandt he was on the level.

"Thank you. You confirmed that Hirsch lived on the premises while he was here?"

"That's right, there's a sexton's quarters at the southern boundary of the church grounds."

"I'd like to see those quarters now, and in the process, conduct a routine search of the rest of the grounds. With your approval, of course."

"Tonight?" Eckhardt flinched almost imperceptibly. "It's getting dark, but certainly. I'll be glad to show you the grounds, and the gardener's residence, myself."

Chapter 23

Brandt retrieved his comrades, and Father Eckhardt lead the detachment across the transept to the rear chapel and out onto the church grounds. A path of timeworn stone pavers led up a steep incline towards the tree line. Fritz Heller fanned out from the grouping and led his agents down to a dirt trail below, while Brandt, Faber and Roth stayed on the winding path behind the steady gait of the priest. The path led them through a wrought iron arch and into the church cemetery. An overhang of trees cast their shade in the dwindling daylight, as the agents snaked their way through the monuments.

"Why do you seek the living among the dead?" Roth smirked nervously, crossing himself.

Brandt returned a thin smile, as the cemetery plots receded into a vast wooded perimeter. After moments of trudging through the dense undergrowth, the canopy of trees emptied abruptly into a clearing on a small hilltop. From this elevated vantage point, Brandt spotted the roof of the sexton's quarters, simultaneous to the emergence of Heller's agents from the wooded footpath in the valley below.

"Halten!" Brandt ordered, turning to Eckhardt. "We'll take it from here, you just stay put. It's vacated? No surprises, right?"

"Of course," the priest nodded.

They edged down the grass-covered slope, which was still

damp from the thawing of the recent dusting of snow. As they drew closer to the old stone cottage, Brandt signaled Heller's men towards the rear entrance, while he led Faber and Roth towards the front porch. One by one, the agents unsheathed their guns.

They crept onto the wooden porch and took sides on either side of the front door. Brandt checked the clasp handle. It was unlocked, and he swiftly pushed it open on its hinges. Before he could enter, Sergeant Roth pushed his way through the door and into the front hall. There was no electricity in the old building, leaving the barren front rooms lit only by the shafts of illumination from the fading daylight. They switched on their flashlights, which offered little assistance at this in-between hour. The trio of officers moved quickly from room to room. Through the walls they heard shouts of *"alles klar"* as the Gestapo agents cleared the back of the cottage. Within moments the units converged in the connecting hallway. *Nothing.*

At the far end of the hall, Brandt spotted an undersized door. *A storage closet? Maybe a walk-up attic?* He moved toward it quickly and swung it open, bending down to peer into the darkness. A rickety set of wooden stairs led down to a level below. *A basement!* Brandt trained his beam down the stairs.

"We have another level down here!"

He felt the other agents crowding towards him, and once again Roth came barreling past, a Gestapo agent fast on his heels.

"We've got this one, Lieutenant!" Roth shouted, as they bounded down the stairs and disappeared into the darkness with their pistols and flashlights drawn.

Always has to be the first one in. Brandt allowed himself

a veiled smile, in spite of the setting, at the young sergeant's unbridled exuberance.

"Alles klar! Nothing but a cellar!" Roth called back from the bottom step. "But someone's been living down here!"

A tunnel wide enough for a single person to pass through had been dug from the dirt floor of the basement, burrowing underneath the back wall, until it emptied out into the wooded yard some twenty meters away. *That's a lot of trouble to go to, to provide an emergency exit from an abandoned sexton's quarters.*

They had also recovered some clothing and a wool blanket. The corner next to the partially below ground window was littered with the remnants of recently eaten food, scattered around a small dugout that had been used to build a fire.

Why hideout down here in the damp and dark, unless you're a fugitive who knows you're being tracked? And who would even know about this place, aside from Hirsch, and whoever had worked here before him?

Brandt hadn't decided whether to take the priest to task for this yet, or not. It was possible that whoever had been using the basement, had been squatting there without anyone at the church knowing. *Had it definitely been Hirsch?* He decided not to mention anything about it just yet.

Brandt and the other agents trudged back up the slope together. He could see that Eckhardt had eagerly been awaiting their return.

"Everything in order?" he asked apprehensively.

"Looks that way," Brandt offered, evasively, as he led the group back onto the wooded path.

Glancing over the priest's shoulder, Brandt noticed an overgrown path. The surrounding shade helped further conceal the walkway beneath a preserved coating of snow. He peered around Eckhardt's unmoving frame. At the end of the trail, there was a gated fence in the distance. He veered in that direction.

"Where does this lead?"

The priest moved into his way, "It's abandoned."

"What's abandoned?"

"The church school," he stammered. It closed with the outbreak of the war. The buildings are just used for storage now, and if you're wondering, it closed long before Jacob Hirsch was assigned here."

The priest's voice was on edge. Brandt brushed past him, noting his change in demeanor. He moved purposefully through the overgrowth and slush towards the fence, and surveyed the buildings through the wrought iron gate. Below the shallow remnant of snow, there was a visible trail of recent depressions in the ground.

This snowfall isn't yet three days old. There's been daily foot traffic to and from these buildings.

"You have the key to this lock?"

"Possibly back in my office, or maybe at the rector's," Eckhardt muttered, searching himself absently. "It hasn't been used for so long."

Brandt removed the Walther from his holster, and grasped the steel padlock. Without hesitation he struck the butt of his pistol forcefully against the shackle. The rusted lock and chain fell to the ground in a heap. He heard a murmur arise from the agents behind him, invigorated with a new sense of purpose. He looked back at the priest, who was pale and visibly beside himself. *What's he hiding?* Brandt forced the gate open, and strode towards the building, calling back over his shoulder for the other agents to join suit.

"We're going to check the school grounds!"

The priest stood rooted to the spot, as the agents pushed past him. They had been inspired by the Lieutenant's forceful decisiveness, and were once again energized by the thrill of the chase. At the center of the schoolyard stood a single-storey clapboard building, flanked on both sides by a series of detached structures of the same design. Brandt stopped at the first entrance, and in a show of deference, allowed Heller and his agents to take the lead in checking the facilities room by room. The gesture earned him a now-familiar twisted grin from his Gestapo counterpart.

A little professional courtesy never hurts. More like tossing the rat some cheese.

Brandt followed after them, crossing over the threshold into the entrance hall. The sound of footsteps reverberated throughout, as the agents shuffled across the hardwood floors from one classroom to the next, as if on the scent of fresh prey. The inside of the complex was an unfinished primary school. The tables and desks were covered with sheets, and rows of unused textbooks were stacked against the wall. There was something haunting about the sight of an abandoned schoolhouse. Interval calls of "alles klar" echoed back to him as he walked towards the rear of the main building.

It looks like this place hasn't been used since the day it was finished, just as the priest said. But why does he seem so agitated by our intent to search a deserted school? And why the depressions in the snow?

The door at the back of the central classroom opened into a small unfinished space. The room had open gaps where rough-ins had been left for a sink and water closet, that had never been installed. Tables and chairs were scattered around the room, and open cabinets lined the walls. *A break room for teachers?* On the back wall, he noticed a small refrigeration box tucked below a bottom row of cabinets. He leaned down to open it. There was partially melted ice on the top rack, and below it an assortment of fresh produce. *Abandoned for years?*

The floorboards beneath his feet creaked as he stood up. He moved around the area purposefully, shifting his weight from foot to foot. There was a wide berth of the flooring that sounded almost hollow below. He walked towards the only window in the unfinished break room. The window overlooked the back of the schoolyard, and a deserted, snow-covered playground. He winced involuntarily at the sight of it. Looking down, he saw the doors of a large storm cellar protruding from the back of the building. *That cellar is directly below this room.*

With renewed intent he strode quickly back through the front entrance, and out onto the grounds. He shot a quick glare in Father Eckhardt's direction, brushing past him as he rounded the corner of the building. The priest looked increasingly pale, as he fell quickly in line behind Brandt muttering something incoherently. At the back corner of the building the storm cellar came into view, jutting out from the foundation. A thin layer of snow covered the overgrowth around the cellar. *But not the doors.*

Just like the main gate, there was a well-worn path of depressions still visible in the melting snow, trampled down by recent foot traffic. Brandt could hear the voices of his men and the Gestapo agents ambling back down the stairs of the entry as they exited the building, their search of the classrooms coming to a close. They wouldn't be far behind him. He could also hear the muted strains of the priest hovering near his shoulder, "Please, Lieutenant, please!"

Brandt drew his Walther again and moved decisively towards the cellar. He crouched down by the doors and looked back one last time. Eckhardt's expression was one of sheer desperation. Out of the corner of his eye, Brandt saw Faber and two of the Gestapo agents moving down the side of the building towards his position. Faber raised his eyebrows inquiringly as they made eye contact, and quickened his pace.

Brandt hesitated briefly, and took a deep breath. *No more holding back.* With a single motion, he unclasped the latch, and forcefully pulled one of the heavy wooden doors open. Its hinges groaned loudly under the extreme weight, and cold. He peered into the darkness of the cellar; his pistol extended. He sensed motion, and quickly steadied his arm to take aim. Brandt involuntarily stepped back in shock, almost losing his grip on the heavy door in the process. His eyes strained to come into focus.

Huddled on the mud floor of the underground cellar were a cluster of bedraggled children. *There must be a dozen of them!* They shivered en masse in their tattered clothes from the exposure to the cold. *Or from fear?* Their eyes looked up the cellar stairs at him in unison in what he could only interpret as terror. Some of the older children held their hands over the mouths of the younger ones to muffle any potential cries.

He turned his astonished gaze to Eckhardt who was palpably beside himself. He could see that the priest was trembling where he stood, and Brandt realized that he was too. In his peripheral, he saw Faber and the Gestapo agents rapidly approaching. He glanced past the open cellar door in their direction. They looked at him intently as they drew close, noticeably concerned by his raised weapon and stance, their view still shielded by the priest's back, and the raised door.

Faber called out to him with concern, "Everything alright, Lieutenant?"

Brandt hesitated an instant. He looked back into the bowels of the cellar. The quivering mass stared back at him wild-eyed, struggling as one not to move or make a sound. He returned his pistol to his holster, and lowered the door back into place, watching the shadows slowly consume the terrified faces as he did. He clasped the bolt back into the locked position, and turned towards his approaching comrades. He took care to wipe away any residue of surprise from his expression, replacing it with one of tangible frustration. He waved the agents, and the priest, back towards the front of the buildings, with a forceful gesture of his hand.

"Alles klar. There's nothing here."

Chapter 24

The tail of his trench coat flapped violently as he walked against the gusts of blowing rain and sleet. He ducked into the shelter of a narrow alley to adjust his collar, pulling it up over his chin to muffle the effects of the unforgiving elements. He shielded himself against the wall and peered around the corner at the rows of dilapidated apartment buildings, each block indistinguishable from the next. The temperatures and frigid precipitation had driven everyone indoors, but even from the dark, empty streets, he could feel the cramped humanity bursting at the seams. He stepped out of the alley, and quickened his pace.

This is the human consequence of the projects Captain Keppler and Major Goertz had been working on. Minister Speer's relocation plans have pushed the Jewish population density in this area to its limits, and now that glut has to be unclogged. Enter the transports. Just ask Rebecca Weiss.

One thing he had learned to be immutably true over the course of his investigation, was that even those government agencies that could agree upon nothing else, were of one accord about the issue of Jewish resettlement. Those Jews who hadn't been resettled abroad, needed to be segregated and confined to a segregated quarter within the city. And this had become that centralized location, Berlin's Jewish district. Any Berlin resident of known Jewish lineage, who hadn't been deported, jailed, or conscripted into the camp system was likely to be found living somewhere within a few city blocks of where he now stood. And if they weren't here, then they were most likely either a fugitive, or had friends in high places. *Or in Jacob Hirsch's case, maybe both.*

Brandt stopped at the corner, and descended a short flight of steps to a basement apartment. He knocked on door #17, and waited. The screen door from the apartment above creaked opened and slammed shut in the wind. He saw the peephole of #17 go dark, and then heard the chain lock slide open.

Rebecca Weiss opened the door wordlessly, and quickly retreated in the direction of a corner table where she had been writing. Brandt stepped inside the squalid apartment, and swiped the rain from his jacket, closing the door behind him. He removed his hat, and ran a hand through his hair, as he surveyed the run-down flat. Weiss had taken a seat at the table beneath one of the apartment's two partially underground windows. He walked past her and looked out onto a muddy courtyard littered with debris. *There are no services to even remove their garbage and waste! The animals at the Zoologischer Garten Berlin have better living conditions.* He turned back to find her staring at him.

"Very inconspicuous. No risk of anyone recognizing you dressed like that," she chided, quickly returning her gaze to the table covered with papers. Brandt glanced at his outfit and smirked, in spite of himself.

"I see the Gestapo has spared no expense in making sure you're comfortable," he said with the hint of a smile.

Weiss didn't look up.

"I understand you've made a contact," he continued.

"I'm nearly certain it's your guy, but he's tried to change

his appearance from the time of your photograph."

She slid her wooden chair back from the table, which scraped sharply in protest against the concrete floor. She reached into a satchel beneath the table, and retrieved a packet of documents. Weiss deftly sorted through them, and removed a small card.

"He gave me the name 'David Hedrich', and this identification card bearing the same. You be the judge," she said, handing him the documents.

"David Hedrich?" Brandt replied, startled. "Do you know that name?"

"It doesn't sound familiar, but then it's a pretty common name."

Maybe on the surface, but there's nothing common about Hirsch using that name!

"That name doesn't wash, and the photograph is of Hirsch."

"He wants forged identity papers under the name Richard Hess, a transportation pass, and an exit visa."

"That's a tall order; he's trying to get all the way out."

The identification papers have obviously been altered, but how did Hirsch come by David Hedrich's identification card? And why provide that name and card to Fraulein Weiss if you're trying to get forged documents in a different name? Is this the same David Hedrich? Do he and Hirsch know each other? Work together?

"I tried to get more information from him. I told him I needed an address for the documents, but he wouldn't disclose anything."

"How about a pick-up spot?"

"He told me he'd be back in touch. And when I told him

it would take a few days, he became very agitated. He offered more, to speed up the process."

"More money?"

"Yes, and these...," she said, again sifting through her packet. "Different types of ration cards. He had sheets of them."

Brandt took the sheets and examined them closely. *They're not forgeries. How did he get these in bulk? He's well connected, but to what? Der Schwarzmarkt?*

"These are government-issued. And you say that he had an endless supply?"

She nodded without looking up.

"So, if you don't have an address for him or a pick-up spot, how does the exchange take place?"

"He contacted me through a third party to arrange the first meeting, and said he'd do the same to arrange the swap."

"Who was the third party?"

"I don't know, I'd never seen him. He was an older man, well dressed, with a grey beard. He approached me outside in the courtyard. He said a *Freund der judischen Germeinde* needed papers, and would be paying me a visit. I thought perhaps the old man was a Gestapo informant testing me, but true to his word, Hirsch showed up the same night. So, I assumed he truly was a friend of the Jewish community after all."

Weiss was distracted by a soft chirping sound, and quickly got up and walked towards the far corner of the flat. There, beneath the apartment's only other window, hung a birdcage. She retrieved a small package from her pocket and emptied the contents into her palm. Opening the cage door, she sprinkled the food in a silver bowl. The bird was extravagant and regal looking, with a bronze head, and a blue-black sheen to its body and wings.

Brandt observed the careful manner with which she attended to her pet.

"That's a beautiful bird."

"Her name's Rachel. She's an archangel pigeon," she answered absently. "One of the few possessions the Gestapo permitted me to keep, despite the ban."

"They've banned birds? What will they think of next?"

"You can laugh if you want, but according to German law it's illegal for a Jew to own a carrier pigeon," she replied, her dark eyes blazing.

He saw the impassioned glint in her gaze, and for a moment caught a glimpse of the pain and anger that simmered just beneath the surface of her studied composure. He nodded his head attentively, and watched as the fire receded.

"Before the Reich passed those laws, my father used to breed pigeons as a hobby," she continued, her tone softening. "These were his favorites though. He called them Erzengeln."

Archangels? "Why are they called that?"

She hesitated. He could sense the internal conflict in her features, as she weighed whether or not to share something of meaning with him. Her eyes drifted away from his towards the belowground window.

"When I was young, my father spent hours showing my sister and me how to care for them, and telling us stories about how they received their name. Our scriptures tell of mankind's attempt to build the Tower of Babel, in an effort to reach the heavens."

Brandt caught himself nodding along. He remembered the tale of the ill-fated ancient tower from his own youth. It had been one of the stories he learned in the basement classroom where his parents left him when they attended church services. *What child hadn't had his imagination captivated by the thought of building a castle that extended higher than the eye could see?*

"According to the legend, when the builders realized they could go no higher, they instead decided to build a temple at the top of the tower, to worship the unreachable God. And every day these pigeons would come and nest in the roof of the temple. When they flew away, they would soar so high that the priests would lose sight of them in the clouds. So, the rumor grew that these birds, who communed with the heavens and returned to dwell in the tower, were the messengers between man and God... His Erzengeln.

Brandt was transfixed by her ethereal, far away tone. She told the story so intently, her gaze fixed on some unseen time and event, as though she was reliving the tale from her childhood. He realized she had stopped speaking, her gaze looking askance at his blank stare. He cleared his throat awkwardly.

"That's a fascinating story."

"Anyway, now Rachel is all I have left of my father, and I like to think of her as the messenger between myself and heaven," her voice became distant, and the momentary luster had faded from her eyes. "Only instead of nesting in a temple at the heights of the earth, she's a caged prisoner in an underground hovel, where she can't even see the sky... kind of like me."

The weight of her words knocked him off balance. *She really had become every bit as much a caged animal as her bird. Like those children shivering in the church cellar.* He averted his gaze, and rubbed his hand across his brow with a wearied breath.

"Sorry, I wouldn't expect you to understand, or care about any of that," she rejoined, the sharp edge returning to her tone.

Her words stung. He quickly realized that she had mistaken his unresponsiveness for indifference, and struggled to steady himself. It was too late to clarify. *What would I say anyway?*

"No, it's not that. It's just been a week filled with cellars and caged animals of different types. I should go."

She made no reply. He suddenly felt very tired. He picked up his hat from the back of the chair, and headed towards the door.

"I'll check on your progress tomorrow. In the meantime, if Hirsch, or anyone acting on his behalf, tries to contact you, you know how to get in touch with me," he concluded, stopping short at the door. "And for what it's worth, I'm sorry about your father."

"Danke," she replied distantly. She remained seated at the table, but he could see that a gentleness had returned to her face. He thought he recognized a tinge of regret in her expression. Then he heard another far away voice, and was surprised when he realized it was his own.

"I lost my father suddenly too. To a senseless, random act. So, I know what it feels like to talk to someone you love one evening, just like you have every other night of your life, only to discover the next morning that, due to something totally beyond your control or understanding, you're never going to see him again... at least not in this world. I'm glad yours at least left you a messenger. Gute Nacht."

He was shocked by his confession, but he didn't look up,

or wait for a reply. He briskly opened the door. He was greeted by the draft from a wintry gust of wind that sent flurries of snow swirling around him. He pulled his jacket up snugly around his neck once again, and walked out into the moonless night.

Chapter 25

"The prisoner was picked up for interrogation late last night, but I didn't get word of it until this afternoon," Faber huffed. If we're lucky, maybe they haven't torn out his tongue yet!"

Brandt shook his head. 'Late last night' he had been at Rebecca Weiss's flat, gathering intelligence on the movements of Jacob Hirsch. His mind drifted back to the encounter. *Why did I lower my defenses with her? Why would I tell her about my family?* He steeled himself against such displays of weakness in the future. *Most importantly, we need to get to the bottom of the connection between Jacob Hirsch and David Hedrich.*

"What have you found out about David Hedrich?"

"Quite a bit about his background, but unfortunately nothing that has us any closer to finding him," Faber replied, as he downshifted and headed north out of the city center on Scharnhorst Strasse. They crossed into the Wedding district and in short order found their vehicle traveling parallel to the Hohenzollern Canal. The canal had been an engineering marvel of its time, constructed nearly a century earlier to help navigate the divide between the Havel and the Spree. The canal's history would be forever linked with the place they were now heading, Plotzensee. The sun was setting ahead of them as they crossed the Kordlsee Strasse bridge, and Plotzensee Prison appeared, looming ominously on the horizon.

The 65-acre compound, surrounded by an imposing system of walls, spread out before them like a relic from another era. And in some ways, it was. The facility had been commissioned during the reign of Emperor Wilhelm I, and had immediately become the largest prison in Germany. Since the Fuhrer's ascension, it had become the home to many high-profile political prisoners. *And the site of numerous executions.* If for no other reason than the prison's working guillotine, it had become one of the most whispered about places in Berlin.

Faber flashed his credentials at a perimeter barrier, and parked in the staff lot. They exited the vehicle and headed towards the front gate.

"If the Gestapo just picked Daschle up last night, why would they transfer him to Plotzensee so quickly?" Brandt inquired.

"I don't know."

"They have an in-house prison filled with interrogation cells right under their own roof, and completely under their own control, at Gestapo headquarters... so why transfer him here?"

Brandt's inquiries were interrupted as air raid sirens began to wail in the distance.

"They've started their runs early tonight."

Brandt nodded, casting a glance skyward. They passed through an external checkpoint at the gates, and quickly became aware of the effect of the twenty-foot-high security wall that ran along the perimeter of the grounds. *Our perception of a wall all depends on what side of it we're on. Are we more concerned with keeping something out, or with keeping something in?* They trudged towards the foreboding

190

brick edifice that served as the entrance to the Plotzensee prison complex. The windows were covered with iron-girded bars.

They navigated their way through the shadowy halls of the cruciform shaped building in silence, until the passage opened out onto the first floor of the main cell block. Loud shouts and sounds of commotion filtered down from above, echoing through the chambers. Looking up they could see the endless rows of inmate cells reaching three stories high above them. They plodded towards the east wing of the cellblock. A vast array of barred windows offered an obstructed glimpse out onto the walled prison courtyard, where prisoners milled about aimlessly.

Beyond the crowded courtyard more of the red brick buildings that comprised the sprawling prison system became visible. Brandt reflexively shuddered as he spotted the brick shed next to prison *Haus III* in the distance, or as it was grimly known, *'the house of the dead.'* This is where the resident prison executioner carried out execution orders. From the cases Brandt had heard about, the process was no more humane than it had been in medieval times: death by guillotine, beheading by axe blow, and even mass hangings from meat hooks. All of this transpired under the watchful eye of the prison's chapel, whose stately spire hovered high above the execution hall.

Brandt was glad when they emerged from the east wing, and descended a short staircase towards a long corridor of holding cells. He cleared his mind, and returned his focus to the prisoner, rather than the prison.

"What charge are they holding Daschle on?" he inquired, breaking the silence.

"The report says he was arrested for 'distributing seditious materials' at the Lodenfabrik. Could that sound any more contrived?"

"So, you think Colonel Schonbern knows about this?"

"Knows about it? Two-to-one says he ordered it. The timing's not a coincidence," the sergeant concluded, his voice trailing off as they approached a clearance desk at the end of the corridor.

A diminutive, bespectacled Gestapo agent glared contemptuously from behind his desk as he watched them approach. Brandt grinned inwardly at the thought of this haughty bank clerk, miscast as a prison guard. *If the inmates ever got their hands on him!*

"Lieutenant Brandt and Sergeant Faber to see the prisoner, Kirk Daschle," Brandt said curtly, producing his credentials.

"Access to that prisoner is restricted to officers with Gestapo clearance, orders of Major Weskamp," the agent replied dismissively.

Weskamp, who else?

Brandt could feel Faber pressing against his shoulder.

"Schonbern's trained monkey, what a surprise." he offered, under his breath.

The Gestapo agent leaned forward trying to overhear, or perhaps trying to intimidate them with his close scrutiny.

"We're here to question the prisoner as part of a joint investigation with the Gestapo, acting under the direct authority of Standartenfuhrer Schonbern," Brandt countered.

He watched some of the smugness recede from the clerk's features at the mention of the colonel's name, and decided to press his advantage further, "I'm sure it wasn't Major Weskamp's intention to contradict his own superior's directives, nor your intention to do so now."

The agent fidgeted with his papers, and after a considerable pause pushed a sign-in log across the desk in resignation. He initialized Brandt's signature, and wordlessly directed them across the stone floor towards a dank row of holding cells. At the end of the corridor, he dismissed a brutish looking prison guard with a wave of his hand, and unlocked the door.

"He's all yours. Good luck, he's the quiet type," he oozed sardonically. The patter of his footsteps echoed off the brick walls, as he scurried back to his desk.

Brandt peered into the murky room, wincing as the putrid odor of the cell washed over him like a blast from a furnace. A listless body was slumped against a mattress in the corner, with one arm awkwardly hanging from a chain on the wall. Brandt inched forward, his mind reeled at the thought that this wretched figure could possibly be Kurt Daschle, the same strapping, spirited worker he had interrogated just the week before at the Loden Werke factory.

"Jesus Christus. See if you can get some water for him," he instructed Faber, aware that his voice had come out as little more than a whisper.

Brandt moved closer, his eyes still adjusting to the darkness. He was surprised to see that the prisoner's eyes were open, and that he was seemingly alert. He could feel Daschle's piercing gaze, even through the severe swelling, that disfigured the man's face.

"You certainly look the worse for wear since the last time I saw you."

Brandt thought he saw the trace of a faint smile form around the edges of Daschle's bruised lips.

"What could you have possibly done to warrant this type of beating?" he continued.

"T-t-talked to you," Daschle labored, his voice was raspy, and his words were distorted by the thickness of his tongue.

"What? Your arrest report says you were picked up for distributing seditious leaflets at the Lodenfabrik?

"*Das ist Scheisse*! A trumped-up charge," he exclaimed, his anger quickly giving way to exhaustion. "This isn't about me. This is about you."

"About me? How so?"

"Ever since they arrested me, all they do is ask what information did I give '*da Kriminalpolizei*... What did I share with you? And then the beatings follow."

"What information do they think you gave me?"

"I don't know, but they want to know about Hirsch."

"What about Hirsch?" Brandt inquired. *Colonel Schonbern's men are the only ones who could possibly know the connection between Daschle and Jacob Hirsch, right?*

"And I'd gladly tell them what they want to hear, just to make it stop," he gasped, his voice momentarily trailing off. "Just to make it stop, only I didn't give you anything."

Faber returned with water, and the prisoner's eyes rolled back in his head as he mumbled something unintelligible to himself. Brandt took the cup and placed it within reach of Daschle's free hand. The prisoner's good hand, was too battered to hold the cup, so Brandt moved closer and held the cup to his mouth. He gulped at it greedily, struggling to hold the water in over his parched, serrated lips.

"How is he?" Faber inquired in a hushed tone.

"He's in bad shape physically, but his mind is surprisingly clear," Brandt offered, turning away from the prisoner. "He

194

says the Gestapo did this to him because they think he's been supplying us with information. What do you think?"

"It's possible. Standartenfuhrer Schonbern is known to use any method of extraction at his disposal. Anything to impede our progress, or further his own."

"The more things change…"

"And if that means trampling this poor slob into the ground in the process, so be it. Plus, Major Weskamp made the arrest, and had him transferred here, and the good major doesn't wipe his ass without Schonbern's stamp of approval."

Brandt smiled. The prisoner's recovering voice emanated from the corner, continuing his train of thought as if he'd never paused.

"Besides, even if I do talk… they're not letting me out of here. No matter what I say, they're not letting me leave here alive."

Brandt walked back towards the hunched body, leaning down close. The man's eyes had closed again in exhaustion.

"Daschle, listen to me. If you have more on Jacob Hirsch, give it to us and we'll try to get you out of here, get you released into our custody."

The slits housing the prisoner's battered eyes darted open, staring wildly. His disfigured face grew animated, his body stiffened against the chain.

"*Fick dich!*" he grunted, his deformed mouth almost spitting the words at Brandt. "I've tried helping you before, and look at where it landed me. Your custody? Fuck you both!"

"*Ficken uns?!*" Faber moved forward purposefully, glowering at the heap on the floor.

Brandt fended the sergeant off with an extended arm, and leaned in uncomfortably close to Daschle's mutilated features.

He could smell the broken man's fetid breath against his skin, and see the bloodied and bruised pores oozing on his cheeks. He leaned closer still until he was pressed against the side of the prisoner's face, speaking directly into his ear.

"I'm not going to press you, but know this: When we walk out of this cell, it's just you and the Gestapo."

He could see the prisoner's facial expression tighten.

"And from the looks of you, I have a feeling you aren't going to survive what they have planned for their next visit, especially when they find out that you've been talking to me again," he concluded.

Brandt stood. He hovered over the prisoner's unresponsive frame for a moment, waiting for a reply. Daschle's face had assumed a pitiful expression amongst his ruinous features, his lips trembling in defiant silence. Brandt and his counterpart headed back towards the outer corridor. Faber had pushed open the cell door leading out into the hall by the time the plaintive whimper reached their ears.

"I can give you Hirsch!"

Brandt's eyes darted to Faber. He walked back towards Daschle slowly.

"You can give me Hirsch?" he asked, flashing an incredulous smile. "Oh, so now you have some new information regarding the whereabouts of Jacob Hirsch?"

"That's right," he nodded desperately.

"You're sitting here chained to a wall, unable to lift yourself out of a puddle of your own excrement, and yet you can 'give me' the most wanted man in Berlin?"

"I know where he lives. Where he holds up."

"How would you know that?"

"I just know."

"That's not good enough. How do you know?"

Daschle's breathing pattern deepened. Brandt could see the wheels turning in the prisoner's head as he weighed the least incriminating way to respond.

"I've known all along. You and the Gestapo aren't the only ones looking for him."

"Who else would be looking for Jacob Hirsch?"

"A worker at the Lodenfabrik was looking for him too. A guy named Hedrich."

"Hedrich!"

"Yes, Hedrich. Says he tracked him down to a Jewish tenement in the Treptow district."

"David Hedrich? How do you know him?" Brandt's mind reeled.

Faber moved closer, a look of shock spreading across his face.

"Don't know his first name. He just got transferred into the factory camp a few weeks ago, and started asking around about Jacob Hirsch. I was Hirsch's supervisor, so naturally he came to me. Said Hirsch owed him an old debt."

"A debt?" Brandt replied. "And is this Hedrich still assigned to the Lodenfabrik?"

"Not sure, haven't seen him since that day," Daschle responded. "Like the rest of the workers with travel passes, he could come and go as he pleased."

Who the hell is this guy? Are he and Hirsch working together? Against each other? Is he the man we should be looking for?

"Why wouldn't you have told me this before, rather than giving me the runaround about the church transfer?"

"Hirsch has never done any wrong by me. He has some

197

ties to der Schwarzmarkt, and even spotted me some extra ration cards when I was strapped. I had no reason to turn on him. Plus, he's not the type of guy you want to cross."

"So where does Hirsch live in Treptow?"

Daschle hesitated. Brandt sensed the captive's resistance to sharing his last shred of leverage, but they had precious little time for delay. He leaned more closely for effect, again smelling the fetid stench of the dried blood and vomit perched on Daschle's lips.

"Your life is only as valuable as this information, Daschle. It's your only currency. In exchange for a word, I'm offering you your life. Take the offer while it lasts."

The desperate man's swollen eyes scanned Brandt's face wildly, searching for assurance.

"These guys are going to squeeze the lifeblood out of you for this information, and then once they have it they're going to discard the hollow shell that's left. The executioner's shed is only a stone's throw from your cell. You've heard of the house of the dead?" Brandt inquired sharply, looking for cracks. "Say the right words to me right now, and I'll have you out of here, released into my custody, within the hour."

The prisoner hung his head, his body silently shuddering.

"He has a flat in the Ras Haus tenement building in Treptow. Supposedly been living there with the foreign workers. *Appartement* 209B," Daschle exhaled slowly, his last shreds of resistance seeping out with the air in his lungs.

Brandt remained crouched next to him, motionless. He silently studied the prisoner's crestfallen expression for a moment, searching for any signs of deception or additional information. *He's spent, physically and emotionally.* Brandt stood, and walked with Faber toward the cell door.

"See if you can find anything to confirm that address, and have Sergeant Roth meet us there with a small squad of uniformed personnel."

"You want tactical back-up?"

"No, that didn't work out too well last time. Let's keep it in the family. Just some uniforms and Roth."

"Right."

"Then inform Colonel Brunner that we have a witness in Gestapo custody, who is central to our investigation, and ask him to pull whatever strings necessary to get him transferred. When we wrap this up, I want officers dispatched back to the Lodenfabrik and a wide net cast to find this David Hedrich."

"Understood."

They heard muffled sobs, and turned to survey the pile of flesh slumped in the corner of the cell. Daschle's swollen eyes were shuttered tightly, and his chest heaved as twin rivulets of water flowed down his discolored cheeks.

Chapter 26

Sergeant Roth met them at the rendezvous point near the street front entrance to the Ras Haus residences, accompanied by six uniformed officers from their precinct. In the shadow of endless rows of dilapidated brick buildings, Brandt hurriedly briefed the unit on the target and scope of their operation. He didn't like to rush into this type of extraction, but there was a crisis of trust in the precinct, and too many unknowns to risk waiting. *Who else knows of Hirsch's whereabouts, and who would have been tipped off if we included other agencies? And how long do we have before the Gestapo, or one of their plants at Kripo, gets to Daschle? We can't have a repeat of the factory raid. It has to be now.*

The Ras Haus had effectively become a foreign village in the southeast corner of Berlin, an industrial housing complex between the neighborhoods of Neukolln and Treptow. The tenement's proximity to the nearby railway lines, and transit stations, made it a natural residential destination for workers of all backgrounds, who were arriving on the trains from the east for temporary resettlement. For those workers fortunate enough not to land in one of the many work camps on the city's outskirts, this became home for them, and in many cases for their displaced families.

It was the middle of the night. *Naturally.* He couldn't recall the last night he had actually been in the comfort of a bed at this hour. The street front was quiet, aside from the muffled hum emanating from the overcrowded facility. Brandt led his small detachment towards Tower Five. The four-story edifice would have been indistinguishable from the surrounding buildings if not for its roman numeral lettered entrance *V*, and the fact that it appeared to span in both directions for half of a city block. He waved several of the uniformed officers around the building's perimeter, as his sergeants and the remaining agents followed him into the main foyer. Debris and discarded clothing littered the entry hall. He tapped his fingers against an aging building diagram pasted on the wall.

"209B."

The unit ascended one level through a shabby stairwell, exiting through the creaking steel door that announced their arrival onto the second floor. They quietly traversed the long, dimly lit hallway that stretched further than the eye could see. They scanned the apartment door numbers between the peeling, faded walls, weapons drawn and at the ready. The sounds of cramped, restless humanity grew more distinct. The agents were startled as #203A cracked open on the right side of the hall as they passed. A young woman peered out at them wide-eyed, before quickly shutting the door. An instant later an infant's plaintive cry resumed from within. They lowered their weapons, and walked on.

#209B became visible to their port side. Brandt motioned with two fingers on his left hand, and crossed over to the opposite side of the doorframe, his Walther raised. Sergeant Faber crossed over to join him with another officer, as Roth and the remaining uniformed agent flanked their position. They briefly held this spot and listened. They heard nothing.

Roth nodded, and raised his pistol to his shoulder. He squared himself to face the door, and stepped back with his right foot to create momentum. The brittle floorboards creaked loudly under his shifting weight. The sergeant hesitated a count. He braced himself and lifted his right leg, kicking it violently towards the door handle. Instantaneously there was a loud report, and then another. Wood splintered from the door, propelling Roth off his feet. He landed across the hall with a thud.

By the time the third shot rang out, its ordinance piercing the door and embedding itself in the wall on the opposite side of the hallway, the entire detachment had taken cover on the ground.

"Stay down!" Brandt shouted, already pulling himself to the spot where the sergeant lay sprawled across the corridor. Roth strained to lift his head, his voice an inaudible gurgle in his throat. Brandt looked in his eyes, and saw only fear, quickly giving way to shock.

"Hold on Sergeant."

Brandt hovered over him, shielding him as he tried to better examine his condition. He pulled the top of the sergeant's jacket open, and could already see a dark pool of blood seeping through his shirt from a gunshot wound below his left collarbone. He placed his hand over the wound. It wouldn't stop. It was near an artery. He checked Roth's pulse. It was ragged and faltering.

"Just breathe, Emil. Stay still, we're going to get you out of here," he said, as calmly as he could, signaling to a young uniformed agent, who was rooted to the ground on the opposite side of the hall. "Call for medical, *schnell*! *Offizier unten*! And let them know there's an armed suspect on the premises."

He leaned closer to try to hear the words Roth was repeatedly mouthing. Faber had sidled up to his shoulder. The shots had subsided. Brandt leaned in still closer, trying to hear the sergeant's faint, rasping voice.

"I'm sorry… I'm sorry."

Sorry?

"It's not your fault, Emil."

Roth faded, the life flickering from his eyes. He went limp. Brandt lifted him further and cradled his head in his arms.

"Come on Roth. Hang in there. Emil. Emil!" he shouted, as Faber moved to intercede.

"I've got him, Lieutenant," he said.

Brandt placed his hand against the side of Roth's head, as Faber and another agent moved in, "You don't leave him, Anton."

"Leave him?"

But Brandt had already turned and crouched towards the door. He felt his heart racing, as he peered through the splintered wood where the door had separated from the frame. His ears were still filled with the muffled hum from the report of the gunshots. Through that buzz he could vaguely hear one of his men appealing that they wait for backup, and Sergeant Faber calling him by his first name. *Konrad!*

With a suddenness of movement that even surprised himself, Brandt lunged, roughly shouldering the door open at its most vulnerable point. It swung open with a resounding crash, as it pulled free from the hinges. He found himself inside the apartment, pistol raised, as he scanned the barren room. In an instant he confirmed that the main living space, as well as the attached bath, was empty. In that same instant, he noticed a flapping movement from the sheer curtains.

Verdammt! The fire escape!

Brandt reached the window in time to see a man descending the last rungs of the escape, one floor below. The man's footsteps were already echoing off the asphalt of the narrow alley between the buildings. Brandt didn't have time, or the angle, to take the shot. In a single motion he holstered his weapon, and vaulted the window frame out onto the landing.

He rapidly began his descent, his feet slipping on the wet metal rungs of the ladder. Nearing the bottom, he jumped free, landing in a crouch on the damp pavement. He could see the silhouetted outline of the fleeing man still visible at the far end of the foggy alley. He regained his balance and pursued, quickly finding his top-end stride. The narrow confines of the alley, and increasing visibility of his target, brought strange focus to his pursuit. He was closing. Brandt knew that he had good speed over short distances. Judging from the suspect's stride, against his own, he liked his chances of catching him before the alley emptied out onto the streets. He decided against pulling his pistol, it would only slow him down at this point. He could feel his pulse begin to pound in his ears.

The suspect's gate slowed. Brandt followed suit, now unholstering his pistol, in case the assailant decided to turn and fire. The man slowed further. *What's he doing? There's at least another 50 meters before the alley ends!* The fugitive made a sudden turn to the right, and was gone from sight. *Scheisse!* Brandt sprinted to close the distance, slowing as he approached the spot where the man had vanished. There was a blind alley. He edged along the wall, peering around the corner in time to see the suspect take a left turn, before disappearing into another alley.

Apparently the long, symmetrical rows of indistinguishable brownstone tenement buildings were bordered by a series of smaller apartment complexes as they neared the main thoroughfares. This created a complex network of small alleys between the buildings. *Ein Labyrinth*!

A nearby air raid siren began to plaintively wail, permeating the cold night air, and his concentration. *Perfekt!* He bent over and huffed heavily, his breath producing a cloud around him. The fugitive had taken a right off the main alley, and then a left. *He's still winding his way towards the main road. That's the only way he can hope to get out of this maze without being hemmed in. But if he reaches the street in time to blend in with people heading to the bomb shelters...*

Brandt's legs spurred him to action almost before his mind could make the decision. He would take the gamble of not following the assailant into the side alleys. Instead, he would run straight through the main alley in hopes that a direct route would put him on the street front ahead of the suspect's winding path. He holstered his pistol and broke into a full sprint. By the time he reached the outlet at the end of the alley, he could already hear air raid wardens blowing their whistles, and the commotion of people being herded towards the shelters.

The alley emptied out near the entrance to the Ras Haus projects, and onto Graetz Strasse. Graetz Strasse served as a busy thoroughfare between the nearby barracks installations and the Treptow district by day, but at this hour of the night it would normally be deserted... *if not for the air raid alert.* Brandt found the street teeming with people spilling out of the surrounding residential buildings, streaming in packs towards one of the several air raid shelters designated for the block. The street was awash in a mixture of foreign tongues, children's cries, and piercing whistles and shouts as weary inhabitants chaotically searched for safety.

The masses on Brandt's side of the street were all being herded in his direction, their width covering Graetz Strasse from sidewalk to sidewalk, as they trudged towards the assigned bunker just past where he had exited the alley moments before. This made his attempts to move in the opposite direction nearly impossible, but it also meant that the suspect would likely be swept in this direction, if he had attempted to exit the alleys further down the street.

Brandt climbed the entry stairs of a nearby building, pushing against the tide of people churning past him, in search of an elevated vantage point. His eyes darted, searching the rows of oncoming faces, then scanning the street from the perimeter of the Ras Haus buildings to the opposite curb. No sign of the suspect, or his grey cap. Or rather, there were tons of grey caps, as workers had grabbed something to cover their heads as they rolled out of their beds and into the wintry nighttime air, not knowing how long they'd be stuck in the frigid shelters. He looked on in vain, growing more despondent by the moment. *Sergeant Roth's shooter can't just slip through our grasp like this!*

Tracers lit up the distant sky, and the report of anti-aircraft fire from nearby flak towers could be heard above the din. Brandt made one last concerted effort to move further down the block, pushing eastward against the flow of people in the direction of the alleys where he had left the trail of the fugitive. *He has to be on the street by now if he continued in this direction.*

Trying to see above the crowd, Brandt became entangled with a tight clump of workers attempting to move past him in the opposite direction. He gave some ground, trying to skirt by them on the far side, hearing grumbles and what he took for foreign epithets directed at him for going against the grain. He found himself enmeshed in a crowd that was being prodded toward the shelter like cattle, and before he could regain his traction, realized he had been moved a dozen paces backwards. He was nearly at the mouth of the bomb shelter before managing to break free. He found himself face-to-face with a block warden who was bringing up the rear, rounding up stragglers on this side of Graetz Strasse.

Brandt flashed his badge at the surprised warden, and pushed past him, surveying the organized mayhem as the dwindling crowds were being corralled into other bunkers. Approaching from the opposite direction on Graetz Strasse, he saw Sergeant Faber moving towards him with several other men in tow. *I told him not to leave Emil's side!* He turned back to the warden suddenly.

"How many public shelters are there on these blocks?"

"What's that, Herr Lieutenant?"

"How many public bomb shelters are dedicated to this block?"

"Just these three."

"Go tell the rest of the block wardens to seal the other two shelters, and that no one leaves until we search them!"

"Pardon me Lieutenant, but that's not…"

"Just do it!" Brandt demanded. "I want anyone trying to avoid the shelters apprehended and brought to me. My men will assist you, starting with this shelter."

"Right away," the warden offered scurrying down the

street urgently in the direction of the next closest shelter.

Brandt felt Sergeant Faber's hand on his shoulder. He knew that he didn't want to turn around and look at his colleague, but he did anyway.

"Sergeant Roth?"

"He's gone. They've already taken him away."

Chapter 27

Brandt stooped over the shattered fragments of wood on the hallway floor. He stared vacantly at the busted doorframe. *Not even an hour ago, Emil was standing right here... and then lying there. Why did I let him go in first? Why didn't I request more firepower?* He tried to push the questions, and the images of his fallen colleague, from his mind. A pair of agents, who had been dispatched from the precinct, shuttled back and forth between the apartment and the hall as they drafted a report of the crime scene. He moved out of their way, and into the flat, where Faber and a uniformed corporal searched through the belongings that the suspect had hurriedly left behind. There had been no signs of the fugitive in the search of the shelters, and the 'alles klar' had since been given for people to return to their homes. Brandt turned his gaze back to the spot in the hallway where Roth had been shot.

What about his wife and little girl! He was a new father...

Faber made his way across the flat, and stood next to him silently. He felt Faber's hand on his shoulder again.

"He was just here..." Brandt whispered.

He could feel his face flush. A mixture of anger and guilt coursed through his veins.

"Why wouldn't I have summoned more backup?"

"You can't blame yourself," Faber countered. There's nothing you could have done differently. We had more than enough men to flush out a single fugitive holed up in a housing project. It's not your fault."

"You told me to request tactical support, but I had to keep it quiet, had to apprehend him myself! I should have been the first one through the door!"

"So you could be the one on the way to the coroner's office in a bag?"

"Better me than him. He has a Frau und Kind!"

"Look, I've known Sergeant Roth a long time, a lot longer than you, and he wouldn't have had it any other way. He always wanted to be the first man in. You know that. The best way we can honor his memory is to get the guy who shot him."

"Lost in the crowds. What a waste!"

"Not a complete waste," Faber said, shaking his head. "He left behind a few items of interest."

"Like what?"

Faber motioned him towards the suitcase laying open on the abandoned apartment's faded yellow sleep sofa. The tattered bag had been packed to capacity; its contents jumbled together in a haphazard fashion.

"He obviously anticipated someone coming for him, and his packing job indicates he wasn't planning to wait around," Faber said. "I'd venture everything he had of value in this world is crammed in here. Including this."

Faber handed him a set of identity papers, all bearing the name 'Jacob Israel Hirsch.' The photo was the same one Hirsch had cropped onto the false documents he had passed on to Rebecca Weiss under the pseudonym David Hedrich. Brandt scrutinized the documents closely. They were authentic.

"So, this is our guy. No more chasing ghosts."

"Right, and with his actual identification numbers, maybe we can search the records and trace his past movements through the system. But that's not all," Faber continued, pushing back a thin layer of clothes and folded jackets to reveal the contents buried below. Brandt moved closer, his eyes widening. The bottom of the suitcase was covered with stacks of ration cards, stamp booklets, several envelopes of cash, and a Mauser pistol.

"He may have lived in squalor, but he's got quite a stash for a fugitive Jew" Brandt acknowledged, picking up a booklet and examining the seals on the ration cards. *From the same allotment that was offered to Weiss in bulk.*

"They're government-issued, and so is the pistol." Faber said.

"So, he either has access to der Schwarzmarkt or a contact in one of the government agencies?"

"I'd say both. Think about it. His name is all over the visitor's log at Captain Keppler's office, and we know Keppler trafficked heavily in der Schwarzmarkt goods."

"Kill your supplier?" Brandt countered. "Not many German Jews are in a position to sever the hand that feeds them, no matter how well connected they are. "

At least this is a solid lead. We finally know who it is that we're chasing. But even if he had severed ties with Captain Keppler, why had he targeted Major Goertz? And what's his tie to David Hedrich? For every new revelation there's a slew of unanswered questions.

He felt the adrenaline begin to pump life back into his tired limbs, and some of the weight lift from his heavy eyelids. They finally had a concrete suspect, and a positive identification, rather than just a name or alias. *But at what cost? Why did Emil have to give his life for this?* His thoughts returned to the image of his fatally wounded colleague, writhing on the floor. A cold shudder passed through his body, and his eyes drifted towards the droplets of rain running down the outside window of the apartment.

"Listen, Lieutenant, it's been a long day, and an even longer night," Faber interjected. "I'll draft the report, and supervise the scene from here. Why don't you go home and get some rest? Lieutenant?"

Chapter 28

"Herr Lieutenant? The rain is letting up."

The words from the back of the car roused him from his waking slumber. He hadn't properly slept since Sergeant Roth had been shot. He hadn't even tried, but at this point that was nothing new. He glanced in the rearview mirror at Fraulein Weiss, who shifted anxiously in her seat. The heavy rain had subsided, reduced to a cold drizzle that pattered against the windshield. He looked at his watch, uncertain of the time, or of just how long he had been lost in thought as the vehicle idled at the curb.

"Good, get your things."

Brandt left the car parked against the curb, and led them towards the high arched gate at the southern entrance to Treptower Park. They crossed over a damp, deserted span of the bike path that ran along the perimeter of the park, and followed the walkway through a thicket of tall trees. Reaching a clearing, they could see that the expansive park sprawled in every direction, to the north, east, and west of their current location. A maze of trails diverged into densely wooded areas, bordered by a series of waterways to the east. Brandt directed them towards a wide walking trail on their left. The path was heavily bordered on both sides by barren stretches of forest, the leafless trees groaning under the weight of the clinging water and ice.

He could see why Hirsch would choose the park grounds as the pickup spot for his exchange with Fraulein Weiss. There was no way to fully seal the porous perimeter, and there were numerous well-covered escape routes within the park's trails system if the exchange went bad. In the event that he evaded their dragnet in the park, there was also nearby water access to the Spree, and an S-Bahn station within a stone's throw of the southern entrance. To top it all off, Hirsch had set up the meeting for nightfall when visibility, and their tracking capabilities, would be severely hampered. Brandt had already seen how slippery Hirsch could be in the cover of darkness, and he didn't want to experience that again.

Will he even show? Did we spook him back into hiding last night, or flush him out into the open? He had a feeling Hirsch would show, now more than ever. The near miss at the Ras Haus would make it seem like the walls were closing in, and force him to speed up his exit strategy. *And just like clockwork, he set up his rendezvous with Fraulein Weiss for the very next day.*

The rain had begun to fall harder. Brandt noted that Rebecca Weiss had pulled her scarf up over her head, and he decided to quicken his pace. A wide stone walking bridge appeared in the distance, with stairs leading up from the gravel path onto one of the park's terrace gardens. They headed towards it. Drawing nearer to the bridge, a large statue of a perched eagle glowered down at them from the terrace level above. *This is the place.* They took shelter from the rain beneath the underpass. Fraulein Weiss lowered her scarf, and suppressed a shiver, as she ran her hands up and down her arms to create warmth.

"This is where you're scheduled to make the exchange,"

Brandt confirmed, scanning the vantage points from the tunnel.

"That's right."

"Hirsch chose this location because it offers concealment, and a variety of ways in and out," he said. "We'll have men posted in plain-clothes throughout the basin of the terrace, all with clear sight lines to this overpass. Try to stand away from the tunnel walls so that you're never obstructed from view."

"I will."

He peered through the steadily increasing rainfall, and motioned in the direction of a small structure protruding from a distant tree line.

"See that building?"

"Yes," she nodded.

"That's about 60 meters away. It's an old ranger station that's no longer in use. The basement has been converted into a bomb shelter. I'll be positioned there with several of my men. From there, we should have a clear view of Hirsch's approach, no matter which direction he's coming from."

But what if we don't? What if he slips past us in the dark? Brandt knew that he could close the distance between the station and the bridge underpass in a matter of seconds, but he didn't want it to come to that. He had put his faith in his physical abilities last night, and they had failed him. *Not again!*

"Alright," Weiss responded, hesitantly.

"We plan to take Hirsch down before he even reaches you," he assured her. "If he somehow makes it to your position without being detected, don't be alarmed. Conduct the exchange as planned, and calmly walk away in the direction of the station, and we'll take it from there once you're clear.

Verstanden?"

She hesitated before nodding, and looked down, but Brandt had already detected a glint of apprehension in her eyes. He felt his throat tighten, and the tone in his voice falter.

"If something doesn't feel right, you just move in the direction of the shelter. I'm not going to let anything happen to you."

"Are you alright, Lieutenant Brandt?"

Am I alright? Her piercing brown eyes looked directly up into his. He felt like she could see straight through him.

"Seems like I should be asking you that question."

"Tell me what's troubling you."

Images from the previous night came flooding back to his mind. He couldn't shut them out. He needed sleep, or at least some downtime to process the whirlwind of events encircling him. He realized that neither of those respites were likely to occur anytime soon. He felt the walls coming down. His walls.

"Last night I lost someone close to me, someone whose life was in my hands," he paused before continuing "and I'm not going to let that happen again."

"I'm sorry," she offered genuinely, continuing after a measured pause. "Though that's not exactly comforting."

This time she was the one who tried to diffuse the tension, but he was in a different space, having already lowered his defenses.

"Why are you doing this?" he asked, abruptly.

"What?"

"After what they've done to your father, to your family. What does the Gestapo still have on you that's worth risking your life for?"

At the mention of her family, he had seen the tears begin

216

to well up in her eyes. She turned away, facing the wall with her head lowered. He hesitantly reached out and touched her shoulder. She was shaking. She remained silent, but didn't move further away. The cold rain pelted the stone bridge, echoing through the underpass.

"They still have my mother and my younger sister," she said in a hushed tone.

She turned to face him. Tears were streaming down her cheeks. Her voice was filled with a tone of resignation, which was belied by the fierce glisten in her eyes. She gazed at him intensely, studying his reaction.

"They're holding the rest of your family?"

"They're imprisoned at a women's camp north of the city, at Ravensbruck. Either I cooperate, or they follow the same route my father did on the transports. Or worse if that's possible."

Is there anyone they don't have their tentacles wrapped around? Anyone whose strings aren't being pulled from behind the curtain? And who is always the puppet master? Schonbern!

"What are they charged with?"

"Being *Jewish*, what else?"

"This is not what I intended, Rebecca" he halted briefly, realizing he had never used her proper name before. "It's not my choice to put you in this situation. We can catch this man without resorting to dangling you out in front of him. "

"I know you can. And at first, I didn't intend to cooperate, regardless of the Gestapo's threats," her voice was suddenly laced with defiance.

"You didn't?"

"Not for a second, I'm not like you Nazis. I couldn't have

the burden of an innocent life on my conscience, even in exchange for the lives of my family. My father wouldn't have wanted that. My mother and sister wouldn't want that either."

Her words stung, and her tone was recriminating, but he understood.

"So, why are you cooperating?"

"Because you brought me the name 'Jacob Hirsch.' That's when I realized I could satisfy both of my obligations."

"What? You told Major Weskamp you'd never heard of Hirsch!"

"My father was the head of the Berlin Judenrat, we knew nearly everyone involved in the Jewish Underground, both good and bad. Jacob Hirsch was a good man, who sold his soul. Men like him are as much a threat to the survival of our people, as any Gestapo agent.'

"Men like him?"

"My father knew Jacob Hirsch had turned Gestapo collaborator. He said such men were like animals who fed upon their own young in order to survive."

"You suspected Hirsch was a collaborator?"

"Yes, and when Major Weskamp showed me his photograph, I knew it was him. I knew this was my chance to perform a service for the Jewish community, and help my mother and sister at the same time."

Brandt was silent. He was amazed at how well she had managed to conceal this information under the stress of interrogation, and at how well she had kept her composure under such duress. Then he recalled the ease with which he had watched her mask her underlying emotions on several occasions. *I can't blame her for holding out on me, she was just trying to protect her family. Who wouldn't do the same?*

"I don't know why I'm telling you any of this," she continued. "I'm probably being naive, but either way it doesn't matter, as I won't help the Gestapo, or you, ever again!"

"I understand."

How quickly her defiance flares, simmering just below her calm exterior. You won't have to help us again. This finishes it!

"I was hoping the rain would let up, but it looks like that's not going to happen," he said, looking at his watch. "Come on, we don't have much time. I'll show you the place we have set up for you in the shelter."

Chapter 29

He waited for her to adjust her scarf, and then walked ahead of her in the direction of the shelter. By the time they cleared the underpass, the frigid rain had begun to come down in torrents. They simultaneously picked up their pace, and within moments had reached the front overhang of the old ranger station. They huddled close together trying to stay dry beneath the sparse covering of the canopy.

He struggled with the rusted latches on the door. In the tight confines he felt her body brush against his side for an instant. They pressed more tightly together. He turned towards her without breaking that delicate contact. She was looking up at him, her dark eyes glimmering through the driving rain. She lowered her head. Her hair was soaked, despite the best efforts of her scarf, and her damp clothes clung to the outline of her body.

He cupped her face in his hands, lifting her chin until she was gazing directly into his eyes. He kissed her softly. He kissed her passionately, with reckless abandon. His arms wrapped around her lower back, pulling her closer to him. He felt her return his embrace. He freed one hand and forcefully pushed the jammed door loose from the latch, guiding them in from the downpour.

They remained entangled as he led them down the narrow hall of the shelter, the weight of his advances pressing her back against the wall. In this manner, they felt their way down the corridor to the room that had been setup as her lodging for the evening. They remained thoroughly entwined with one another. He pulled away briefly, struggling to undo the wet buttons of her clinging, soaked blouse. He leaned in to kiss his way up her neck, and pulled her blouse open roughly. She gasped softly, as they descended, as one, onto the mattress on the shelter floor.

Chapter 30

Brandt stroked Rebecca's hair, as her head rested against his chest. He ran his hand across her bare shoulders, stopping to touch a key shaped locket dangling from her neck. Her eyes opened, and returned his gaze. She opened the locket, exposing a minuscule black and white photo.

"That's my family," she said, softly. "My mother gave it to me before we were separated."

"It's beautiful. It must make you feel close to them."

"It does. The locket belonged to my grandmother. It reminds me that I can't change the past."

"How so?"

"When my grandmother died suddenly, my mother couldn't accept the loss. After the funeral, she actually went to my grandmother's house and padlocked all the doors, as if she could preserve everything just as it had been."

"Some things can only be preserved in our memories."

He felt her nod in agreement against his shoulder. It was a lesson he had learned from personal experience. He couldn't help but think of his own reaction to the news of his father's death. He hadn't been there to see his father's body until the day of the funeral. He couldn't bring himself to believe that it was true, even after he saw him from afar in the casket. *That couldn't be my father!* He wasn't going to view the casket up close. He didn't want to see his father like that. Just before they closed the casket for the service, he had changed his mind. He had touched his dad's cold face, and stiffened chest, and he had said *'Auf Wiedersehen.'* And he had wept. All of this came flooding back to him, as Rebecca continued her story.

"We told my mother that she had to come to terms with it, that you can't just lock reality into a compartment and hope that it goes away."

"Why did your family decide to stay in Germany?"

"Partly because my father wanted to help the community, but a lot of it was my mother's denial. Berlin had been her family's home for generations, and she insisted nothing bad could befall us here. She couldn't see the storm clouds on the horizon because she wouldn't allow herself to look."

None are as blind as those who will not see. Self-deception is always the deadliest deception of all. Another lesson I've learned the hard way.

"The first time the Gestapo arrested my father it was in the middle of the night. He was gone for a week. My mother suffered a nervous breakdown. Her illusions of safety had been shattered. The day my father returned home, she went to my grandmother's old house and broke all the padlocks. She went through all of my grandmother's belongings, and sold or got rid of everything that wasn't precious or nailed down. And she came out wearing this..."

"In the shape of a key."

"It never left her neck again," she paused, stifling tears. "Not until the day she gave it to me as she was being loaded into the back of a Gestapo truck."

He could see tears starting to roll down her cheeks. Her body shuddered quietly, but she refused to weep. He put his arm around her shoulders to comfort her, unsure of what to say.

"It's alright. I'm sure your cooperation is going to help secure their release. What about your father? Why didn't he use his connections to help your family emigrate?"

"Everyone in the district urged him to flee, but he couldn't bring himself to do it."

"Why not?"

"He had a sense of obligation as one of the community's spiritual leaders, and he had responsibilities on the evacuation committees."

"Evacuation committees?"

"I'm surprised you don't know," she said searching his face questioningly. "When mass deportations began this fall, the *SS* needed leaders within the Jewish community to help with the transport schedules."

"Why would Jews agree to assist the *SS* in deporting other Jews?"

"They didn't have much of a choice. But when the community leaders saw that this was happening with or without their help, they decided to cooperate. That way they could ensure that the deportations were handled as humanely as possible."

"Humanely?"

"It's all relative," she shrugged. "At least having a voice in the process allowed them to identify who was the most fit to travel, to keep families from being separated from one another, and to help people prepare for the transports with dignity, rather than being hunted down and rounded up like cattle."

"But if he was cooperating in this way, how did your father run afoul of the Gestapo?" he asked, immediately sensing her wariness. "Don't worry, I'm not exactly in the

Gestapo's good graces right now."

"I sensed that about you from the first time I watched your interactions with Major Weskamp," she said, visibly flinching as she uttered the major's name. "My father also used his position of influence to shield as many people in the Jewish community as he could."

"And how would he shield them?"

"Each case was different. He would sometimes take in a family who was on the roundup list until they could find a way out of the city. On other occasions he helped people avoid the dragnets, or pulled strings to speed up the passport process for those trying to emigrate. He felt this was his calling. This was how he knew Jacob Hirsch."

"What do you mean?"

"Hirsch had originally worked in *der Untergrund* movement, trying to smuggle Jewish families out of the city, but then he disappeared for a few months last year. When he returned, he wasn't the same. Rumors circulated that he'd spent time in one of the camps, and was now owned by the Gestapo. Anyone who tried to work with him from that point forward, came to a bad end."

"Any idea what camp?"

"No."

"Did your father ever work with him again?"

"Not after that. He thought Hirsch was involved in the disappearance of other community organizers who had gone missing, like Schuman and Hedrich, so he never trusted him again."

"Wait, Hedrich was a community organizer?" Brandt said, sitting up.

"That's right."

"David Hedrich? From Kurische Strasse, in the Friedrichshain district?"

"We all lived in Friedrichshain."

"The same David Hedrich whose identity papers Hirsch presented when he approached you? You told me you didn't recognize his name!"

"I'm sorry, but I had little reason to trust you, and with my family in danger I couldn't afford to take any chances."

Fair enough. Look where cooperating with us has gotten her so far.

"I need you to help me understand this connection. Why would Jacob Hirsch have had David Hedrich's identity papers? And why would he try to pass them off as his own?"

"I've been asking myself that same question for days, but I don't know how he would have acquired them. As for why he used them, perhaps because he knows that David Hedrich's name carries clout in our community, whereas his own name is tarnished? Hirsch must have thought I didn't know him, or David Hedrich, by sight, and that Hedrich's name alone might grease the wheels of our transaction?"

"Is it possible Jacob Hirsch suspected you were working with the Polizei?"

"I don't know, but when I saw David Hedrich's name on those papers, I cried. It confirmed my worst fears about what had become of him and his family."

"Did you know his family well?"

"Not well, but I knew of them. I only remember seeing David Hedrich once or twice, when he came by the house to meet with my father. He made an impressive appearance. He was tall with a noble, military bearing, but he had a kindness in his eyes. I liked him. He was well regarded as a leader of der Untergrund emigration efforts among the Friedrichshain community. He was known to have arranged the escape of numerous area families facing deportation before his own family went missing."

"When did they go missing?"

"I'm not exactly sure, but it was around the same time as my father's arrest. It's been less than a month. But what does all of this have to do with apprehending Hirsch?"

Brandt slipped his shoulder from beneath her head and looked at his watch. In a single motion, he stood up and grabbed his shirt from the floor.

"I'm not sure but you should get dressed. We need to get you out of here."

Chapter 31

Extricating themselves from the park, and inconspicuously dropping Rebecca off at the edge of the Jewish district, had taken far longer than he had hoped. He could feel his internal clock ticking, his stress elevating with each movement of the hands. *Rebecca said Jacob Hirsch had been a benefactor to the Jewish community before turning collaborator during a stint in the prison camps? But what is his connection to the ghost that was David Hedrich?* He had a vague, gnawing anxiety that matters of gravity were transpiring in his absence, and that his prolonged truancy had not gone unnoticed. Returning to the office amidst the stop-and-start of the late afternoon rush had done nothing to calm his nerves.

As he feared, Sergeant Faber had been awaiting his return outside the Magazin Strasse entrance of the Kriminalpolizei precinct house. The sergeant anxiously dragged on a cigarette standing beneath the building overhang, though the rain had mostly stopped. Faber flicked the butt into the street, as Brandt pulled the vehicle to the curb. He could see the agitation etched on the sergeant's weathered face as Faber approached the passenger side window.

"Where have you been? I've had dispatch trying to reach you for the past hour."

"I was at Treptower Park, taking Fraulein Weiss on a walk-through of the exchange route, but there's been a change of plan."

"I hope you enjoyed your walk in the park!" Faber chided. "But never mind that. Der Priester, Pfarrer Eckhardt, called the precinct asking to speak with you immediately. Said it was urgent."

"Whom did he talk to?"

"Yours truly. When you couldn't take the call, it was transferred to my office."

"Did he say what he wanted?"

"No, but he seemed agitated," Faber indicated. "He wouldn't go into detail over the phone. He asked that I relay the message only to you. That's why I've been pacing the halls for the past hour!"

"My mistake."

"It's alright, you were obviously busy. You want me to come with you?"

"Get in," Brandt assented.

He reached over to unlock the door, and the sergeant nimbly hopped into the passenger's seat. Brandt swiftly steered the vehicle back onto the southbound side of the intersection, in the direction of the Neukolln district, and St. Michael's Kirche.

"I've got some news, but first things first," Faber continued. "Are you alright? You seem a little rattled."

"How could I not be? Aren't you a little rattled after the events of the past 24 hours?" Brandt replied, quickly recognizing the defensiveness in his voice.

"Naturally," Faber concurred. "But why the change of plans with the Jewish prisoner?"

"Because something doesn't add up, and I'm not going to risk anymore lives until we have better intelligence."

"Alright, what's troubling you?"

"Well for starters, judging from the contents of his briefcase, Jacob Hirsch has access to a high-level government supplier."

"Right? We already suspected that."

"So, why would a guy that well-connected need to use Rebecca Weiss to get exit papers?"

"I'd be lying if I said that same thought hadn't occurred to me, but maybe access to his supplier has run dry?"

"Perhaps, but I need more than that before dangling another innocent life out in front of him."

"That's your call, but the Gestapo's going to be none too pleased," Faber warned. "As far as they're concerned this is their operation now, and using the Jewess is the directive."

"I'll take responsibility for how we use Rebecca Weiss."

"You developing a soft spot for her?" Faber chided.

"Take it easy, Sergeant," Brandt frowned, in no mood for ribbing.

"Just be careful, that's all I'm saying."

"Speaking of Rebecca Weiss, she also mentioned knowing of David Hedrich, and that he had gone missing just over a month ago."

"You read my mind."

"What do you mean?"

"That's the news I had for you," Faber responded. "We've learned that the same David Hedrich whose house Major Goertz had purchased, also served on the Judenrat relocation committee here in Berlin that was disbanded in October."

"Is that right?"

"And do you know who headed up this committee for the Jewish community?"

"Who?"

"Rabbiner Samuel Weiss, Rebecca Weiss's father."

Just like she said. Maybe Rebecca is finally telling me the truth. The entire truth.

"She indicated that her father and David Hedrich had worked together."

"Wait, there's more. Guess who oversaw this committee's activities on behalf of the RSHA department of Jewish Affairs?"

"Theodore Goertz?!" Brandt replied, the realization striking like a bolt of lightning out of a clear blue sky.

"That's right!"

It makes sense. Major Goertz was head of the department whose primary responsibility was the relocation of Jews from designated areas of Berlin. Why hadn't I thought about this angle before?

"But why was the committee shut down in October?"

"For a few reasons. First, Reichsmarschall Goring issued a ban on Jewish emigration in October. As the committee's primary role was in coordinating services for the emigration of Berlin area Jews, their committee became obsolete, except for in facilitating the deportation process."

"So, when the option of emigration was removed, those who had facilitated it became expendable."

"Correct," Faber confirmed. "But this particular committee remained active for a while, to assist with mass deportations. It was only disbanded after it was accused of activities undermining the deportation process. Rabbiner Weiss and Herr Hedrich were among those cited."

"Perhaps this was the offense that got Rabbiner Weiss deported?" Brandt posited. "We know he died in transit, but what about Hedrich? Was he deported too?"

"We haven't been able to confirm that yet."

"Come on, Anton! Major Goertz was living in this guy's house! Of course, he was slated for deportation! Fraulein Weiss said as much. But these guys kept meticulous records of transport schedules, so where's David Hedrich's transport order?"

The sergeant shook his head. The last kilometer of their drive ensued in silence, as they processed this new repository of information. Brandt turned onto Annen Strasse, and the spires of St Michael's appeared above the tree line. He brought the vehicle to a rest along the side of the road.

Walking towards the church their attention was drawn to a series of broken windows around the perimeter of the edifice. They entered through the narthex. The inside of the church had suffered extensive damage. In the nave, pews had been overturned, stained glass windows had been shattered, and artwork had been pulled from the walls. Brandt's eyes drifted to the barren wall where the tapestry of the boy in the well had been pulled to the ground.

A short, balding man, dressed in church robes scurried through a scattered logjam of pews. He bowed as he approached them, identifying himself only as Diakon Forster.

"We appreciate you coming, Offiziere."

"What happened here?"

"I'm afraid the church has been vandalized," he whispered. "Father Eckhardt would like to speak with you."

Vandalized? That makes it sound like the harmless antics of some neighborhood gang, and we all know that's not the case.

The deacon wordlessly guided them through the disarray

of the defiled sanctuary, in the direction of Father Eckhardt's office. He waved them towards the open door, where the haggard priest sat reclined in his chair, staring up at the ceiling.

"He's waiting for you," Forster said, receding back into the shadows of the sacristy.

Eckhardt sat up apprehensively as they neared his office. His face was pale and drawn, its features etched with concern.

"Herr Inspector, Sergeant Faber, I'm glad you're here." he said, standing to greet them.

"Who did this?" Faber inquired.

"Do you really need to ask?"

Not really. They've wreaked the same brutal havoc on this building that they inflicted on Kurt Daschle's body.

"The Gestapo?" Brandt offered as a formality, turning to Faber. "This seems to be the treatment afforded to anyone who talks to us."

"Perhaps that's the reason, but that's not why I called you…" the priest interjected.

"Then why did you?"

What could be of greater concern to a priest than the destruction of his church?

"Sergeant Faber, would you mind excusing us?" Eckhardt inquired.

"Anton, give us a minute."

Faber nodded, grudgingly. He closed the priest's office door with added emphasis to register his wordless protest.

"Thank you. There's something you need to see," the priest said, leading them out by the exterior door on the other side of his office.

They walked silently through a saturated garden path, towards the south of the property. As they diverged onto a wooded trail, Brandt recognized the route from his initial search of the church grounds, the week before. The priest somberly led the way, the only sounds emanating from a set of keys that rustled against the sash he wore around his waist.

"I wasn't sure whom to contact about this," he said. "Any course of action I take places the church in a precarious situation…"

"How much more precarious can it get?"

"The church I'm speaking of is more than a building, but I'm glad that you and your partner came alone."

He removed the key ring and moved towards the locked gate that led to the abandoned church school grounds. The broken lock and chain that Brandt had severed, had been replaced.

"Father Eckhardt, if this is about your situation with the refugee children, I really don't have the time for this right now."

The priest shook his head dismissively, without speaking a word. He proceeded across the yard towards the back of the main building, and stopped a few strides short of the same cellar where Brandt had uncovered the children.

"Please, Inspector!"

Brandt wasn't sure how to react. He could see the priest's hands shaking. He moved slowly towards the cellar, and bent down to lift open the wooden doors. They seemed heavier, and creaked louder than ever, in their waterlogged condition. He crouched into the opening, and squinted down into the darkness.

"What the…?"

A body was lying prostrate on the wet dirt floor of the cellar, contorted into a cramped position. Brandt moved down the short set of steps, to get a closer look at the lifeless figure. A thick rope, tied into a noose, still hung from the neck of the battered corpse. He pulled the victim's twisted body towards him, trying to get a better look at his face.

Jacob Hirsch!

The cellar floor seemed to spin around him.

Hirsch? A suicide? Or made to look like it? But how? Who could have...?

He reined in his reeling thoughts. His initial wave of shock quickly gave way to dismay.

"Was in der Holle happened here?" he cursed, glaring up at the priest.

Eckhardt stood motionless, silently shaking his head from side to side.

"Did you find him in this condition?"

"Yes."

"When?"

"Shortly before 4:00," Eckhardt stammered. "Deacon Forster and I had arrived at the church for afternoon prayers, when we came across his body hanging from the arch of the south gate."

"He had been left out here in broad daylight?"

"Apparently. We don't have much staff left, and it's a remote part of the property."

"And the deacon helped you move the body to the cellar?"

"That's right."

"How long before you called me?"

"We took the body down, and moved him here. We were appalled to store the body in a place we've used as a shelter for so many...

"How long?"

"Not more than half an hour."

"And you've contacted no one else? No one else knows?"

"No, just myself and Deacon Forster."

Brandt's mind raced through scenarios, even as he questioned the shaken priest. He was livid at Eckhardt for too many reasons to number. *But I can't focus on that now. Hirsch? I have to figure out how this happened, and what to do about it. I can't do that alone.*

"I want you to go back to the sanctuary and send Sergeant Faber to me. Stay in your office, and speak to no one about this."

"Herr Lieutenant, I had hoped that you would keep this…"

"From my partner? Keep another one of your secrets from my colleagues?" Brandt fumed. "Just get him for me now! And make sure that the deacon doesn't leave the premises until we've talked to him too."

Chapter 32

Brandt didn't wait for the priest to leave before ambling down the remaining stairs. The cellar was filled with a damp, putrid smell. He placed his arms under the deceased's armpits, and carefully dragged the body up the steps to better examine it in the waning light of day. Rigor mortis had set in, making it a difficult endeavor to move so much stiff, deadweight up to the ground level. He had crouched to loosen the noose, and examine the victim's neck, when he heard the sergeant approaching. He moved to the side, allowing his partner a clear view.

"Seems that the prodigal has turned up in a rather unexpected manner."

"Hirsch?" Faber said, his shock quickly turning to skepticism. "A suicide?"

"I don't think so, either. For someone suicidal, he sure seemed intent on self-preservation when we had him cornered a few nights ago."

Brandt further untied the noose from Hirsch's neck. He lifted his head to remove the rope altogether, and then lowered it back to the damp earth. He adjusted the top buttons on the victim's shirt collar, further exposing the trauma to his neck. Faber crouched next to him to get a better look.

"Besides, do these look like markings, consistent with a voluntary hanging to you?"

Faber shook his head, "Not unless he strangled himself with barbed wire first."

Brandt resumed his examination of the corpse. There were fresh abrasions on the deceased's face and torso, and the types of scratches on the hands and arms that indicated a struggle. Brandt could see where Hirsch's fingernails had likely clawed away at his assailant's skin. He patted down the victim's clothing and searched through the pockets. *Empty? He had nothing on his person? A guy with a stash that would make King Midas blush?* He felt a small protrusion from a side pocket below the victim's waistband. He reached his thumb and finger inside, and drew out two plastic, oval capsules. He separated them, and smelled the powder inside.

Bitter. Cyanide.

"A cyanide capsule," Faber observed, looking over his shoulder.

"Quick and painless."

"A lot of fugitive Jews carry them. They find it more palatable than being sent to the camps. And, in case there was any doubt, you don't put yourself through the torment of a hanging, when you have those at your disposal."

Brandt nodded in agreement, as he continued to check for any further signs of coercion or trauma. A marking visible below the cuff line of the deceased's left sleeve caught his eye. He unbuttoned the cuff, and pushed the sleeve further up the victim's forearm. There, starting on the tendons of his left wrist, the victim had a tattoo, of a skull encircled by a set of garlands. *I've seen this before.* Further up his forearm, Hirsch had been marked with a six-digit numerical code, the kind used to catalogue prisoners who had spent time in the concentration camp system. *Rebecca was right, Hirsch had done time in the camps. Around the same time as his initial disappearance?*

238

"Have you seen these markings before?" Brandt asked, drawing Faber's attention to the victim's wrist and forearm.

"I'll be damned! That's the 'death's head and laurel wreaths.' Everyone in these parts knows that insignia," the sergeant responded, ominously. "That's Reinhard Becht's crest! This guy belongs to Brigadefuhrer Becht... or did."

Brandt hadn't thought about Brigadefuhrer Becht again since the night of the promotion gala. *But that's not where I've seen this symbol, is it?* He racked his brain.

"What do you mean 'belonged to him?'"

"I mean he's sealed. Bought and paid for. Whatever he does, he operates under the protection of Brigadefuhrer Becht."

Bought and paid for?

"Seems like his protection only stretched so far. How would he work for Becht? As ein Informant?"

"Suppose he'd been arrested for some offense and sent to one of Becht's camps. If he proves useful, maybe Becht commutes his sentence, and has him released in exchange for his services as a snitch."

Just like Rebecca's father suspected. A colleague gets apprehended and sent to a camp, and switches his allegiances to gain his freedom. Then he gets reintroduced into the community as an informant, and begins to rat out those he had previously been working with. Had Hirsch been the one who blew the whistle on her father? On David Hedrich?

"So why the tattoo? He's already got a prison number on his arm."

"Maybe Brigadefuhrer Becht had him branded as a reminder of his indebtedness, and as a warning to any Gestapo patrols that pick him up to steer clear, because he's covered."

"Someone didn't get that memo," Brandt rejoined. "But

that could explain why all of Hirsch's files had been pulled. Someone as high up the ladder as Brigadefuhrer Becht could make Hirsch, and any criminal record he may have had, disappear."

"Right. But in that case, why not go to Brigadefuhrer Becht for protection?" Faber replied.

"What?"

"If you're Jacob Hirsch, and you're covered from on high by one of the most powerful men in the Reich, why not go to your protector, when your life is in peril, rather than going Untergrund?"

"I don't know, maybe that bridge had been burned?"

"Or maybe it was burned for him?"

They pondered the problematic issue. Like so many previous developments in their investigation, Hirsch's death had created more questions than answers. However, now the clock was ticking. Darkness loomed on the horizon, spreading across more and more of the vacant church grounds. Brandt stood up, slowly removing his gloves.

"I'm going inside to see what light his former 'employer' can shed on the matter. Can you arrange the transport of the body to the medical examiner's office?

"Of course."

"And let's use one of der Kriminalpolizei coroners for this one, and have the body tagged as an unidentified for now. I don't want the Gestapo, or anyone else, knowing that we have Hirsch yet, not even Colonel Brunner."

"Herr Nomen Nescio, hmm?"

"Exactly. A man without a name."

Chapter 33

Brandt retraced his steps along the path leading back to the church in the dark. He attempted to catalogue the host of unanswered questions that were vying for his attention. *Who had done this to Jacob Hirsch? Who would have had the motive? The ability? The access? Who even knew that he was here? Had Hirsch still been living in the sexton's quarters without them knowing all along? Or was this his fail-safe after we had flushed him out at Ras Haus? Eckhardt!* He needed to examine the sexton's quarters again, and search the rest of the church grounds, in order to gather more information about the struggle that led to Hirsch's death. *But first, the priest!*

He re-entered the church, finding himself back in the long interior corridor that led past Eckhardt's office. The office was empty. He proceeded down the corridor in the direction of the nave. It was easy to get turned around without a guide. At the end of the hall, he found a columned archway leading back into the main sanctuary. He could hear the sound of voices nearby. Peering around the row of columns, he saw Father Eckhardt and the deacon engaged in a heated conversation, as they cleaned up broken glass and debris from the floor. They spoke in hushed tones, but beneath the surface of their whispers, the vehemence of their disagreement was evident.

Brandt crossed the sanctuary in their direction, stepping over an overturned lectern that had shattered against a row of pews. At the sight of his approach, their clandestine conversation abruptly came to an end. The deacon bowed his head deferentially, and silently took his leave. *Always scurrying away. I'll deal with him later.* He turned his sights on the priest, wasting no time launching into his line of inquiry.

"You two trying to get your stories straight?"

"What?"

"How long had you been harboring Jacob Hirsch on church property?"

"We've done nothing of the sort."

"And yet, here he is!"

"I'm as surprised as you are. Prior to the shock of finding his body this morning, I hadn't seen Jacob Hirsch since his abrupt disappearance months ago."

"So you expect me to believe that a week after we conducted an extensive search of these grounds, a search where you withheld the presence of other Jewish refugees, Jacob Hirsch just happened to turn up dead on the premises?"

"Lieutenant," the priest held up his hand, on the defensive. "I realize how it appears."

"Do you? Because 'how it appears' is that you've knowingly been harboring a suspected murderer!"

"I've already told you, everyone in this parish viewed Jacob Hirsch's presence with suspicion. He was no more trusted during his time here, than he was missed during his absence.

"So you say."

"I have remorse that you feel misled, just as I have remorse that something drove him to the point of taking his own life."

"Remorse!" Brandt shouted, feeling his face flush. "You

knew this man was the subject of a massive criminal manhunt, and a suspect in several brutal murders. Two nights ago, he shot and killed one of my best, young officers. And you feel remorse? What is that even supposed to mean?"

"Please Lieutenant."

"My only 'remorse' is trusting you."

"I had no idea. I'm sorry."

"I don't want your sympathy! All I wanted was an honest account of his whereabouts. I thought that turning a blind eye to your operation with the refugee children was harmless, that it was the right thing to do. Or at the very least, that it would be met with some cooperation."

"It was appreciated, and I've tried to cooperate."

Brandt shook his head, "Perhaps if I hadn't let that infraction slide, I wouldn't have had to explain to my partner's wife why her husband won't be coming home from what should have been a routine arrest!"

"I am sorry about the loss of your comrade, but I didn't mislead you about Hirsch."

"Then what is he doing here? "

"Take a look around you, Lieutenant," Eckhardt pleaded, raising his voice for the first time. He waved an open palm towards the wrecked sanctuary. "The Gestapo is looking for a reason, any reason, to shut our doors, and silence our dissent, permanently."

"What's that have to do with your lack of cooperation with Jacob Hirsch?"

"Everything. You've seen firsthand what we're trying to do with the displaced and orphaned children here. It's a task we're literally willing to risk our lives for, no matter how petty you may find it. Do you really think I'd jeopardize that by harboring a known criminal and fugitive?"

Brandt felt his anger begin to recede as he considered the priest's rationale. He took a deep breath, allowing the tension to de-escalate, and his mind to shift out of attack mode. He studied the priest's tired, haggard face. *He always seems genuine, but where does that leave us? How can I account for the fact that Hirsch was here, and that someone with a motive to kill him, knew he was here?* He felt exhausted by the endless cycle of seemingly impenetrable questions. He took a seat on the steps to the altar, drained by the wild range of emotions of the past 48-hours. The priest took advantage of the lull to drive his point home.

"I have a lot of innocent people relying upon my ability to weather this storm. We're all going to have to answer for the grievous way we've neglected the persecuted in their hour of need, but the first step towards making atonement must be the protection of the innocent. And I'd never compromise our mission here, for the sake of a man like Jacob Hirsch. You've always had my full cooperation, whether you know it or not."

Father Eckhardt walked past him back towards his office. Brandt let him go without looking up. He heard the rustling sound of the priest's robes come to a sudden stop, and move a few paces back in his direction.

"You know, Lieutenant Brandt, that used to be the calling of your profession as well, 'the protection of the innocent.' You shouldn't forsake that duty, as it's the only thing separating you from your barbarous counterparts in the Gestapo," he concluded, this time decisively turning to take his leave.

Father Eckhardt's voice had been soft, almost melodious, as it wafted across the barren stone sanctuary, but the priest's words had struck a chord deep within him. Brandt closed his eyes, and saw wave after wave of buried images. Images he rarely saw in a waking state. He felt himself shudder, but his body was still. Something churned deep inside of him, something that felt as though it would burst like water through an overflowing dam. It welled up behind his eyes, and in his throat. Then he heard another distant, detached voice reverberating off of the stone walls, and quickly recognized it as his own.

"There was this 10-year-old boy, Erich Nagle. One night he doesn't come home from *Schule* with the rest of the Kinder in his class. Two days later, his body was found in a basement, hanging from the pipes in the Schule boiler room. He had been violated, abused, and when he no longer had the strength to amuse his captor, he had been strung up and left for dead."

He heard the priest moving back towards him, his slow footsteps scuffing against the cobblestone floor, but Brandt didn't look up. He stared straight ahead, at some imaginary focal point in the distance. He could see the child's lifeless body before him, even with his eyes open.

"When did this happen?"

"It was my first homicide case. I had been assigned to the Munich Gestapo, fresh out of the Akademie. On a tip, I found out that the Schule superintendent was a stern disciplinarian with a predilection for young boys. Maybe just disciplining them wasn't enough to do it for him anymore. So, one afternoon while he's conducting class, I go and toss the guy's place. I mean, I really turned it over good," Brandt recalled, shaking his head. "In a vent above the laundry room, I found the boy's bloodstained underwear, and Schule uniform, in a plastic bag along with some pornographisch materials. The superintendent wasn't really trying to hide them. He hadn't discarded them. He was keeping them as part of his collection, as a reminder of his conquest."

"Mein Gott," Father Eckhardt whispered.

Brandt looked up at the priest, as if seeing him for the first time. His face was attentive and earnest. There was a sorrow behind his eyes.

"I went to Mein Kapitan with what I'd found, knowing that the depravity of the crime more than justified the way I'd acquired the evidence. Plus, the Gestapo wasn't big on evidentiary procedure. So, I briefed my partner, and waited for the word to go takedown this predatory scumbag. Problem was, this wasn't just any scumbag, he was a somebody in the local Nazi ranks."

"I see," Father Eckhardt nodded, understandingly.

"In his spare time, he was an organizer and local party boss. That night I get a call from Mein Kapitan saying that the Schule half-witted janitor, Albert Lohman, had been arrested for the rape and murder of Erich Nagle. He had 'confessed' during his interrogation. Never mind he had the mental faculties of an infant, and the physical strength to match. He was mentally infirm, and a Jew, that being grounds enough for a conviction right there. And after all, the superintendent was a 'good party man'."

"What did you do?" the priest asked, taking a seat next to him on the altar steps.

"Everyone in our precinct knew it was a frame-up. Even the kind of guys who have no moral reservations about beating confessions out of a helpless retard don't like to see a murdering pedophile walk. Just the same, the superintendent was transferred to another Schule district with little more than a slap on the wrist, and Albert Lohman? As a token of Gestapo justice, and as an example to the rest of the Jewish community, he was hanged, without trial, from the steel bars on the Schule playground."

Brandt lowered his head and closed his eyes. The recurring image that had haunted his dreams for longer than he could remember played out before his mind's eye. For the first time, the haze had subsided, and he could see it clearly. Albert Lohman hung from a steel crossbar in the vacant schoolyard. Two black uniformed Gestapo men stood watch at the janitor's feet, shielding themselves from the rain that fell from the grey, overcast skies. Brandt pressed his face against the glass of the second story window, helplessly looking on at the execution he couldn't prevent. *It hadn't been foggy that day at all.*

"I'm so sorry, Lieutenant Brandt," Father Eckhardt offered.

"And I went along," Brandt continued, shaking his head slowly from side-to-side. "I told myself that it was an isolated miscarriage, that the good I could do in other cases outweighed the bad, and I went along. But the thing is, each time you bury an injustice below the ground of serving a greater good, your skin grows a little bit thicker, a little bit harder, a little less sensitive, until you can't even feel the difference between right and wrong anymore."

Brandt lowered his head again, and rubbed his brow with his hands. The bursting sensation behind his eyes had subsided, and had been replaced with fatigue. A moment passed in silence, a moment in which Brandt could feel the vastness of the dark, empty nave. The vastness of a dark, empty world. He felt the priest lean closer to him, gently placing a hand on his shoulder.

"That's the good thing about skin, Lieutenant, it's meant

to be shed, and regenerated. It's when what's inside of you starts to harden, that you need to worry."

He could feel the priest hover over him briefly, whispering something inaudibly, before taking his leave. A moment later he heard Father Eckhardt's receding footsteps, followed by the office door quietly closing behind him. Brandt remained seated on the altar steps. He felt a sense of relief, as if a weight had been lifted. That seemed ironic, given the muddled state of the investigation, *but it goes deeper than that. And what about Eckhardt? What weighs on him the most?* He stood up and walked back towards the priest's office, gently tapping on the door before opening it. Eckhardt looked up inquisitively from behind his desk.

"One more thing, Father. Those children you had hidden in the storm cellar... what's their story?" he asked, immediately sensing the priest's reluctance. "This is confidential, just between you and myself."

"As a result of the war, and the Reich's policies, many children have been separated from their homes and families. Most are children whose parents have either been deported, conscripted into forced labor, or killed."

"Are most of the ones you take in Jews?"

"Most of them. With the *SS* closing Jewish social services and orphanages in the city, the situation has turned into a humanitarian crisis. If we can't help these children, then nothing awaits them except misery and suffering, and ultimately, death in some ghetto or camp. And unlike some of my brethren, I can't abide that they merit such a fate, simply because they were born Jewish."

"But how do you do it? You've said yourself that you're under constant surveillance," Brandt inquired. "How do you manage to move so many children through here undetected?"

248

"There's too much at stake to disclose the details, but they don't all come through this property. We have a network of contacts in numerous fields, who are sympathetic to our cause, and who facilitate getting them across the border."

"A network of contacts? How about the name David Hedrich? Does that name mean anything to you?"

"I don't recognize it."

"Please, don't hold out on me," Brandt replied. "Could David Hedrich be a benefactor behind one of these networks?"

"I'm not familiar with him, but it's possible, as the dangers of the process demand anonymity for many who are involved."

Brandt reached across the priest's desk to a loose stack of blank paper. He hurriedly scrawled information in small, discrete lettering on the top right-hand corner of the sheet. He tore the page at the boundary of the writing, and folded it, before placing it in Eckhardt's hand. It was his turn to lean closer to the priest, confidingly.

"There's a young Jewish woman at this address. Her name is Rebecca Weiss. Her father gave his life for the same principles you profess. If you send for her using my name, she can be ready at a moment's notice," he said, staring at the priest imploringly. "I want your word that you'll get her across the border."

"That's a great deal to ask, Lieutenant."

"Her family has all either been killed or sent to the camps, and the only thing keeping her alive was her usefulness in tracking Jacob Hirsch. Once word of his death gets out," Brandt paused. "I want your word that you'll get her out. This squares us, wipes the slate clean."

He could feel Father Eckhardt's scrutinizing gaze searching the very depths of him. Finally, the priest nodded solemnly, and placed the folded paper in the pocket of his robe.

Chapter 34

What was that old adage about never returning to the scene of the crime? Did it apply to detectives as well as criminals? I hope not. Brandt had spent the early evening driving in circles around the neighborhoods of Friedrichshain, but his car always found its way back to the home on Kurische Strasse. He had been having an internal debate over the pros and cons, always knowing which would win out. Once the decision had been made it had been easy to gain access to the sealed off residence. The steel latticework had made for a slippery climb, but the balcony doors had been easy to pry with his utility knife. It had actually been his father's knife, one of the many ways he was still with him.

He had made sure to leave no sign of entry, or of unnecessary site disturbance, as Colonel Schonbern had made it excessively clear that the property was off-limits. *And why was that? Why had the colonel been so adamant about keeping us away from the vacant home of a deceased major who was central to our investigation anyway? Had Schonbern pushed us time and again in the direction of Jacob Hirsch, all while acting as if he was being pulled along?* Regardless, he knew that if he ran afoul of the colonel's orders one more time, he'd likely be off the case for good. *Or worse.*

Major Goertz's den had been just as they'd left it. He'd spent nearly an hour scouring the main row of filing cabinets, sifting through the contents of 'klassifiziert' Gestapo files, before he needed to take a break. He had wandered the halls to clear his mind of the mountain of transport schedules and labor assignments. One thing was certain from the files, the Reich's deportation apparatus was much more vast, than he had ever imagined. Anyone of Jewish descent destined for the territories in the east had little hope for survival.

During his break, he had taken care to steer clear of the gruesome master bedroom, but had wandered through the other upstairs rooms for the first time. They had been bedrooms and playrooms dedicated to the previous occupant's young children, filled with trains and stuffed animals and story books and toys. Framed pictures of a happy family; *David Hedrich's family*, still adorned the dressers and bookcase shelves. *This may have been Major Goertz's last known residence, but it had never been his home. Where was this family now? On the transport trains I just spent the last hours reading about? If they'd been lucky enough to survive the transit, it only got worse.*

He had finally returned to the den, less concerned about preserving the scene, and intent on finding the link he had been looking for. Behind the main row of files, there had been stacks of moving boxes, cluttered on and around a solitary wooden filing cabinet. He had run his fingers over the file's imprint, immediately recognizing the symbol engraved on the cabinet's wooden drawers. *A death's head encircled by a laurel wreath! That's where I had seen Hirsch's tattoo before, not here, but in the crime scene photographs of the filing cabinets that had been removed from Captain Keppler's office! Just like everything else, Keppler and Goertz had a matching set! Only someone forgot to remove Major Goertz's cache.*

He had again used his knife to pry the locked drawers open, pulling the tightly cramped files out in bunches, and tossing them aside in frustration when they were more of the same. That's when he had seen the telltale seal engraved into the bottom shelf of the cabinet's empty lowest drawer. He had tapped the handle of his knife against the wood, producing a hollow sound. *A false bottom!* He had used the blade to lift the thin wooden cover, revealing a shallow cavity below. The lone inhabitant of the concealed space had been a sculpted marble box. When he had lifted the lid, he immediately knew that he had hit pay dirt.

Chapter 35

A rapid procession of knocks disrupted the silence that had descended over the room. It was not the first time this evening that his prayers had been grounded before they even took flight.

"Excuse my intrusion upon your meditations Father."

"It's no intrusion. What's troubling you, Brother Heath?"

"This arrived moments ago from the order."

The clergyman's hands shook as he retrieved the folded paper from the pockets of his robe, and handed the sealed missive to the priest. Father Eckhardt broke the seal, and read the simple handwritten inscription: 'The shipment arrived safely.'

"Danke, Father," he whispered. "Don't despair Brother, the Lord still protects those who seek refuge in Him."

"I'm afraid that's not all Father. There are a number of men here to see you from the Gestapo," he stammered. "I managed to keep them in the narthex by telling them you were in confession. But you should dispose of that."

"You can tell them I'll be with them presently. And Brother Heath, don't forget to ring the bell for evening vigils. We'll praise Him even in the midst of our darkest hours."

Father Eckhardt folded the paper, holding it over the open flame of a candle, before dropping its smoldering remains in the repository below. He took a deep breath, and walked to the outside corridor in the direction of the narthex. He saw a group of uniformed Gestapo agents huddled by the walkways at the northwest corner of the church, and was surprised to see Colonel Schonbern among them.

"Herr Standartenfuhrer, I wasn't expecting a call from you at this hour."

"That's where we differ, Eckhardt," Schonbern replied, extricating himself from his agents and advancing towards the priest. "I was expecting a call from you. A call you instead decided to make to Inspector Brandt."

"What?"

"A call regarding the death of a man you knew was being sought by the Gestapo!"

"Hirsch? I assumed Inspector Brandt was the appropriate party to contact in this matter. Your own men had indicated deference to him."

"Drop the pretense, priest! We're aware of the operation you've been conducting within the church."

Father Eckhardt's heart sunk. From his peripheral, he noticed Deacon Forster nervously pacing back-and-forth behind the small detachment of Gestapo agents. Their eyes met, and the deacon slowly shuffled towards him. The priest fought against the growing pit in his stomach. The betrayal felt like a knife plunged into his chest. Denial would be futile. Forster knew everything about their operations.

"Brother Forster? What's going on here?"

But he already knew.

"Forgive me Father, but I couldn't let this continue," he said, drawing close in a whisper. "I couldn't let you jeopardize the church any further. We can't sacrifice our sacred calling for the sake of outcasts and Jews!

"Brother," Eckhardt exclaimed sadly. "Comforting the helpless is our sacred calling."

The deacon looked perplexed. At a nod from the colonel, a Gestapo agent interceded to escort him away. He stared over his shoulder at Father Eckhardt as he was removed through the throng of agents towards a parked staff car.

"We're fortunate to have men like Deacon Forster. Men who exhibit loyalty to the church, as well as to the Reich, are we not Major Weskamp?"

"We have a true believer among us," Weskamp smirked.

"Let's forego the charade, Father Eckhardt. We've tolerated your vocal dissent towards Reich policy, but assisting in the escape of Jewish criminals?"

"Criminals? They're children."

"They're Jews! We've granted you so many chances, and now we find you harboring a man wanted by law enforcement, and conspiring with Inspector Brandt?"

"Conspiring? You placed Inspector Brandt here, just like you most likely planted Jacob Hirsch!"

"Be careful, Father!"

"If one of your men has gone rogue on you, Colonel, that is none of my affair. As for my cooperation, I've tried that, and what has it brought our church except persecution and destruction at the hands of the vandals you call Polizei?"

"I've warned you, priest," Schonbern growled, moving closer menacingly. "To use your own language, your church is resting on a foundation of sand at the moment. So, it's in your best interest to disclose everything you know right now. Anything less, and believe me when I say that your church hasn't begun to experience persecution. Do you understand my meaning?"

"Your attempts to threaten me are in vain," Father Eckhardt replied. "I live by Christ's command, 'Do not be afraid of those who kill the body, but cannot kill the soul. Rather, be afraid of the One of who can destroy both body and soul in Hell'."

"I can do both, I assure you! Hordes of Jews facing unbearable labors, famine, and the fires of incineration in the East, can attest to that!" he paused abruptly, as the bells of St Michael's began to toll for evening prayers.

Schonbern fell silent. He was visibly perplexed, as he looked around, first at his men, and then at the priest. It wasn't often one witnessed the colonel incriminate, much less censure, himself. Father Eckhardt smiled inwardly, and thought to himself: *The truth always comes out. Gott protect those who find themselves in the path of the destruction this man has set in motion, and grant me the strength to stand against whatever evils he intends to unleash.*

"Nevertheless," Schonbern continued, somewhat rattled. "I need to know any information that you have about the death of Jacob Hirsch, and the complete contents of your discussions with Inspector Brandt. And I would suggest we discuss this in a more suitable place, perhaps the privacy of your chambers?"

Chapter 36

Brandt found a booth tucked away in the corner of the dark tavern. He sat facing the door. The pub was mostly empty, aside from a few on-leave soldiers at the bar, vying for the attention of the blonde barmaid. At the other corner of the room, a smartly dressed man in a suit and tie sat alone, an open section of newspaper lay next to his untouched beer. He looked out of place.

Brandt felt the binding of his newly obtained evidence grating against the skin of his stomach, and shifted in his seat. He looked at his watch. *Where is he?* Just then he saw the silhouette of, Faber through the street front window. The sergeant quickly scanned the room, and made his way over to the table.

"Lieutenant, what's going on?"

"Have a seat. I needed to talk to you away from the precinct."

"Why? What's happened?"

"I've come across some information that casts an entirely different light on the murders we're investigating, and I'm not sure what to do with it."

"Let's hear it."

"First, I want to let you know that this reaches high. Just knowing about it is going to change everything, and you may not want to wade any deeper into this."

"That's a hell of a thing to say to me after everything we've been through! I'm already in this as deep as it gets!"

"No, you haven't reached the bottom," Brandt cautioned. "You may think you have, but once I share this with you, there's no going back."

"I think you know my answer," Faber countered without wavering. "I've never held out on you. I've broken rank with orders from Colonel Brunner and the Gestapo, and I've buried my partner. I intend to see this through, no matter where it leads."

"You're right, I'm sorry. I just wanted to give you the option."

"Now you know where I stand."

"Very well. Remember when you asked me at St Michael's, 'Why wouldn't Jacob Hirsch go to Brigadefuhrer Becht for protection if he was in trouble?'"

"Yes."

"Well, what if Becht, or someone associated with him, was the one trying to have you killed?"

"What? Why in the world would Brigadefuhrer Becht want to do that?"

"Just listen. I've gained access to some classified documents."

"Gained access?

"Don't start with me," Brandt continued, undeterred. He reached below his shirt to retrieve a ledger from his waistband, and placed it between them on the table. "This was stashed beneath a row of transfer files in one of the filing cabinets in Major Goertz's den. The ledger's contents were maintained by Goertz, himself."

"You've been back to the Goertz estate?"

"That's right."

"How could you have…"

"And while we're at it, it's not the Goertz estate. It was the home of David Hedrich, before Major Goertz had him and his family displaced and most likely killed. So, if we're going to be honest, let's call it what it is."

"Alright, alright, I don't know what's gotten into you," Faber assented. "I'm the one who sat in the driveway of that estate, and told you what Major Goertz and his cohorts were capable of, and you wanted no part of it. Remember?"

"You were right. I should have listened to you."

"That's water under the bridge, but what about the ledger?"

"I'm not sure how to interpret all of the entries yet, but in essence, it records the flow of confiscated property, assets, and currency to a number of Reich officials."

"Was it authorized?"

"Definitely not!" Brandt confirmed. This much is clear: Captain Keppler, Major Goertz and Jacob Hirsch were all involved in a large-scale extortion ring. And it appears that they were all working for Brigadefuhrer Becht."

"How is that possible? They all worked in different agencies."

"Different agencies, but all with one common area of oversight."

"The relocation of Berlin Jews," Faber concluded.

"Correct! And they used their different agencies to access the Department of Jewish Affairs in an effort to target affluent Jews, expropriating their victims' funds and property as they assigned them to the transports. Then the ring would divide the spoils amongst themselves, or move the funds to predetermined locations throughout the country."

"Predetermined locations?"

"The bulk of the confiscated assets were converted to marks or gold, and then disseminated through a web of smuggling channels to different provinces throughout the Reich. Each of the provinces consisted of a designated safe house for storage, but I haven't figured out all the nuances of that part of the operation yet."

"Incredible! How did a small fish like Jacob Hirsch fit into the equation?"

"Just like you thought, as an informant," Brandt replied. "His familiarity with the Berlin Jewish community helped keep them one step ahead of other Nazi agencies, while he kept them informed about the plans of those Jews who were trying to illegally flee."

"What about those other agencies? The *SS* and RSHA couldn't have known about this, and couldn't be happy about it if they did."

"Exactly. The extortion ring made sure there was still an ample harvest left to be reaped by the other agencies, but not before they took their prime cut."

"This is all detailed in the ledger?"

"It shows everything," Brandt responded, looking around the tavern, before discretely pushing the book closer to Faber. "Deeds of trust, parcel plot numbers, stock holdings, even maps of the asset smuggling routes, not to mention a running handwritten tally of the proceeds allocated to each member of the ring, from Captain Keppler all the way to the top."

"Mein Gott! They thought of everything."

"And it's all in Major Goertz's handwriting. He apparently doubled as the bookkeeper for the ring. And do you know where I found it?"

"Do I want to know?"

Brandt granted Faber the hint of a smile.

"It was hidden in a file cabinet engraved with the mark of the skull and laurel wreath, at his estate, below a drawer with a false bottom. A drawer filled with money, property titles, black-market items, you name it. Including the deed to his own home."

"What do you mean?"

"I mean, regardless of what the Interior Ministry says, that house was still titled to David Hedrich. A man that Major Goertz apparently worked side-by-side with on the evacuation committees, and then had deported for his home and possessions."

"Right in plain daylight!" Faber marveled. "Was that the case with all of the Jews they shook down?"

"Everyone, dispossessed and deported, shortly afterwards. Some of the more well-heeled targets even offered bribes in an attempt to avoid, or at least delay, the transports."

"Can't imagine that tactic was too effective?"

"Not often. The ledger shows a few stays of deportation in exchange for payments promised, but in each case, once the bribes were accepted, the targets were deported anyway, and their possessions were confiscated."

"So the bribes only purchased a temporary reprieve."

"That's how it worked," Brandt affirmed. "The ring would use the promise of 'protection' to get the victims to disclose the location of hidden funds or assets, and once they received the goods, they'd remove the shield."

"Brigadefuhrer Becht's crest, the same one we found branded on Hirsch's arm, is all over these pages," Faber indicated with a tap of his index finger. "Is he ever mentioned by name?"

"Not that I saw. In the ledger entries, he's identified by his crest insignia every time. And there looks to be another member high up the food chain, who is only identified by a crest too," Brandt replied, turning back several pages. "A death's head encircled by a snake eating its own tail. Look familiar?"

"I don't recognize it."

"Well, whoever 'the snake' is, he's on nearly the same rung of the ladder as Brigadefuhrer Becht. That crest appears near the top of almost every major column, receiving a big share of the cut."

"Perhaps another one of his camp commandants?"

"Perhaps. So, what do you make of it?"

"I don't know what to say," Faber marveled. "I knew that the confiscation of Jewish possessions was commonplace, dating back to at least Kristallnacht. But I couldn't fathom it was happening on this scale, and to this level of organization."

"Yes," Brandt agreed. "The scope is hard to comprehend. Thousands upon thousands of Berlin residents displaced, and millions in assets and currency confiscated."

"But why would Brigadefuhrer Becht try to wipe out the cogs of such a lucrative scam?"

"That's the question. I'm not even sure that's what's going on, but the membership of the ring is quickly dwindling, and that's not by coincidence."

"Generals typically don't like to get their hands dirty like this."

"True, but generals also don't like to get caught with their hands in the till," Brandt countered. "With his recent promotion, Brigadefuhrer Becht's star is on the rise with the Reich brass. Getting caught in a scandal of this magnitude, much less skimming from the higher-ups who promoted him, could derail everything."

"And this isn't just the fleecing of some wealthy Jews. They're shortchanging some pretty powerful agencies in the process."

"You think men like Obergruppenfuhrer Heydrich or Reichsfuhrer Himmler would turn a blind eye to the millions of reichsmarks in currency and land, intended for their coffers, being smuggled out of Berlin by their own subordinates?"

"Hardly. They'd have your head removed from your shoulders, courtesy of the Plotzensee guillotine, just for looking at them wrong."

"Right, so maybe Brigadefuhrer Becht is eliminating anyone he thinks can tie him to this ring?"

"It's hard to imagine."

"He certainly has the motive and the capability," Brandt posited. "Maybe he called in his debt from Jacob Hirsch, ordering him to dispatch of Captain Keppler and Major Goertz, and then had Hirsch blotted out to tie up the loose ends?"

"It's possible."

"Not many people are going to raise an eyebrow over the killing of a disgraced Gestapo Captain, or a Jewish snitch with a record."

"But what about Major Goertz? A Cabinet Minister?"

"That's right, he's hardly low profile. Offing someone as visible as Goertz would be a riskier proposition, not to mention the way he was murdered."

"So, what's your other take?"

"The possibility that Brigadefuhrer Becht isn't alone at the top of the ring, and that his involvement doesn't include anything other than the extortion activities listed."

"And?"

"Well, if that's the case, the suspect list increases," Brandt acknowledged. "I've run through countless scenarios in my head."

"Such as?"

"Perhaps the victims are being wiped out by members of another agency they've wronged or encroached upon? Perhaps someone else has uncovered their transgressions ahead of us, and is already exacting punishment? And that doesn't even take into account anyone this ring has fleeced, who had the means to seek revenge."

"So where does that leave us?" Faber sighed.

"The one thing we know for certain is that Brigadefuhrer Becht is the only known member of the ring who hasn't been killed. So, perhaps rather than predator, Becht is the prey."

"You mean he could be next?"

Chapter 37

The rental flat at Granseer Strasse felt no more like home, than it did the first time he had laid eyes on it several weeks prior. Then again, he hadn't had much time to acclimate to his new home. He stared at his reflection in the dresser mirror. It had been a long stretch since he'd had a moment to survey his condition. The darkness below his eyes had spread, as had the growth of stubble along his neck and jaw line. He almost felt as though he was looking at a stranger. Had he become so absorbed in his surroundings that he was losing touch with who he was. A large bruise had appeared above his right shoulder, where he had dislodged the door at Jacob Hirsch's apartment complex. He unbuttoned his shirt and tossed it on the floor.

Who had known where to find Jacob Hirsch after he fled the tenements? And more importantly, why couldn't we have found him a couple of days earlier? Before Emil...

He noticed a soft glow coming from the window, and crossed towards it in the dark. A black sedan idled across the street. *Is Schonbern having me followed?* A mixture of rain and ice had started to fall, illuminated by the low watt street lamps below. He lowered the blackout curtain, and returned to the dresser.

Brandt picked up a clean, white shirt. This was his first fresh shirt in days. He had forgotten what a luxury clean laundry was. He put the shirt on, slowly buttoning it from top to bottom, before tucking the hem into his pants, and fastening the button. He threaded his gun belt through his belt loops, and attached his leather holster at the protrusion of his left hipbone. He picked up his Walther PPK from the dresser, and stared at the compact black barrel. He loaded the six-round magazine, and holstered the weapon. *Will this be enough?*

He opened the top right drawer of the dresser. Moving a surface layer of clothes to the side of the drawer, he withdrew a Mauser M1914. The pistol's nickel finish gleamed in the soft lamplight. This had been his father's firearm, *but tonight it will be my backup weapon.* He pushed the slide lock back, and loaded its eight-round magazine, before placing the pistol in the rear holster attached to the back of his waistband. He put on his jacket, and slid the ledger inside the fold of the coat liner.

He had made his decision; the only question was whether or not to inform Faber. He stared at the phone on the bedside nightstand, uncertain whether to pick up the receiver or rip the line out of the wall. He opted to make the call. The extension rang until he was almost ready to hang up, and then he heard the sergeant's raspy voice on the other end.

"Hello? This is Faber."

Did I wake him? He doesn't sound himself.

"Anton? It's Brandt. I'm sorry to call so late, but it couldn't wait until morning."

"What's going on?"

"Listen, I want you to forget everything we discussed tonight…"

"Forget? "

"There's no reason for both of us to be involved in this

mess."

"Konrad, listen to me," Faber interrupted. "You need to take this information to Colonel Brunner or Schonbern. You're in way over your head."

Konrad? Faber had never used his first name before, nor had he ever sounded so concerned. *Not even when Emil was shot.*

"Schonbern? That's the last thing I'd do. Even if he's not aware of the extortion ring, he's not going to let someone as close to him as Brigadefuhrer Becht take the fall."

"Then what? You said it yourself, there are no alternatives."

"I know."

"What? What do you mean you know?"

"As soon as I read the ledger, I knew there was no way out. Either I sit on the information and watch as more killings and corruption go unchecked, or I put my own head on the block by implicating an untouchable like Brigadefuhrer Becht," Brandt concluded. "I've been down both of those avenues before, and I won't do it again."

"There are other ways, Lieutenant. I'll back you all the way, but you have to bring this evidence into the precinct."

"I can't bring it in. There's only one place to go."

"Lieutenant? You can't be thinking about going out there on your own? Lieutenant? Konrad!"

Faber heard the other end of the line go dead. He held the receiver out away from his face and stared at it in disbelief, until an outstretched, black-gloved hand relieved him of it.

Chapter 38

Brandt skirted the government district on Muller Strasse, before merging onto Reinickendorfer. This throughway headed north out of Berlin, and at the city limits would become *Deutsch Strecke 96* towards Oranienburg. The town of Oranienburg lay approximately 30 kilometers north of Berlin, and his travel time would be further slowed on the dark, icy roads. But the drive would give his racing thoughts a chance to do something they had so far been unable to accomplish in the city, to slowdown and process the twists and turns of the past several days. *What is it about being in motion that brings such clarity?*

From the point of view of his investigation, all roads now led to Oranienburg. Just outside the town line was Sachsenhausen, the camp that had imprisoned, and then released, Jacob Hirsch back into circulation. Hirsch had worked in the camp's brickworks, one of the largest in all of Germany. It provided materials for both construction and war projects in Berlin, and throughout the Reich. Sachsenhausen was also the site where Brigadefuhrer Becht had gotten his start. First as a camp commandant, then as an admin at the nearby camp headquarters, and finally as Chief Inspector of the entire Reich concentration camp system. More importantly now, it was where Brigadefuhrer Becht still kept his private residence, a mere stone's throw from the camp's perimeter walls. *Like Sergeant Roth would have said, Becht apparently isn't one who minds bringing his work home with him.*

Brandt was astounded at how a cataclysmic series of events could be set in motion by a single word. The Fuhrer had wanted to transform Berlin into the centerpiece of a new Europe, the capital city of the thousand-year Reich. Germania it was to be called, and its glory was to eclipse that of ancient Rome.

And so, his chief architect Albert Speer had set out to accomplish the Fuhrer's vision. Large swaths of land within the city had been reclaimed by the government. Multitudes of residents had been resettled, or in the case of the city's Jewish inhabitants, dispossessed and deported. A small army of forced labor had been conscripted to clear the way, and break the ground. And at a host of camps out in the wilderness, away from the prying eyes of the civilized world, an invisible nation of 'slaves' had started their daily trek to the rock quarries, and gravel pits and brickworks to provide the materials.

Pharaoh had commissioned the pyramids, and the slave drivers had sprung into action. But Pharaohs lived in palaces. If you wanted to find the slave drivers, you didn't go to the palaces, you went to the rock quarries. And Reinhard Becht had undoubtedly become the Reich's chief slave driver.

What if Minister Speer's implementation of the Fuhrer's vision had also inadvertently spawned this killing spree?

Brandt exited *D.S. 96*, a few kilometers south of Oranienburg and followed the road signs through a series of winding, wooded back roads towards the main camps. He downshifted as the surface changed from pavement to gravel, his tires skidding as they tried to generate traction. He finally emerged at a clearing below the high stone walls of

Sachsenhausen. In the distance he could see an inconspicuous, solitary house that sat back at the base of the hills, away from the road. *Brigadefuhrer Becht*'s *residence.*

Brandt slowly pulled his car onto the siding, 100 meters or so from the general's driveway. His tires came to a crunching halt in the accumulating sleet and snow. He cut the lights and let the engine idle, as he observed the property. A sedan, and a staff car were parked in the drive, but there were no signs of life from the house. *What would I expect at this time of night?* Brandt checked his watch. It was nearly 4AM. *Or better yet, morning. The sun won't be up for another 3 hours.*

He exited the vehicle, staying close to the cover of a wooded tree line along the perimeter. This cloaked his approach to the house, until he could reach the gravel driveway. Both vehicles were Mercedes with government-issued plates, and Inspectorate decals. A couple of inches of wet, heavy snow had accumulated on the automobiles overnight, and there were no signs of tire tracks or footprints leading to or from them.

Brandt estimated that the snow had been falling at a rate of about an inch an hour. At that pace the snowfall would have masked any tracks, even if Brigadefuhrer Becht had departed or arrived earlier in the evening. He scanned the front of the house from behind one of the Mercedes. There was a very dim glow visible from the front windows. *Possibly from a light in the front hall? Is Becht even in there? What if I've risked everything and he isn't even here? Better yet, what am I going to do if he is?*

In a sense, it didn't matter. Brandt had already decided he was going in either way. Either he would confront the General with his findings if he was home, or he would search Becht's quarters for further evidence if he wasn't. Despite the enormous risk of this gambit, he felt a sense of peace in having already determined his course of action. The die was cast. There was no turning back.

Brandt quickly covered the distance between the driveway and house. He attempted to peer through several windows into the darkened interior, but in each case the curtains were pulled, and windows were locked. Rounding the side of the house, he could see a narrow shaft of light shining out onto the snow-covered yard. It emanated from a small, ground level window. *There must be a basement, but why would a pitch-black house have a basement light on?*

Brandt drew closer, and crouched down on one knee next to the window. He thought about Emil Roth. He drew his Walther, and chambered a round, the pistol's signal pin offering him instant confirmation. The window was partially underground, and he realized he would have to lie flat in order to see into the slender framing. He felt the damp coldness through his clothing as he lowered his body against the frozen earth, and then the prick of ice and snow against his cheek as his head followed suit.

He peered through the frosted half window. His view was distorted by the condensation on the glass, and the narrowness of the pane. He strained his eyes, making out parts of an unfinished, dirt-floored basement. The only source of light seemed to be a single bulb that hung between the exposed wooden support beams on the ceiling. Something caught his eye. There were tracks and patterns on the dirt floor, as though a person had been dragging something heavy across the surface. *Or someone?* He was startled by a nearby crunch on

271

the frigid ground, and scrambled to get back to his feet. He looked up just in time to see, but not avoid, the blow from the butt of the pistol, and everything went black.

The blackness temporarily receded into a grey haze. He felt a warmth oozing from his left eye socket, an island of heat, surrounded by the other frozen regions of his face. A sharp pain blared through his skull. He became aware enough of his surroundings to realize that his arms had been bound, and that he was being dragged by his collar through the snow, and then down a flight of frozen concrete stairs. The sharp pain intensified into a throbbing mass spreading unchecked across his entire head, and he blacked out again.

Chapter 39

Brandt came to, his head resting against the cold ground. Through blurred vision, he could see the profile of a bearded man in a long, frayed greatcoat and boots washing his grime-encrusted hands at a sink in the far corner of the basement. *Or was it blood?* On the near side of the sink basin, an unsheathed dagger rested beside Brandt's confiscated Walther PPK. He squinted to better make out his assailant's features in the poorly lit corner, and winced in pain as he tried to contract his left eye. He couldn't discern the man's face with any clarity, and the mirror above the sink was too dust-covered and cracked to offer any assistance. The man was too absorbed in his scrub down to notice that Brandt was awake. He wrestled quietly against his restraints, but felt little movement.

Brandt heard a muffled sound behind him, and eased himself gently over onto his back. He was suddenly overcome by the sense that someone else was in uncomfortably close proximity to him, and quickly completed his roll to the opposite side. He shuddered as he found himself face-to-face with a man who had been bound in the same manner. *General Becht!* The general's gaze was watery and distant, and his body showed signs of multiple stab wounds around his shoulders and torso. Brandt instantly recognized the wounds as fatal. The general had entered an advanced stage of shock, and was now hovering between life and death.

"Brigadefuhrer Becht?" Brandt whispered.

Becht's empty stare remained unchanged, but his lips moved almost imperceptibly. His breathing was shallow and sporadic. At such close distance, Brandt could see his dilated pupils, and thought he could see fear in the general's eyes as they drifted upwards. *His eyes are rolling back in his head.* That's when Brandt realized that he no longer heard the water running in the basement sink. The general's eyes hadn't rolled back, but had rather drifted upward and settled behind him. Brandt felt a long shadow fall over him, and jerked his head quickly to look over his shoulder. The tall figure of his assailant towered over him, his bearded features obscured by shadows.

"I won't preside over an investigation which tramples innocent women and children, in pursuit of the guilty," the man uttered, slowly drawing out the last words.

Brandt involuntarily winced at the intensity of the man's voice. He thought for a moment that he vaguely recognized the words as his own. Through the pain in his head, he searched for a connection. The man crouched towards him, partially emerging from the shadows. Despite the frigid temperatures, his face was covered in a pale, cold sweat. His beard was matted down with moisture, and blood.

"Noble sentiments for someone so comfortable in the company of thieves and butchers! How do you reconcile that in your mind?" the man snarled, menacingly.

The assailant jerked him forward by the back of his neck, and for the first time Brandt could see the man's face clearly. *Mein Gott!* Brandt could also see that the man was brandishing a dagger in his right hand. *It's SS issued, like the one used in the Keppler and Goertz murders.* His mind subconsciously processed the information, even amidst the imminent threat, as his muddled faculties tried to fight through the dense cobwebs. He remained silent.

"You do remember me?"

"The Lodenfabrik," Brandt stammered. "You were the factory worker who intervened in the Gestapo raid."

Brandt recalled the image of the fallen laborer, looking up at him, dazed by the blow to the head. They had switched places. But as he closely scrutinized the man's face, he realized there was more to it than that. *It's David Hedrich! Not a ghost at all, but very much alive.* He could vaguely recognize the similarity between the photos from Hedrich's home, and the bedraggled man who stood over him now. He decided to keep this knowledge to himself, until he could piece everything together. *Or until I have no other choice.* David Hedrich might be alive, but the man whose smiling countenance he had seen in numerous family photos, and whose stories of sacrifice he had heard of from Rebecca Weiss, bore no resemblance to the raving captor standing astride him right now.

"Among other places," he continued, loosening his grip. "Our paths have crossed a number of times. But on that day, you stepped in to save my life. Why?"

Where else have our paths crossed?

"You were unarmed, and trying to protect a mother and child. I was just doing my job."

"Your job!" the man scoffed. "Well that would make you a rare breed, then, but I'm not that naive. You have no mercy on women and children, I know that firsthand."

"How would you know that? And what were you doing at the Lodenfabrik in the first place?"

"I was doing my job!"

Your job? I scoured those transfer files, you were never assigned to the factory. And yet, there you were, right under my nose.

"And what is your job?"

"This," the man said, wielding the dagger so close that Brandt could see the patterns of the bloodstains on its blade. "Bringing the guilty to reckon. But it seems you have a habit of seeking out my next victims, almost before I can do so myself. How is that possible?"

"Your victims?"

"How are you always just one step behind?" he continued, threateningly. "Unless you're an accomplice? Are you protecting them, trying to cover-up their atrocities? Is that what the Polizei are now, the whitewash for government sanctioned murderers?"

Brandt struggled to mask his confusion, but his silence only seemed to fuel his captor's rage. He fumbled with the knots behind his back. His assailant stood suddenly, moving in the direction of the motionless general. Brandt noticed him grimace as he straightened out of his crouch.

"Were you there? There the night this bastard and his cohorts…" he stammered, gesturing wildly towards Brigadefuhrer Becht with his dagger.

He stopped short. The general's eyes were glazed over in the fixed stare of death. This inconvenience caused him to turn his full fury back towards Brandt, lifting him roughly off the ground by the collar of his jacket.

"What night?" Brandt inquired, frantically squirming against his bindings. He could see the murderous intent in Hedrich's eyes.

He pressed the dagger forcefully against Brandt's throat. The edge of the blade dug so tightly against Brandt's skin that he could feel his pulse pounding against it. He couldn't force a reply over the applied pressure.

"No? Then what are you doing here? What could you possibly be doing searching the General's private residence at this hour? Unless you knew I'd be here."

Brandt realized that any hesitation could mean instant death, but he also realized that this wasn't a time to reveal that he knew Hedrich's identity. Against the sharp tension of the blade, he uttered the first thing that came to his mind, which just so happened to be the truth.

"I'm investigating Brigadefuhrer Becht."

"What? I don't believe that!" Hedrich bellowed, even as his knife pressure loosened.

"Becht's the target of a criminal investigation into charges of extortion and conspiracy."

"Don't lie to me! You're not investigating the General for extortion," he growled. "You don't understand, I've seen you at the Fabrik, and at the St Michael's Kirche. I know you're an inspector, and that you've either been tracking me, or the bodies I've left behind."

At St. Michael's?

"No," Brandt said, shrugging his head towards the general's lifeless body. "We thought the casualties were left in his wake. That Brigadefuhrer Becht was trying to eliminate anyone who could connect him to the extortion ring. All of the victims had collaborated with him in an extortion racket."

Hedrich's grip against the back of Brandt's neck released, allowing his head to fall back against the support post. Their eyes broke contact for the first time. Brandt allowed himself to exhale, even though the assailant remained within striking distance. A still silence settled over the basement. As Hedrich began to speak, Brandt resumed his subtle work with the knots.

"How did this so-called extortion ring work?"

Disclosing the details of the case is my best chance to divert his attention. Need to keep him talking.

"The main graft involved targeting wealthy Jewish families for deportation, and confiscating their property and assets when they were on the way out the door."

"I know all about the transports, that's not news. What made this ring any different from the government agencies involved in this legalized extortion?"

"Becht's ring was engaged in these activities *before* legal emigration ceased and the transports began, unbeknownst to the other agencies. And, another angle of their racket was the solicitation of bribes from families of higher means, in exchange for the promise of protection."

Hedrich visibly winced.

"Protection? What manner of 'protection' can a predator offer its prey?"

"For those who could afford the cost, it purchased a temporary reprieve from the evacuation process."

"'Evacuation process?'" he howled. "Is that how you ease your conscience? By telling yourself that these people are just being evacuated? Then what?"

Is it? Is that how I soften the blow?

"Once they bled the target dry, the protection was withdrawn, and the victims' names were returned to the transport schedules. Then the ring would have the assets converted into marks or gold bars and smuggled out of Berlin to line their coffers at different locations around the country."

"How could I have not known about this?" his captor mumbled to himself. "Is it possible that the people I thought I was helping, were only having their agony prolonged?"

Hedrich's voice had grown hollow, and distant, as if he was alone in the basement talking to himself. A mercurial change had occurred in his demeanor. The menace had disappeared from his face, and had been replaced by an expression of despair. The murderer who had hovered, glowering over Brandt moments before had drifted away, leaving a shell of a man in his place. If possible, Brandt thought his assailant had grown even paler than before. He wicked the perspiration away from his twitching brow with the dirty cuff of his sleeve, and slowly unfurled himself from his crouched position. He eased himself down onto the ground, until his back rested against the opposite cinderblock wall.

He had grimaced again at the change of position. Brandt watched as he pulled back the left flap of his coat, and lifted the bottom of his stained top. A balled-up undershirt was tucked into his waistband on the lower right side of his abdomen. The fabric was soaked through with blood. His shaking hands pulled the garment away, slowly inspecting the angry wound below. *He's been shot!* A bullet had entered the lower quadrant of the man's abdomen.

Mein Gott! No wonder he's pale and fevered. How long ago had this happened? Did the bullet exit through his back, or is it still lodged inside of him?

The man lifted his gaze from the wound, and stared at Brandt. There was a vulnerability in his eyes for the first time.

"That's not looking good. You need medical attention."

"What do you suggest, checking myself into the concentration camp infirmary?" he smirked. "I hear they have an extremely low recovery rate among Jewish patients."

"I only mean…"

"You should concern yourself with your own welfare!"

But the edge to his voice was gone, like a switch had been flipped to the 'off' position. Brandt watched as the man discarded the soiled shirt across the dirt floor, and replaced it with a handkerchief from his jacket pocket.

That's not going to do him any good.

"An unforeseen consequence of trying to take the General alive. He was my last source… my last chance to discover what became of my family."

His eyes settled intently on Brandt's. The fire had returned to them, but his posture remained at rest.

"Your family? Not the woman and child you were protecting at the Lodenfabrik?"

That wasn't his family. There was no record of David Hedrich ever being assigned to the Lodenfabrik. The woman and child at the factory didn't look like the family pictures anyway. Rebecca suggested that his family had been deported, and Sergeant Faber thought the same. Does Hedrich really not know?

"The night they came for my family, I wasn't there to protect them."

This is my opening.

"Who came for them? What's your name?"

"I no longer have a name," he replied absently. "I am only Herr Nomen Nescio."

"The man without a name…"

"You've dehumanized us, erased our identities, and destroyed every shred of dignity which gives a name its meaning. There are no more Jews with names in Germany!"

"I understand, David."

"You do know who I am, you lying…"

"Yes, I know your name, but not from hunting you. I know you're name because you're someone who likely lost everything to the same ring that I'm investigating."

"How would you know that?"

"Because, David Hedrich resided at 428 Kurische Strasse with his wife and children. A home he sometimes used to shelter Jewish fugitives seeking to flee the transports, before Major Theodore Goertz appropriated the estate for his own uses, that is."

"Goertz!" Hedrich seethed, but he remained motionless, as though glued to the wall. "Don't say that name! That was our house! The home of meine Familie!"

All of those family photographs, snapshots of this man's previous life. Closed off rooms filled with toys and children's books, never to be played with again. His whole life gone!

"I know. Rebecca Weiss told me that you were an honorable man. That you, and her father Rabbi Weiss, risked your lives to help others escape. Is that why your family was targeted?"

"Don't think you can soften my resolve by dropping a name," Hedrich replied. "She's just a pawn, another innocent whose family you, and others like you, most likely helped to destroy."

"She's more than that," Brandt bristled. "But what about your own family? What do you know about what's happened to them?"

"What could you possibly care? You're in with these butchers up to your eyes."

Maybe I am? Have I been corrupted too?

"We may find each other's methods repulsive, but we're both looking for the truth," Brandt offered, sensing that his captor's resolve was waning, along with his strength. "There's a good chance neither of us is going to live to see the outside of these walls. So, let's finish this, here and now. Why don't you tell me; what happened to them?"

Chapter 40

Hedrich stopped fidgeting with the makeshift dressing on his wound, and silently stared at the barren dirt floor. For the first time, Brandt could feel some slack in his ropes. His arms tingled from the lack of circulation, and his wrists ached.

"I couldn't see things clearly then," Hedrich began. "I was too close to the situation. My wife and I had heard stories of the numerous judischen Familie vanishing into the oblivion that the Gestapo benignly termed 'evacuations.' But I felt insulated, particularly, because of my position on the emigration committee, and because of my relationship with Theodore Goertz."

"What was your connection to Major Goertz?"

"I'd known him for years. We worked together in the Order Police, before Jews were purged from the ranks."

"You were with Orpo?"

"Yes," he nodded, absently. "Goertz managed to conceal the fact that he was a *Halbjude* himself, when the *SS* came recruiting him for a promotion."

Goertz was a half-Jew? The man had a hand in the deportation of most of the Jews in Berlin!

Even after my purge from Orpo, I wasn't concerned about the growing persecution," Hedrich continued. "Why should I be? I wasn't even a practicing Jew. I was a German. I had served my country in the first war, Spezialkorps, and afterwards as ein Polizist.

Special Corps? No wonder he's so skilled with a dagger, and so difficult to track.

"How long ago did you serve with Major Goertz at Orpo?"

"I left the force after the purge in '35 to become a defense contractor. I had plenty of money, and connections. In my mind, the Gestapo might come for others, but my family couldn't be touched."

"So what changed?"

"Goertz was deployed to der Ostfront last summer in Operation Barbarossa," Hedrich fumed. "He was attached to a special unit, and when he returned, he was a different man."

The einsatzgruppen! Faber indicated that Major Goertz had trained and led einsatzgruppen detachments, and that they had engaged in atrocities abroad. The files in his office confirmed as much. If those allegations are true, you can't take part in that type of mass slaughter and remain unchanged.

"I've heard about them."

"I'm sure you have," Hedrich snarled. "Regardless, at that time the doors to emigration suddenly slammed shut, and within days the mass evacuation orders began to arrive in the Friedrichshain district."

"By order of Reichsmarschall Goring."

"That's when we began to understand the gravity of the situation," Hedrich concluded. "Once we started to be able to put faces to the names of the victims, we felt compelled to try to help in any way we could. When the persecution became severe, I sought help, and Goertz offered my family... 'protection.'"

The word hung in the damp basement air like a foul odor.

"I initially thought he offered it out of genuine concern for us, out of a sense of loyalty. But soon, it came with a price tag attached."

"That fits the method of operation of Becht's ring perfectly."

"I knew right then that we had to get out, and that it was only a matter of time before the facade collapsed. While I tried to find a means of exit for us, I decided to use my position of influence to help other Jews facing the crisis. A penance for my past indifference."

"How did you do that?"

"In the Friedrichshain district I worked with leaders like Rabbiner Weiss on the evacuation committees," he confirmed. "On the surface we showed cooperation, but behind closed doors we organized a network that offered services to Jewish families and refugees trying to evade the extensive round-ups; shelter, safe houses, money, extra ration cards, whatever we could provide."

"According to Rebecca Weiss, this activity is what cost her father his life, was your situation the same?"

"Samuel is dead?" Hedrich inquired, shaking his head, and running his hands through his matted hair.

"He died in transit."

"Those swine," he sighed. "I realized that our exit visas were kaputt, and that I'd need forged documents in order to get my own family out of the country. I was put in contact with a grifter who was known to members of the Judenrat for his ties to der Schwarzmarkt."

"Jacob Hirsch."

"Yes, Jacob Hirsch," Hedrich grimaced. "I didn't know him personally, but he apparently knew of me, and of my activities helping Jews who had gone untergrund."

"He should have, he was Brigadefuhrer Becht's personal informant," Brandt responded, nodding towards the lifeless corpse lying across the floor.

"I didn't know. Others within the network had used him to obtain forged papers, and vouched for him. At the time I had no idea he was playing both sides."

"He spent time right here, languishing in Sachsenhausen, until Brigadefuhrer Becht had him released in exchange for his services as a snitch."

"The Bastard!" Hedrich spat. "At least he paid the price for his crimes, and gave up General Becht's name with his dying breath."

Brandt flinched at the thought. He recalled Jacob Hirsch's twisted body lying in the underground cellar. *The man sitting across from me right now has been on an adrenaline-fueled, close range killing spree for days! I need to keep him talking. I can't forget what he's capable of for a second!*

"Hirsch sought out wealthy targets for extortion," Brandt resumed. "So, it was no accident that you were put in contact with him."

"It wasn't an accident at all. It was Theodore Goertz who first gave me his name," Hedrich revealed. "Within the week he had come through with forged passports and exit visas, and asked for my identity papers in exchange. They were perfect forgeries."

That's how Hirsch had acquired Hedrich's papers!

"They should have been; they were probably created on government equipment!"

"I couldn't see any of it then," Hedrich continued. "The day before we were scheduled to depart, I made the error of leaving my wife and children to arrange for transportation."

"Where to?"

"Hirsch had put me in touch with a contact of his in the Weissensee district, and while I was there, I was apprehended in a mass round-up by the Gestapo.

"Apprehended for what?"

"At the time I thought it was a random sweep, being in the wrong place at the wrong time. Consorting with the wrong people."

"There are no coincidences when it comes to the Gestapo."

"That's when I began to wonder. Everything that happened was perfectly contrived against me. Was this any different?"

"Not likely."

"I even had authenticated papers declaring I wasn't of Jewish descent, but the Gestapo wouldn't release me," he shook his head. "I was questioned, then moved from group detention, to solitude in the basement of a Gestapo jail."

"That seems premeditated," Brandt concurred. "Brigadefuhrer Becht's group certainly had the heft to pull those strings, but it's odd that they would use a Gestapo unit and jail."

"Why is that?"

"They didn't have an active member of the Gestapo in the ranks of their extortion ring."

"Nevertheless, there I sat in an isolation cell. A man without an identity, and with no means of contacting the outside world," Hedrich lamented. "The hours became days when time was my most precious commodity. In the darkness of that gnawing solitude, I thought of only of *meine Familie*.

287

Had they used the exit visas in my absence? I prayed for a daylight that seemed to never come."

"The Gestapo just left you there?"

"For a time. Intermittently, I'd be taken to a holding cell where I'd be questioned and beaten."

"How long were you there?"

"My confinement only lasted four days, but I didn't even have hours to spare."

"If this was part of a plan to expropriate everything you had, and deport you and your family, why would they release you?"

"They didn't."

"What do you mean?"

"The last night of my detention, an allied bombing raid caused a lot of commotion in the area of Weissensee where the Gestapo jail was located," Hedrich replied. Nearby electrical stations and gas plants were hit, causing widespread power outages in the district, including the jail. And after days of continuous struggle, I had managed to loosen my shackles against the rock walls of my cell."

Brandt self-consciously ceased his wrangling. *I wonder if he's considered that I may be engaged in the same activity right now?* But Hedrich seemed too involved in his tale to be concerned.

"I had noticed before that this particular guard who worked the graveyard shift, though strong as a bull, was careless. He'd come in twice a night like clockwork to administer beatings," he said, wincing at the recollection. "That night I decided I would be waiting. I sat by the door as the air raid sirens faded, and waited to hear the creaking of the metal cell door, but instead I was knocked off my feet by an explosion."

"What? A bomb?"

"No. I wondered the same at first, but the ordinance wasn't nearly that large," Hedrich replied. "It had to be a flak shell that didn't detonate at altitude, from one of the anti-aircraft guns mounted on the nearby flak towers."

"Mein Gott."

"It must have somehow landed in the courtyard right next to my cell, and exploded on contact, blowing a hole in the stone wall, and knocking the guard in the hall unconscious. I walked out of that jail into the courtyard, and up to the street level where I blended in with the chaos of the air raid evacuations."

Jacob Hirsch wasn't the only fugitive whose escape was aided by the frenzy of the bombing raids, and the ensuing evacuations.

"That's incredible."

"I was glad to be free, but was terrified at what awaited me back home, as I began my trek back towards Friedrichshain."

A grimace spread across Hedrich's grey face. He pulled his shirt up to look at his wound. The kerchief was already soaked beyond its meager capacity to absorb the slow, steady flow of blood. Brandt realized that the man was growing weaker by the moment, and that his condition was worsening right before his eyes. Hedrich sighed deeply. His breathing was increasingly ragged and labored, and his body was shaking slightly.

"You've lost a lot of blood, that's a bad combination with this exposure to the damp and cold," Brandt interjected. "You really should let me get you out of here."

"You said it yourself, Inspector," Hedrich gasped. "Neither of us is leaving here."

"Then tell me what happened when you returned home."

"The night I returned home," Hedrich continued, closing his eyes. "I remember coming through our back doors, the same way Daniel and I would come in when we had chopped fresh wood for the fire. But everything was different. There was no life, no sound of my children playing, none of the activity of Helen flitting from room-to-room straightening up after them. There was just an empty stillness, and piles of boxes. I knew right then that my life had changed forever."

Brandt thought of the children's bedrooms he had seen back at the estate. He could see the pain in Hedrich's expression as he mentioned his wife and children. He could also see that the man's mind was now miles away, more present in his old home than in this room. His eyes twitched and stared wildly, as though he was reliving the events as he recounted them.

"I anxiously searched the main floor calling out their names, but there was nothing. That's when I heard the sound of running water coming from upstairs, from my own bedroom. I raced up the stairs, past my children's rooms. I can't describe what I felt when I saw someone else's uniform hanging from our bedpost. That was where we slept, where we conceived Daniel and Emily. I searched the pants pockets for identification, but then realized to my horror that I recognized the uniform. I took the attached *SS* dagger and pulled it from the sheath. I heard the familiar creak of the hot water handle turn as the spray stopped in the shower, and a shudder ran through my entire body. A moment later, Theodore Goertz emerged from the bathroom wearing my robe. I felt something turn in me, a fury like I had never known washed over me."

"I can't imagine."

"A rage that I didn't know I had inside of me, burst forth uncontrolled. Goertz saw it too. His eyes widened, and without speaking a word he went for the handgun he had sitting on the nightstand. And the rest… is a blur," Hedrich concluded, abruptly.

"A blur?"

"Yes."

"You can recollect the events with that much detail, but you can't remember actually killing him? Or you won't let yourself?"

"I remember bits and pieces, but the rage that consumed me was like a blackout. I remember his head shattering the glass, his pistol discharging, and the struggle for control of the dagger."

"I think you remember more than that. You bathed in this guy's blood, and used it to write on the walls. You had him subdued before you killed him — did you even give him a chance to tell you what had happened to your family?"

"Of course!" Hedrich responded, angrily as the floodgates of repressed memories opened again. "When he wouldn't talk, I pistol-whipped him with his own gun. He swore he didn't know anything about their whereabouts, just that they had been scheduled for the transports, which I already knew. We all had been. I could see the deceit in his eyes, and the fear, but he wouldn't tell me anything. I felt the sting of betrayal, and imagined the cries of meine Frau und Kinder, as I pressed the blade against his throat, and felt the warmth of his blood spill over the blade."

"And then? "

"Afterwards a calm came over me. I decided that as long as I had breath in my lungs, I would pursue the men who took my family from me... the men who stole my life! I would use any resource, any connection, any asset I had at my disposal."

"With Major Goertz unable to provide you with any information, how did you know where to turn next?"

"Das Schwein had moved his work files into my own study!" Hedrich fumed. "I pored over them until I was able to trace the deportation order for my wife and children to the office of a Captain Keppler, where I discovered a connection between him and the very man who had betrayed me at my most desperate hour."

"Jacob Hirsch."

"Yes."

"You were able to uncover a lot. And yet, you still don't know what happened to them?" Brandt asked.

"Who?" Hedrich seemed confused.

"Who?" Brandt countered. "Your wife and children. You still don't know their whereabouts?"

"No."

"At this point, is that even what you're still looking for?"

"What are you saying?"

"I'm saying are you even still searching for your Frau und Kinder, or has your search been replaced by revenge? Has killing become your way to numb the pain, and fill the void?"

Hedrich turned his head sharply towards Brandt, as though physically struck by the words. The distant stare had vanished from his eyes. He moved to stand up, with an agility that belied his condition. *Perhaps I shouldn't have antagonized him!* But Hedrich's stride was halting, and Brandt was not his destination. He slowly limped across the basement floor to the corner sink.

Brandt suspected Hedrich was going to clean and dress his wound, but then he saw the man's gaze fixate on the dusty, cracked mirror that hung above the basin. Hedrich moved towards it as if drawn by an unseen force, setting his dagger on the ledge next to Brandt's handgun. He leaned his head forward, placing both hands on the sink. The first light of dawn was filtering into the basement. From his spot on the floor, Brandt watched as Hedrich closely scrutinized his own reflection in the broken glass. Hedrich's eyes pored over every detail, as if he was seeing himself for the first time. Brandt recognized the familiar sensation. *The man staring back has become a stranger. How long has it been since David Hedrich has truly seen himself?*

Chapter 41

Brandt used his captor's distracted state to intensify the struggle to free his hands. He managed to work them below the hem of his jacket. He felt the butt of his undiscovered Mauser against the back of his hands. He worked to loosen the rope enough to pivot his right hand clockwise from palm to wrist. Each time he made this turn, the rope loosened a fraction more. *Come on!*

He looked up to gauge Hedrich's awareness of his progress. The man remained rooted to the glass, his hands moving across his bearded features, as though looking to find himself beneath them. Hedrich's right hand reached out towards the mirror, and touched the dust-covered reflection. Brandt heard him repeatedly murmuring something under his breath.

"Im, weiter und weiter weg."

Farther and farther away? From what? From finding his family? From himself? From what he used to be?

Brandt heard a shuffling sound, and turned his head suddenly. It came from the opposite side of the basement. A resounding crash followed, as the basement door flew open. The door pried loose from its hinges, and skidded to a halt across the dirt floor. Brandt saw the blur of a black uniform simultaneously burst into the room.

Major Weskamp?

"Stoppen Sie," Weskamp shouted, his pistol trained on David Hedrich's hunched figure. "Show me your hands!"

Another voice followed closely on Weskamp's heels.

"No sudden movements! I have no qualms with shooting you where you stand, Herr Hedrich!" Colonel Schonbern exclaimed, ducking through the low basement doorframe. "I'd just as soon scrape pieces of you off this floor, as I would take you in."

Hedrich had turned away from the sink in shock. He glanced at the dagger and pistol sitting on the ledge an arm's length away.

Don't do it!

After a moment's deliberation, he raised his hands in resignation, and slumped against the basement wall. Major Weskamp quickly descended upon him.

"Herr Colonel?" Brandt inquired, unable to hide his surprise.

"Rest easy, Lieutenant," Schonbern insisted, as he loosened the last of Brandt's bindings. "Sergeant Faber told us you had reason to believe the suspect might target Brigadefuhrer Becht's quarters. Of course, you should have told us as much yourself, as we've been tracking Herr Hedrich as a potential suspect for some time."

"Sergeant Faber?" Brandt asked.

"Was Brigadefuhrer Becht already dead when you arrived?" Schonbern inquired, leaning down to examine the general's lifeless corpse.

"You've been tracking David Hedrich?" Brandt continued, struggling to mask his confusion.

"Lieutenant, the Brigadefuhrer!?"

"Yes, he was mortally wounded and already in shock

when I first saw him."

"He wasn't able to tell you anything about what happened here?"

"About what happened?" Brandt repeated. "No, Colonel. I was knocked unconscious, and he was uncommunicative by the time I came to."

Weskamp had roughly subdued Hedrich in the far corner and shackled his hands. The wounded prisoner had been too weakened to offer more than token resistance, and muffled grunts of pain. The major had moved him to the basement door, where he now stood slumped against the shattered frame, with his head lowered. The colonel stood up from examining his fallen comrade's lifeless body, and dusted himself off.

"Major, I'd like you to call this in, and then accompany Lieutenant Brandt back to Berlin to be checked out for his injuries," Schonbern ordered. "I'll take the prisoner to the camp infirmary, then return to secure the scene until backup arrives."

"Immediately!" Major Kaufmann chirped.

"With due respect, Colonel. I don't need to be checked out." Brandt interjected.

"That nasty gash above your eye says otherwise, Lieutenant Brandt," Schonbern said, with a withering glare that indicated the matter was decided.

Schonbern turned away, briskly taking possession of the prisoner from Major Weskamp, and leading him by the shackles towards the outside stairs. Weskamp and Brandt followed in tow climbing the icy staircase slowly behind the colonel and his staggering captive. The dawning daylight was still sparse, but there was enough of a glare to cause Brandt to squint. He felt a rush of pain to his eye socket. The major directed him towards an idling Mercedes in the drive, as Schonbern veered off towards a path that led into the woods in the direction of the camp. *Nothing feels right about this.*

"Colonel Schonbern!" Brandt interceded, moving in the colonel's direction. "Why not have the prisoner accompany us back to Berlin to receive medical attention? He can be remanded into your custody afterwards."

"This path connects die Kommandanten quarters to the camp, where he can receive immediate treatment at the infirmary."

"The severity of his wound requires a fully equipped medical facility, not a camp infirmary," Brandt countered, pushing ahead despite his better judgment. "Our ability to resolve this case depends on his survival, so why not place him at a hospital in Berlin under your oversight?"

"I'll determine what's most expedient regarding the prisoner's condition, and the resolution of this case, Lieutenant!" Schonbern growled. "Sachsenhausen offers the closest combination of medical attention and maximum security. The camp doctors are more than capable."

"But Colonel…" he continued, noticing that Hedrich was now watching him, as well.

"That will be all Lieutenant Brandt!" Schonbern concluded sternly. "You are to immediately accompany Major Weskamp to the hospital, and then to Gestapo headquarters for debriefing. I'll expect to see you in my office upon my return."

"Yes Colonel."

He watched as Schonbern led his stooped and staggering prisoner across the snow-covered yard, and into the wooded path beyond. He stood there as they receded into the forest, until he felt an insistent tap on the shoulder from Major

Weskamp.

"This way, Lieutenant," Weskamp instructed.

Brandt followed the major towards the vehicle. A familiar mixture of gloom and foreboding settled over him. In fact, everything about this felt far too familiar. *How did the colonel know where I was? Faber would never willingly cooperate with him would he? And how did Schonbern know about Hedrich? Why would he come out here in person, anyway, with only Major Weskamp for backup?*

As they arrived at the vehicle, Brandt turned again towards the back of the property. The visibility of the colonel and his wounded counterpart had diminished until they could barely be distinguished from the coverage of the woods. *There's nothing more I can do now.*

Major Weskamp reached to open the rear passenger door of the idling Mercedes staff car for Brandt, and waved him in the direction of the back seat. The gesture caused the sleeve cuff on the major's left arm to rise slightly above his wrist. Brandt glimpsed a familiar imprint, on the outstretched tendons of the major's left wrist. He had a small tattoo, of a skull encircled by a snake eating its own tail.

Chapter 42

Colonel Schonbern pulled roughly on the weakened captive's manacles, coercing him to pick up his pace. They trudged on wordlessly to the sound of water dripping, and branches breaking all around them, as they wound their way through the crystalline woods. Their boots crunched sharply through the frozen top layer of snow that covered the trail. The incline grew increasingly steep, and their progress slowed, as the prisoner's legs buckled under the strain. Schonbern pressed the barrel of his pistol hard between Hedrich's shoulder blades prodding him on.

Up ahead, a smaller path diverged from the main trail, in an eastward direction. The colonel halted briefly, looking back towards the general's quarters. The house and property had completely receded from view. They recommenced their march, with the colonel steering them onto the narrow trail, which led deeper into the more densely wooded area. After a few minutes of steady progress, they emerged at a clearing. The clearing was littered with the frost-covered stumps of trees that had been felled by hand, their trunks dragged into groupings around the perimeter. In the distance, there were signs of freshly dug trenches, which had since been draped with a layer of snow.

"We're not headed towards the camp," Hedrich mustered weakly, breaking the frigid silence. "Why the deception? Do even your own men find your actions too repulsive to condone?"

"Things would have gone much better for you, and your family, if you hadn't chosen to flee," Schonbern replied.

Hedrich wrestled against his cuffs at the mention of his wife and children, but his waning strength was quickly subdued as the colonel hoisted his chains upward until his arms were at their breaking point.

"What would you know about my family?" Hedrich panted, in resignation.

"I likely know more about their last moments than you do, you pathetic *Judenschwein*!" Schonbern sneered, peering over the prisoner's shoulders to see the effect of his words. "You may have managed to kill a few of my unsuspecting colleagues, but I'd venture you're none the wiser than you were the day you started."

"You don't know what you're talking about."

"Of course, how could you have learned anything about the fate of your precious wife and children? None of the people you killed were present the day they were apprehended."

Hedrich froze in his steps. He peered over his shoulder at his captor, with an expression of horror.

"But I was," Schonbern concluded.

A shadow descended over Hedrich's pale face. He summoned every last ounce of his strength and struggled furiously against his bindings, in vain. The colonel forced him roughly to his knees, digging the muzzle of his pistol into his neck, below the base of his skull. He held this position until his captive stopped flailing.

"Burn in hell, you demon" he gasped.

"Relax, Herr Hedrich, there's no need to bring hellfire

into it," Schonbern cooed. "You'll be reunited with them soon enough, and by the same hand."

"No!"

"I believe our relationship, though destined to be brief, can be mutually beneficial," Schonbern resumed, dragging the limp prisoner towards the center of the clearing. "You see, you've unwittingly been of great value to me"

"Value to you?"

"True, you needed some assistance along the way, but once I decided not to inform Major Goertz of your escape, and saw what you were truly capable of..."

"What?"

"I sometimes wonder how much more complicated things might have become if I hadn't ordered my tactical team to 'stand down' when they had you in their sights," Schonbern continued. "But then I realized, that if I just left you to your own devices, that you could be immensely useful to my objectives."

"You couldn't have..."

"Your military training undoubtedly served you well, and you certainly weren't lacking for motivation," the colonel proceeded, relishing in his captor's building anguish. "All I had to do was subtly divert attention away from you. I scrubbed every personnel file that ever hinted at your existence, and pointed every asset I had towards Brigadefuhrer Becht's Jewish lap dog, Jacob Hirsch, knowing all along that once you were on the scent of Hirsch's trail, he'd lead you right back here to the General!"

"How could you have possibly..."

"But other than that you deserve all the credit. Just drop the breadcrumbs, wind you up, and let your blinding rage do the rest."

"You didn't wind me up."

"Nevertheless, you've managed dirty work I never could have accomplished on my own. And do you know why? Because there's no more reliable assassin than the one who doesn't know whom he's working for."

"I didn't kill for you, I was avenging my family, trying to find them."

"Ah, yes, your wife and children, I had almost forgotten about them," Schonbern scoffed. "Rest assured, each of the men you killed had a hand in their fate and many others, but you were my special case."

"You evil bastard!" Hedrich shouted, struggling wildly against the restraints.

"Such anger. I see where your son got it from," Schonbern sneered, watching the prisoner's agonized expression at the mention of his child. "I do have to admit though, he acquitted himself courageously for a member of your mongrel race. He was very protective of his Mutter and Schwester, in your absence. It actually earned him my admiration, though it also earned him a bullet."

"No!" Hedrich gasped through his tears, shuddering as his body slumped to the ground.

Schonbern dragged the limp prisoner closer to the ledge of the trench by the scruff of his neck. He leaned close to whisper in his ear.

"After that, your wife and daughter were much more cooperative," the colonel hissed venomously. "At least until they were no longer useful. Perhaps if you had been present that day, your family's fate could have been different!"

"*Gott, bitte nicht!*"

"Your God can't hear you," Schonbern said mockingly.

"As much as I abhor the thought of a Jewish cur spilling German blood, I must confess that your rampage helped me dispatch of several comrades whose indiscretions threatened to entangle us all. The scope of our endeavor was always much larger than they could grasp."

He lifted the prisoner onto his feet, dragging him towards the lip of the first trench.

"Now then, just as you've helped me, I've helped you learn the fate of your family. And now I'm going to reunite you with them."

The finality of the colonel's words broke through Hedrich's benumbed senses. He straightened himself and opened his eyes to peer over the edge of the dugout. A heap of mangled, lifeless bodies were strewn across the trench, piled together in snow-covered tiers. He looked at the frozen collage of insensate faces in the mass grave with unabated terror.

"I'm going to make this painless for you," Schonbern sneered, tracing his pistol against his captive's neck. "A single shot to this soft spot between the base of the skull and neck severs the nerves, bringing instant death."

The colonel swiftly kicked at the back of Hedrich's knees, causing the prisoner to slump to the ground. Schonbern pulled him up roughly by his collar into a kneeling position. He placed the muzzle of his pistol firmly against the captive's neck and cocked the lever. A shot rang out, and Hedrich tumbled forward over the frozen ledge and into the pit, propelled forward by a weight greater than he could resist. He landed face down on the frigid mound of corpses. As the pain of his hard landing receded, he quickly realized two things: He hadn't been shot, and he hadn't fallen alone.

Chapter 43

Brandt emerged from the tree line, and quickly crossed the frozen terrain of the clearing, his Mauser raised and trained on the obscured precipice. He crept towards the edge, unprepared for the horrific sight that stretched out before him. As he struggled to grasp the abhorrent scene, he recalled Faber's description of the mass graves and killing fields on the eastern front. *But this is Germany! Only a short distance from the capital, German citizens are being murdered and discarded like debris at the city dump!*

He quickly reigned in his careening thoughts, and trained his eyes on the two living persons resting atop the icy sea of corpses. David Hedrich had fallen into the pit face-first but had successfully managed to roll over onto his back. His eyes stared wildly up at Brandt. To the left, a flailing motion drew Brandt's attention, as Colonel Schonbern groped for his lost pistol, while awkwardly trying to find his footing on the unfamiliar terrain of frozen human flesh. A red stain spread out from the hole in the colonel's jacket just below his right shoulder. *The bullet went straight through.* Schonbern stopped scrambling and looked up at Brandt, his marred face a mixture of surprise and contempt. Brandt lowered his weapon.

"You'll hang for this Lieutenant!" he gasped.

"I'm not planning to face any charges, Colonel," Brandt responded. "You knew about everything, all along. You pulled all of the strings, orchestrated all of the killings. Or at least let them happen."

"That's nonsense!" Schonbern shouted up at him. "What reason would I have to allow a filthy Jew to run roughshod through the ranks of my own colleagues?"

"I can think of several," Brandt replied calmly. "Not the least of which would be covering the tracks of your extortion and smuggling ring. You are after all die Schlange — the snake!"

The colonel winced visibly at Brandt's mention of the snake moniker.

"You don't know what you're talking about!" Schonbern yelled defiantly, glancing around the pit for his weapon. "You only have the word of a dying Jew, and a murderous one at that."

"No, I've got it all right here in black and white," Brandt confirmed, pulling the ledger from his jacket liner. "I imagine Reichsfuhrer Himmler would be very interested in a subordinate who extorted millions from him, smuggled it out of the capital, and then plotted the death of his fellow officers to cover up his activities."

The colonel's eyes widened at the sight of the ledger. *He recognizes it!* Schonbern's expression and tone were instantly transformed by the appearance of the notebook, and by Brandt's accompanying threat.

"Warten jetzt ein Minute, Herr Lieutenant" Schonbern held up his hand. "I know of a way we can resolve this to everyone's advantage."

Where have I heard that before? And what is to everyone's advantage anyway?

A flood of thoughts cascaded through Brandt's mind in an

instant. He thought of the last time he tried to bring charges against a Nazi official, and of Albert Lohman swinging from a schoolyard beam. He thought of Emil Roth dying at the hands of an informant that they should never have been chasing. He thought of the dying man staring up at him now from his back, and the family he had been deprived of forever. He thought of Rebecca Weiss, and of her family. *Where is she now? Will I ever see her again? Will she ever be reunited with her family? Are they even still alive? Where does it all end?*

He raised his pistol and saw the colonel's eyes widen in terror as he fired. The bullet hit above Schonbern's brow line, toppling him headlong back onto the pile of frozen humanity that he had built.

Brandt tucked the pistol back into his waistband and shuttled down the slope into the trench. He quickly examined the colonel's lifeless body, and the gaping hole in his forehead. As he snatched a set of keys from the dead officer's belt, he glimpsed the familiar hexagonal gold patch of the spider on Schonbern's sleeve, now saturated in the colonel's blood. *Today he winds up in the same place as all the other infected limbs he sought to purge.* Brandt turned towards David Hedrich. The wounded man's head was raised, unblinkingly watching the exchange in disbelief. *Or has his body entered full shock?* By the time Brandt reached him, Hedrich had closed his eyes, and his head had come to rest on a heap of bodies that formed the trench floor. His face was pale, and his eyes and lips had begun to assume a bluish tint at the corners. Brandt unlocked Hedrich's cuffs and freed his hands from their strained position, feeling his wrist for a pulse. He could barely find a heartbeat. He lifted Hedrich's filthy shirt to examine his wound.

"We've got to get you out of here," Brandt said, beginning to raise him up by his shoulders.

Hedrich opened his eyes and shook his head slowly.

"No, please don't."

"What?"

"There's nothing you can do for me."

"I can't just leave you."

"We agreed earlier, I'm not leaving. Remember? There's nothing left for me here."

Hedrich struggled to control his movements, as he tried to pull back the flap of his jacket and reach into an inside pocket. A packet of papers tumbled out onto his chest. There, among the documents, were four exit passports. He opened them one by one, holding the photographs close to his face, his hands trembling. Tears formed around the edges of his eyes. He let the other papers fall and held out his own forged exit passport to Brandt.

"Take this, perhaps you can use it," he whispered, laboring over each word. "Leave me here, I'm where I belong."

He looked back over his shoulder at the mound of frozen bodies, as if he was searching for something, or someone, and then his eyes were still. The shallow heaving of his chest stopped. Everything was quiet.

Brandt stood up and removed his jacket. Much like David Hedrich, the pockets of his own jacket also contained the items he held most dear. He removed the ledger from its lining, and then reached inside the right flap pocket to retrieve the silver locket Rebecca Weiss had somehow managed to place there the day that they had made love at the shelter. The ledger had come to represent his only remaining leverage, and his last chance to get at the truth without compromising. *And the locket? What does it represent? Hope.*

He knelt down and slowly covered David Hedrich's face and body with his jacket. He looked out over the tundra of dead bodies, capped by the recent addition of Colonel Schonbern. *This is the foundation the Fuhrer, and his architect Minister Speer, are building their thousand-year Reich upon! A foundation of human misery.* He turned to walk back towards the trail.

The early morning sun pierced the dark clouds, as he emerged from the wooded path. The general's residence was quiet and still, except for the black Mercedes staff car that still idled in the driveway. Brandt opened the driver's side door, where Major Weskamp's body sat slumped over the steering wheel. He started to toss the ledger over the major's lifeless body onto the passenger seat but thought better of it. *No reason to discard the only exculpating evidence of this entire sordid mess. Never know when it could prove useful.*

He tore out a single, incriminating sheet from the ledger, and placed it on the dash. He closed the door behind him. *An extortion ring that took the life of everyone in its path, and then had suddenly gone extinct itself. Greed always consumes itself in the end, just like a fire that can never get enough oxygen, or like a snake eating its own tail.*

He walked briskly back to the spot where he had left his car earlier that morning. He climbed in and started the engine. He pulled down the visor and stared hard at his reflection in the compact mirror. The gash above his eye was swollen and bruised, but that wasn't why he was looking. He took his Kriminalpolizei badge off of his belt and removed his pistol from his waistband, and placed them both in the glove compartment. He pulled onto the unpaved road, and headed back in the direction of the main route. He braked as he reached the entrance ramps for highway *D.S.96*, only pausing an instant before taking the roundabout and accelerating north, away from Berlin.

There's nothing left for me here, either.

Made in the USA
Las Vegas, NV
14 August 2021